FIRST AID KIT GIRL

Lynsey Rose studied BA Writing & Publishing at Middlesex University and is now a charity magazine editor.

She is a member of The Willesden Green Writers' Workshop, and her poems and short stories can be found in the award-winning anthology, 'The Monkey's Typewriter' and its follow up, 'What we were thinking just before the end'.

She also writes the blog, 'Exitainment' in which she rants enthusiastically about TV, music, books, feminism and film and can be found at lightupvirginmary.blogspot.co.uk, as well as 'Extol' which showcases her poetry at extol-lightupvirginmary.blogspot.co.uk and makes her look a little less crazy.

THE GREEN PRESS

First published in 2013
by The Green Press, London, U.K.

ISBN 978-0-9562351-2-1

www.thegreenpress.co.uk

Cover by Lee Batchelor
www.leebatchelor.co.uk

To contact the author, visit about.me/lynsey_rose or email
firstaidkitgirl@live.co.uk

Thanks to Anne Mullane, Stephen Moran and everyone at the
Willesden Green Writers' Workshop who helped to make this book a
reality.

Lynsey Rose

FIRST AID KIT GIRL

THE GREEN PRESS

For James,
who read this book before he even met me
and understood
everything

Wembley, 2005

Part 1.... Same Shit, Different Day

Monday

My arm is throbbing.

I walk calmly from the toilet to the kitchen, always on the lookout. There's no good time for what I do, no time of day when no one is around, but you fall into patterns of ways to avoid people. I just roll my sleeve down and play it cool.

This is my cigarette, my beer after work. It's no different. I'm no different.

There. On the wall is my nicotine patch, my box of tricks, my Alka-Seltzer. Nothing is permanent. All things heal; well, almost.

I like the First Aid Kit at work. Actually, 'like' isn't right. Need? Love? Own? None of these are quite it, but one thing's for sure, the First Aid Kit understands me. And I want what's inside it.

I slide open the white catch, and run my fingers against the hard green plastic. The front pops forward and I stare wide-eyed at the little world inside, white boxes full of different ways to hide. I unroll a bandage, glamorously-titled 'Propax', and blot the cream fabric onto my skin. Red rushes up like a wave, drizzling down the gauze, exploding like roses in bloom, my own stop-motion animation. Anyone could walk in and witness this tiny horror, but I feel totally separated from the normalness, from the smooth beech surfaces of the kitchen around me.

I am seeing stars.

I lean on the wall, feeling my breath rise and fall in my chest. The pain confirms my existence.

This is my secret, the one thing I have that they don't. The one way to make it all stop, just for a second. Yet this is the bottom of the wave. After this, it's back to normality. I go back to the grey haze.

I return to my desk, and The Capricorn looks up at me. The Capricorn always looks in case she can catch me eating something. She is French and skinny, French and observant, French and cool. But not in that way. She will stare at me whilst I eat as if I'm a cell on a glass slide. But I am not eating, I never do any more, not in the office, so she forces herself to look back at her screen. She has a giant plastic thing that looks like a locust on her monitor. Why? It stares at me too, with black eyes.

'I'm Not Being Funny, but...' walks up and down, up and down, dishing out the post – a dealer of letters, flyers and invoices. She is in charge of the stationery and the mail. She walks like she has a stick up her arse. I won't make eye contact. She never says hello, and starts every other sentence with her faux disclaimer. She's right, though, she's not being funny. She's just a cunt.

Her second favourite thing to say is 'Can I just say something?' Why not just say it? Is it possible to say 'Can I just say something?' without it being followed up by something you don't want to hear? I suspect not. If you have something acceptable to say, you don't need to frame it with that. Has anyone ever said 'no' to someone who said 'can I just say something?' I'd like to. I'd like to be the first, set a trend.

At lunchtime, I go to the newsagents and buy the Daily Mail, a lottery ticket, and a box of matches with a picture of some kittens on. I hate buying the Mail but I can't be arsed to read a broadsheet. I hate feeling ashamed of reading this shit. I want to tell the newsagent it's OK, I'm not a Tory, I don't believe in it, I just find it amusing. I don't care about illegal immigrants, or lightbulbs, or the BBC, and I don't hate gays, or Muslims, or women, especially as I am one. But I like the spiteful columnists and pompous letters. They make me laugh for the wrong reasons. I don't think the newsagent really cares. But you never know. He might. He could be disappointed in me.

I don't need matches, I just like the kitschness of the kittens and I can make use of them somehow; perhaps I'll set fire to The Capricorn's desk or Bowser's cheap polyester shirt. I consider buying some biscuits for the afternoon in a generous gesture to my fellow workmates, but feel too paranoid about The Capricorn's potential for judgement and calorie notation. She's probably got a spreadsheet with the calories she eats on. She is turning out to be quite a diet aid.

The lottery ticket is just a cruel fantasy. But is that pound worth it, for that five seconds of hope? Probably, just about, for me, scraping 25K and living in a £750 a month one bedroom flat (alone). Probably not for those stupid fuckers who spend their last tenner on tickets, every Wednesday and Saturday without fail. For them it's just another tax, a bind, another way to keep them down. Putting the price up on cigarettes doesn't make poor people stop. It just makes them poorer. But they know that, of course. And besides, the sooner poor people die the better for the Government.

The sooner we all die the better.

I walk the five or so minutes to McDonald's. I like McDonald's; filthy, cruel, capitalist McDonald's – another thing to be ashamed of, obviously – but I don't eat it every day. There's not a plethora of choice when your office block is situated on a retail park. The Capricorn views McDonald's as the jaunty younger brother of nicotine or crack. I remember when I was a kid, it wasn't that bad; it wasn't the enemy. It was just a plasticky treat, a brown-orange place to eat fries every once in a while. Of course, Ronald has always been a freak, but the Hamburglar and his cronies had a certain charm. It's not my fault that things that were OK once, aren't any more. It is actually a form of cruelty, changing the rules like this.

And I do feel guilty for eating meat. I know it pisses Morrissey off. I know pigs are as intelligent as three-year-old children. It's just willpower's not my strong point.

I should make non-cruel sandwiches, but then I'd have to sit in that beech kitchen, surrounded by people talking about *things*. The kitchen is best when it is silent, empty.

I touch my arm, reassuring myself that the bandage is still on and I'm not going to start haemorrhaging through my jacket. I have enough blood on my hands with the Daily Mail, and now skulking into Maccy Ds. What was I going to do next, kick a tramp to death?

Why is everything I enjoy doing socially unacceptable?

I am a pariah.

I suffer through ordering, and then I eat two hamburgers and large fries, liberally showered in salt. I don't eat salad. I don't like to talk to people at lunch – or ever – so I put my headphones in my ears, in case someone from work comes in. I don't bother pressing 'play'.

I try not to look up.

I eat.

I walk back.

After lunch I manage to turn my brain off for at least an hour, folding letters and sliding them into envelopes. It is almost meditative. I can see white spots shaped like half moons drifting down my line of vision, yet when I try to focus they are gone. I wish I could dissolve like that.

I like it when the sun shines in through the window onto my computer screen, because if I can't see it properly, nor can other people. I get annoyed when The Capricorn rolls down the blinds, tutting.

I can't stop yawning, either. The Capricorn is getting pissed off with me. She looks at me over her glasses and shakes her head like I've been up all night raving or shagging. Why am I so tired? Maybe there's something wrong with me.

Maybe I'm dying.

I can hear creepy music coming from somewhere. It's someone's ringtone but it sounds like the Psycho theme tune.

I finish the letters and take the lift up to the post room. As I approach the door, the Fit Guy is there behind the glass, having problems with his key card. I can see his face for at least two full seconds. He is stubbly; I have never seen him this way before.

I swipe my card, and hold the door for him.

'Struggling, were you?' I say, and smile. Well, my lips move, if that counts. I realise he's embarrassed and I had the upper hand for a second. I can't relate to this feeling. I go back to my desk, thinking of his stubble.

I wonder what he smells of.

Jim sits behind me, engaged in personal phone calls, in between making and then drinking endless cups of coffee and tea. His idea of a joke is to stick a Post-it on your back calling you a slapper. Still, at least he knows what a joke is. He also single-handedly broke the brand-new photocopier this morning, so you have to give him credit for that.

Two hours to go.

The guy opposite me, Mitesh, tries to start conversations every so often; he offers cups of tea in exchange for a kind word. He's about as tall as me, which isn't very. He gets routinely picked on by his 'team leader', a gargantuan Toad, but he sets himself up for it. On the phone to his kids, I hear the results of this bullying – he takes it out on them. He is always saying he's going to leave, get better pay, sort his life out. I am struck by his tragedy, but fully aware that I am scratching at the lid inside the same coffin.

Depressed by this thought, I force myself to think of this morning and the green box, my safe haven. In the First Aid Kit, plasters are called 'Airstrips'. That word astounds me. Little strips of air, so medical, clean and and sleek. 'Plaster' sounds clunky, like it's masking the wound, not healing. Americans call them Band-Aids. I don't want to think of Bob Geldof when I'm in my happy place, thanks very much. Fuck Band-Aids and fuck plasters, too.

I like Airstrips, I like the name and I like the feel of them against my skin. I like running my fingers over the spongy surface and the dimples. I like knowing what's underneath when no one else does, my secret, like my clothes covering up the brutal truth of what lies beneath.

If only they knew.

I'm uglier than they could ever imagine.

Talk around me turns to food. People talk about food constantly here; it's not just The Capricorn who's obsessed with it. It's not a subject that interests me too much as I live on white bread and fried potatoes. My parents didn't cook and I hadn't found that path myself as an adult. It wasn't the only one.

The Toad loves food. She loves Thai and Indian, but not Chinese. She loves stuffed mushrooms and chicken and pastries. She loves Baileys in the evening. She doesn't like Jaffa Cakes. She thinks they should make them with milk chocolate, not dark. I think she should learn to love them the way they are, or just stop fucking eating or something before she has a heart attack.

Mitesh has started to repeat himself. He says to me, 'I work in Credit Control but I can't even control my own credit.' He said this to me last week, too. I smile weakly and The Capricorn rolls her eyes at him. Will I become like this, a caricature of myself, reeling out the same old clichés year after year if I don't escape?

But I don't have a catchphrase. I barely have a name.

My car is in the garage, so I catch a lift home with Jim and Kate, who live in Dollis Hill, just around the corner from me. I want to get the tube, but they insist and insist, and I struggle to say no. The journey that takes fifteen minutes in the morning takes thirty at night. They talk about what they are having for dinner and their two weddings, as I sit in the back seat, impassive. They drop me off on the corner, and I say 'thanks'.

<u>Tuesday</u>

It's Jeans for Genes day today so we get to pay a pound for the privilege of wearing clothes that we don't actively despise. It's good for me; there are more pockets in my jeans than my office clothes. I can squirrel things away for comfort. I'm a misanthropic hamster, or a barren kangaroo that hides something else in her pouch for comfort. I've got hidden panels; secret compartments.

Unfortunately own-clothes-day also means I have to look at everyone's attempts to be fashionable, which are tragically inept. Jim looks like he has man-boobs in his too-tight T-shirt. It is one of those generic logo ones, with patches sewn on the sleeves, a random number stuck on the breast (69 in fact, ho ho) and a whitewashed-looking eagle stretched grotesquely over his belly. It tries to be individual. And it is.

Kate is just as bad. No, Kate is worse. She dresses like a fifty-year-old, despite only being 21. She once told me her favourite shop was M&S. I started laughing, until I noticed she wasn't, then I had to pretend I was laughing at something else, which made me look insane. It's adult 'mufti' day and she's still wearing nylon black trousers and this frilly vile blouse. Like, what the fuck?

The Capricorn just looks like she has normal office stuff on, too; her jeans are so uptight she could wear them to a job interview. Her waistband makes Simon Cowell look like he's into hipster jeans. The Toad, also in my line of vision, looks like her outfit shrunk in the wash, or she picked up her daughter's dress by accident. Why else would she be spilling out of it in every direction? I think of a Play-Doh machine I had as a kid, where you mash in the Play-Doh, then push on the lever and it splurges out in an ungainly coil. That's basically The Toad's body. Play-Doh encased in man-made fibres. Yum.

I'm not saying that I look good or anything. I'm just saying that they look worse.

The Martyr's hands are shaking badly today. I answer directly to her. I used to ask her if she was alright, but like an abused dog or child, I learnt fast. She'd either grunt at me or downright ignore me. I knew from bits I'd picked up (tears, slammed-down phones, leaving early) that she was going through a bitter separation. But her divorce seemed stratospherically acrimonious. She made regular acrimony look like the first flush of love.

I ponder what it takes to turn undying love into cut-throat hate. Probably not that much. Probably just one lie, one foot out of line. One word, even.

I don't know who I feel sorrier for, The Martyr or The Martyr's estranged husband. Oh, yeah, I do. Her daughter. The referee. I remember that performance myself – but that was eons ago.

The Capricorn picks up the phone. 'How can I help you?' That poor caller. The short straw.

The sandwich lady comes at 10am every day. She rings her bell and there is an undignified stampede. I never buy from the sandwich lady. I don't do breakfast. I look forward to lunch and like to eat it early, to avoid the scrum.

Some people always buy from her: Jim, The Toad, Bowser. All the fat people, basically. They come back like kids from the fair, fingers curled around their prizes; a manky pasty or sausage roll, a full-fat Coke. I pity them. Don't get me wrong, I'm fat, too, fat enough, anyway. But I don't advertise my eating. I'm not proud of it. It's something to be done away from others, in private, like all the best things.

I feel the underside of my arm, gently.

The Toad comes back fuming. 'Those pasties have gone up by ten pence! I didn't have the right change...' Mitesh meekly offers her a 50p piece. She stomps off again.

The Toad treats her team with about as much respect as a drunk ordering a kebab at 2am. No, a little less respect than that.

There is a felt-covered board separating their team from our team of four. We sit in blocks, like packs of beer. I wish the board was higher, so I couldn't see Mitesh's face or The Toad's struggling rolls of Plasticine flab. It's weird because I am sitting right next to them but The Toad wields no power over me. There is an invisible line where her power begins and ends, thank God. In a way I feel worse because of it because I witness the low-level demoralisation but I am powerless to stop it. I can do nothing but look on, glad it's not me, like someone watching a stranger getting their head kicked in on the street below from the top deck of a passing bus.

One seat in their block is vacant so it is just

The Toad ruling over the two men. They are gentle people; both remind me of boys in a way. Mitesh is irritating, desperate for attention and too touchy-feely, but there's little bad in him. He talks too fast, and trails off into a mumble when The Toad confronts him. I am desperate for him to stand up to her, but he never will. He wouldn't get as far as her tits. The other guy, Clint, is mixed-race with braided hair and a UV smile. He is so young-looking I thought he was my age when I met him. In fact he's a father of three, and now I know him better, he seems more jaded by the day. He tries to remain laidback, but he seems beaten. I see the pain in him and I can't help but feel it, too. No one wanted to do this when they left school. Every one of us – a broken dream.

I'm Not Being Funny, but... comes over. She has a puckered ring for a mouth, the grooves planed by years of nicotine kisses.

She says, 'Someone from your team has to come learn how to use the new multi-function device.' I think she means the photocopier.

Clearly in our case this should be Jim, as he broke it, but he's conveniently gone awol. He's probably taking pictures of his dick on his mobile in the toilet. The Capricorn is still on the phone so I'm nominated by default.

The woman who has been sent to teach us is a bubbly blonde (i.e. an overweight bitch) who doesn't look like she'd know how to work a toaster. She is wearing that peach shade of lipstick that you can only wear once you're over 50. It must get issued at that age, like a telegram from the Queen, 50 years early.

Mitesh has been sent from his department and he stands way too close to me. He pats me on the back to say 'hi' and I recoil, wondering if he can feel the sweat underneath my top. I hover back behind him, hoping if I stand still enough I'll disappear from view, like an anorexic behind a lamppost.

It's not nice when she presses the buttons because she has long acrylicy nails. I like pressing buttons with my soft, stubby bitten fingers. My fingers do not click against the plastic like cheap high heels.

Copierbot talks about paper jams with a zealousness that would seem over-enthusiastic for a first-time mum showing off baby photos. I am distinctly underwhelmed. I am disintegrating under the onslaught. I can feel panic rising up in me because I want to run away screaming rather than listen to another word from her mouth. I try and tune my brain out by running song lyrics through my head but I forget to smile and nod in the right places so she catches me out.

'Can you see alright there?' she says to me, meaning 'are you listening?' Mitesh turns and grabs my arm to pull me closer. I can feel his breath on me, and it smells like zombies, like horror-films. It is all I can do not to head-butt him.

'I'm fine!' I say in a non-fine voice. Copierbot flashes me a vampiric smile.

'Believe me, photocopiers are not my favourite topic of conversation,' she lies. 'But you'll be glad you listened when you get an error code 00432, I promise you.'

'Right...' I look over to our side of the office

and see Jim strolling back to his desk, oversized mug in hand, oblivious to all. I can hear my phone ringing from here but he's clearly hearing-impaired, or possibly brain-damaged, because he doesn't react to it. If he goes for lunch and leaves me here... I'll kill him.

'Finally,' Robocopierbitch says, pushing a long square nail against the control panel. 'If you press this question mark icon, it explains everything I've just told you.'

ARGH!

I scurry off in case she changes her mind about leaving. My chest feels tight. I start thinking about a wider escape and panic builds up. I try and stuff it back down, but my mind is racing forwards, thinking of ways to get out.

I shouldn't do it today. I only did it yesterday.

This is an awful start to the week. There is nowhere to go but down.

I won't do it until next week after that, I tell myself.

This may or may not be true.

Probably not.

I rummage in my bag for my tin. It's a battered old tobacco tin with a sticker of a monkey and a rainbow on the front, which I stuck over it to hide the gigantic cannabis leaf which originally decorated it — it had actually never had any in it, I just bought it from a hippy shop and preferred it to the ones with sexy nymphs on. My jeans (for genes) are baggy so it slips easily into my pocket.

I head for the door.

In the toilets, right above the cubicles, a part of the ceiling is missing. There are exposed white and purple wires, and silver pipes the size of tree trunks. I always think a workman or a nimble psychopath is going to appear there and catch me. I reason that it could never happen as that would be a sort of sexual assault, peering at women in the toilet. I tell myself this, but am still disturbed by the hole. My one hope of privacy compromised.

I take off my red cardigan and open the tin. Only two blades left. I shake the packet and it gives a satisfying rattle. I only have a vest top on underneath. I used to wear shirts to work on regular days but sometimes the blood leaked through before I could put a bandage on. No one saw but it gave me a fright. I should get the bandages first, prepare, but I like the ritual of the way I do it. It seems wrong to have the cure at hand whilst I'm still feeding the disease – like cheating.

The First Aid Kit is for later. I like running the gauntlet, that second when I could be discovered, but am not. It's a part of it.

I open the packet and shake out a razor blade. My skin looks grey under these lights. I only plan to do one, but three are there before my brain can object. I like doing three, it's my favourite amount. My hands are quick and the blade is sharp, cutting vertically and symmetrically. There is a rush of blood to the surface, leaking over my precision lines. The pain stings lovingly, and for one second I am at peace. The floor glitters like a lake.

No one can take this from me.

I breathe in and out, in and out. In my head, it is white. In my head, I'm somewhere else.

I am someone else.

There is a noise like a cat coughing and I jump, inadvertently looking to the ceiling. I realise it is just the air freshener; it goes off intermittently, mechanical and sinister, intruding on my calm. A second later I can smell synthetic pine and I cough, too.

My moment is over. I drop the soiled razor blade into the sanitary waste bin, imagining what it looks like inside, the full abject horror of it. I imagine the blade that was perfect and clean ten seconds ago, falling into that dark and dirty space, with no hope of retreat.

<u>Wednesday</u>

Along with the food bullshit, every day The Capricorn comments on what I'm wearing. It's what she doesn't say that really irks me though. She says, 'Green today!' or 'Purple today!' depending on the colour of my top. What is she insinuating by this? Is it an eyesight test? No, it's just a creepy mind-fuck. I feel like saying 'Die today!' but I don't. The pressure of thinking things and not daring to say them makes my head feel like it might spontaneously combust at any second. I pick up a drawing pin and dig at the skin around my nails. I like watching the strips of skin come up. When they scab, I just dig them up again. It bleeds but it doesn't hurt. It's fun. It pisses The Capricorn off, too. She thinks it's disgusting and my fingers might fall off. I know better. I know that you can peel skin off pretty much anywhere on your body and it will grow right back, like magic.

And no, I haven't tried Stop 'n Grow. Because I don't want Little Miss Perfect Nails. I want scabs. I want the truth. I want you to have to look at it.

Mr Happy comes over. 'Morning! Hi, everyone! How you doing?' His smile would put Hollywood starlets to shame. I try to reciprocate but it feels like a grimace. He doesn't notice. He is high-fiving one and all, and offering cups of tea. I'd rather bathe in shit than high-five someone. How does he do it? It *must* be an act. He probably goes home and beats up his wife. Jim said once that Mr Happy reminded him of a preacher. Maybe Mr Happy could lay his hands on me and save my soul. More likely he's just a vacant waste of space.

The phone rings and rings for The Martyr. Fortunately, the only thing she ever asks is 'what's the time?' or 'what date is it?' despite having a calendar, a clock, a phone with a calendar and clock, *and* a computer with a calendar and clock on it, all at her fingertips. I still tell her the time and the date, though. It's easier than trying to force-feed her some common sense. Some people are born thick, and others chose to remain clueless because it suits them. Either way, you're stuck with them.

The Martyr isn't around, anyway. Her eyes were red again today, so it's possible she's off crying in the shredding room. She made a big fuss of coming in on Saturday and Sunday to 'catch up'. If she'd actually sit at her desk for longer than five minute shifts between panicking or wandering off with Rita, another team leader, then she wouldn't have to work at the weekend. Instead, she spends the day in a state of white-knuckled anxiety and then comes in on Saturday for a bit of 'peace and quiet'.

We do *not* get paid for working overtime or weekends. It is almost inconceivable that she has nothing better to do. Even I have better things to do (just don't ask what, I'm a rubbish liar). But she loves it. She loves doing things and then complaining about them, and then crying again. Meanwhile, I keep paddling along, trying not to suffocate. I feel ill every day: like I have a brain tumour, or cancer, or I'm going to have a heart attack. But no one would even notice if I dropped down dead. Probably not even me. If they did notice, they'd probably just stuff me in a cupboard and get on with it.

There is a letter opener in my drawer. What sort of person uses a letter opener? Maybe in some old film or something, but it's something that should never have been invented. The Dragons would tell you to hop it if you turned up in the Den wielding that. The letter opener looks a bit like a saw, utterly lethal, but deceptively so. I run it across my skin under the desk so The Capricorn can't see, but it's quite blunt, really. Still, I fantasise that it's really sharp. You could stab someone with it, probably. If you did it really hard it might be alright. In the eye would be your best bet.

I try stabbing my legs with it under the desk, trying to bury it deep into my upper thigh. It's rubbish, though, it's about as sharp as a rubber. I want it to go all the way through, and out the other side. Impale me.

The morning descends into platitudeville. Someone comes over with invoices and says, 'I can't keep away!' Someone else says 'You don't know you're born!' and ten people comment on the weather – it's raining. I grit my teeth and fake smile in the face of this relentless adversity.

The big *big* boss is called When Animals Attack. He comes over and says 'Ahoy there!' He always says this. I think about replying 'Hello, sailor!' but it probably wouldn't go down too well. The Martyr thinks When Animals Attack looks like Harrison Ford. Maybe after he's been buried for a month. I think he looks more like Robert Kilroy-Silk.

Sometimes When Animals Attack says, 'Hello troops!' which is just as irritating in its own special way. He is the boss of all the other bosses, but he tries to remain hip and funky by regaling us with stories of street-fighting as a youngster and how he really likes some awful pop music that his twelve-year-old lobotomised kid likes. Sometimes I walk off when I see him coming over because I can't face pretending. It hurts my face too much. I go and sit in the kitchen until he's passed, like someone dodging the ticket checker on the train.

An email pops up from Jim. We get on pretty well, in the same way you get on with your faintly annoying older brother. He thinks he's the last word in cool; I think he's the first letter in lame. I should be grateful he's here, really. Still, I'm not.

The email title is, **Look at this: it's a cracker!**

I double click and laugh as I see a picture of a Ritz cracker.

He smirks at me over my shoulder.

I think for a second and then Google image search a rocking horse. I send an email back to Jim saying, **Open this, it rocks!**

I'm already Googling spinning-tops for my next trick. A reply pops up. **This rules!**

Oh he's not gone for the ruler, I think. Too predictable.

I open it and there's a picture of the Queen. **You win!**

Bastard.

This feeling of sharing a joke and connecting does not last long. Kate comes over and looks at his screen. She obviously sees my name in his inbox, because she turns a bit nippy.

'Do you two do any work?' Then quieter, to him. 'You haven't emailed *me* this morning.' I am secretly amused. Kate's name isn't really Kate. I only discovered this recently; she changed it to an English name when she moved here from South Africa. Her lack of anchorage within her own culture, or respect for her own identity, astounds me. And now she's lost her surname, too. She's just Mrs Jim Townsend. Her old self completely annihilated. Perhaps that's when she had her personality removed, too.

'Are you coming to the meeting?' she asks me.

'What meeting?'

'You're your team's representative.'

'Am I?' Aren't I always?

I look to Jim. He shrugs.

Kate tries to herd me along to the glass-walled meeting room at the end of the open-plan, cardboard cut-out office. You can't even get a spot of privacy during a meeting in this place. It's really shocking.

'Let me get a pen...' I say, grabbing a notepad, too. At least let me doodle. At least give me that much, you android.

I slouch reluctantly down the corridor after her.

A few other unlucky freaks are assembled around the beech table in the meeting room, including Mr Happy from the call centre. I try not to catch his sinister, relentless eye. People cluck round, helping themselves to tea and coffee.

On each wall of the meeting room, is Blu-tacked a 'motivational' poster. Such a thing is obviously obscene and the enemy of all that is right. The one directly in front of me is of a bunch of penguins and says DETERMINATION in large letters. Underneath it says, 'The will to succeed can overcome the greatest adversity.' I wonder how much will to succeed penguins actually have. They just looked like ridiculous waddling, flapping cartoons to me.

I wonder about the kind of sick fucks who design motivational posters, but worse, the people who buy them and think they actually inspire.

What's the opposite of inspired?

Mr Happy asks a question and I'm forced to look at him out of courtesy. I note that he is seated under the ATTITUDE poster, which features a tiger striding moodily through some water, like a sultry male model in an aftershave ad. Apparently 'Attitude makes the difference.' This isn't worth pondering on for too long, I feel, although I try and make an anagram out of the sentence, which passes a few seconds before I give up. I'm not very good at Countdown.

What *is* the opposite of inspired? Defeated? Broken?

Kate starts writing things on the whiteboard. There is the obligatory pen-running-out moment and polite laughter. I start stabbing my notepad with my biro, then I realise this is actually quite loud, so I stop.

Kate says:

'Stop me if I'm using too much jargon.'

Kate says:

'Bear with me.'

Kate says:

24

My name used to be something else but I wiped out my own history to fit in. I'm soulless. I'm a sell out.

I notice Kate is standing under ACHIEVEMENT. This has a fucking polar bear on it. What did a polar bear ever achieve bar almost getting itself extinct due to global warming? I don't see it putting a stop to that. Not them, nor their determined penguin neighbours. Not in the face of our almighty carbon footprint, motherfuckers.

Just thinking the words 'carbon footprint' makes me want to choke myself to death.

ACHIEVEMENT lies: 'Believe in yourself and anything is possible.'

I imagine a poster saying TRITE with Kate's face on it. I imagine posters saying DIAL A CLICHÉ and GO FUCK YOURSELF. Or better still, simply: DIE. More effective. I could be on that one.

Mine would say underneath, 'Spending your life in an office is unimaginative.'

Mine would say, 'Is this really what you wanted?'

Mine would say, 'Run for your life.'

The other poster says, SUCCESS.

Kate does that fucking inverted commas thing with her fingers.

Kate uses the word 'bespoke'. I hate this word, despite not being entirely sure of what it means.

Kate says, 'We're not reinventing the wheel here,' and I try not to throw up.

I am finding this meeting *challenging*.

I'm Not Being Funny, but... is a freakish

busybody at the best of times, and asks loads of stupid fucking questions, which extends the meeting beyond all conceivable belief. She is from Northern Ireland, and her accent makes me want to car-bomb myself.

I draw something that ends up looking slightly vaginal (hello, Freud) and cover it up by making it look like a bug sitting on a deckchair. I'm quite pleased with it. I notice Mr Happy has doodled Pac-Man on his own pad, and feel relieved. Doodling implies you do have a soul, some creative inner part of you. Something I could cling to, if the walls fell in on us right now, and we were trapped for days under the penguins and polar bears in the South Pole.

Kate moves her hands like a weathergirl, whilst I twitch in the corner, gnawing my fingers. If I ever see someone else biting their nails, I think they look like an animal. But I can't help it.

In solitary confinement, you can always escape into your head. They can't catch me in here. In my brain I can have sex, or write a poem, or go on holiday. I don't have to be here. They can't make me.

I always think that my face must give me away. Surely I'm not that good at acting?

I notice the only other thing on the wall apart from the posters is an acrylic orange circle suspended with steel wire. It looks like a clock, with no hands. How evil! It looks like it should be on the wall in McDonald's. But not the new fangled McDonald's, now they've made it all groovy and chi-chi. The orange and brown old-skool McDonald's. Before they brought in the hypocritical dietary advice.

Why am I so obsessed with *McDonald's*?!

I pour a glass of fizzy water, which I hate, but it's the only bottle near me, and I'm not standing up and drawing attention to myself. The reason I hate it is that I expect it to be lemonade or fizzy wine when the bubbles hit my tongue and then the pay-off is just nothingness. I pull a face as I swallow a mouthful. I should be used to a pay-off of nothingness, really.

Kate talks about 'intellectual capital' which apparently means 'people'. Why not just say 'people' and not sound like a cunt?

Kate says, 'Does anyone have any questions?' and escape is palpable. I give everyone the death stare.

'Right, we'll leave it there then. See you next month.'

If only it was that long.

When I get back, The Martyr is actually at her desk for once. The fire alarm goes off every Wednesday at 4pm. Every single time without fail The Martyr jumps like her chair has been directly doused with petrol. I have stopped telling her it's a test. She realises when it stops after 30 seconds.

The phone rings and I can tell it's her little daughter by the fact that all the warmth has been sucked from her voice. I can feel my stomach curling up like burning paper as they speak. Her mood swings startle me. A rep or contractor will come over and she will act like he's her childhood sweetheart come back from the dead. And it's not fake warmth, she actually responds to these men like they are old friends. Yet if her own daughter or son call, they get talked to like they're a distraction, a waste of time.

But actually it's something worse than that. I try not to think about it.

Down the other end of the office Bowser is moaning at people for having the heating on too hot in an area in which he doesn't even sit. I marvel at this. I can see everything from my desk. I can survey the whole stage.

But I'm just another speck of dust.

I get in the lift on my own at lunchtime; a lucky break. There are mirrors on three sides so I can't help but look. I feel like banging my head against the glass but I worry there's a camera in here. Unlikely, but you never know. So I just stare myself out. The reflection is cruel, but I know it tells the truth. My skin looks like tracing paper and my top makes me look like an escaped convict. I pull it down a bit over my belly, but it's like trying to hide a ferry behind a frog. And my hair won't stay straight. My hair is the consistency of tinsel. How could I even think that *he* would look twice at me?

Of course, I didn't think it.

The lift speaks. It says 'ground floor'. I don't reply. I can feel myself nearly running as I get to the revolving doors and disappear into a wheel of glass.

Thursday

Another day in dystopia.

I think I have Alzheimer's today. Alzheimer's or Parkinson's. My nervous system could fall apart at any point. I think about people with multiple sclerosis, or locked-in syndrome, struck down, trapped in their own bodies. I am selfish. I have my body, moving arms and legs. How come it's always the people in wheelchairs who find the strength to become great athletes whilst able-bodied people sit rotting on sofas? That's irony, Alanis, not those 10,000 stupid spoons.

The lights above my desk are too bright; I stare at them sometimes just to feel something different to nothing. It is never winter or summer here, the temperature alternates between freezing and boiling at the touch of a switch, but it's never just right. As soon as the doors lock behind me I am in this strange eco-system, a guinea pig in this false glare.

There are grey rectangles everywhere, the lights, my computer screen, the filing cabinets, my telephone; like paving slabs over my body. The whole office is pixelated like a computer screen. Would I feel differently if everything was purple and round?

Bowser won't shut up today. He is in charge of the call centre down the far end of the office. He is Australian, which means his voice is annoying at any volume, and he lollops round, bald head shining, knuckles dragging on the ground, stopping only to administer orders. He had a 'quiet word' with Clint this morning because he was late, but Clint answers to The Toad, not to Bowser. The Toad said nothing, but I suspect she was secretly fuming. Bowser keeps staring at me because The Martyr is in late and he is clearly fretting that I am sitting here slacking off, which I am. But he can't see my screen. It is a small victory for me. I win this battle.

Jim is eating a packet of crisps. It sounds like he is eating a bag of ice. My hackles rise, then fall.

I spend the rest of the morning scanning things and then stamping them. I can't be bothered to rotate the pictures on the viewer so I spend half the time with my head cocked to one side, so much so my neck hurts. I enjoy stamping the paper. I stamp hard. I like the way the stamp spins round like an acrobat from its pool of ink. It waits upside down, undisturbed, then tumbles round to spell out URGENT in big red letters. I like the contrast of the red on the white. I like disturbing the balance.

I notice the stamper is called 'Sprinty'. This seems far too jaunty a name for such a serious stamp. I don't like it.

When Animals Attack comes over. He has the sense of humour – and looks, come to think of it – of a police sergeant. The Martyr is in at last and plies him with Viscounts and Hob Nobs. It's sad to see her bow and scrape. I can't imagine actually being in fear of losing my job. What a strange sensation that must be. I'm always hopeful I might lose it at any given time.

'Comrades!' When Animals Attack declares. 'Viva la revolution!'

I try not to look too embarrassed for him. He blusters on. 'You don't know about the 70s and the revolution, do you?'

'Not at this time of the morning,' I reply. It's the nicest thing I can think of to say.

'Not at any time!' He says cheerfully and wanders off.

I never really understood the notion that you have to treat some people with more respect because of their position of power. I treat everyone with an equal level of respect.

None.

No, that's not true; I treat all people equally. I treat them like they treat me. It is tiring wishing this much death on people.

Once the coast is clear Kate comes over to ask if I want to go to lunch with her. I don't, but as she's still giving me a lift in the mornings, I feel obliged to grease the wheels (literally). Kate frightens me. She seems to have no natural curiosity about other human beings; she doesn't like music or art or jokes. Sometimes I think it's a cultural difference as she's South African, but that seems unfair on cultured South Africans. After all, it would be unfair to judge the English nation after one meeting with me.

But probably not that far off.

She talks over the table in McDonald's about the wedding; their second in fact, as they've already married once over here as she needed a visa. Now they are marrying again in Johannesburg where her family are. I have no clue where they get the money for two weddings plus jet-setting, and I don't ask. I can feel her words floating past me like cigarette smoke. I feel guilty because I don't care about what she is saying, but then she's just talking *at* me, so what's the difference? She has never asked me one thing about myself in the whole time I've known her. And I'm not about to start telling her my life story voluntarily.

Besides, I don't have one.

When I first came to work here, she used to come over every five minutes and drape herself over Jim in case I was really slow and hadn't realised they were together. I didn't like to tell her I didn't fancy Northerners in their mid-thirties with beer bellies, bad manners and attention-deficit disorder. Bless her for thinking he was a catch. Well, he was of course, for her, as she needed that visa.

Oh, cynical me. Naughty me.

Kate goes on about some DIY programme she watched last night. Kate talks about getting a mortgage in London with a frown on her forehead because of house prices. Kate talks about low-fat diets. I want to tell her I don't care. I want to tell her that the McDonald's salad is saltier and fattier than a Big Mac. I want to tell her that at 21 she shouldn't be married, not even for love, or a visa.

Yet they do seem in love, some comfortable, controlling love. So who am I to say anything? What the fuck do I know?

I wonder what Kate's life was like in South Africa. She doesn't understand many of our cultural references. She didn't know who Jarvis Cocker is, she doesn't think of Gordon the Gopher when she sees Phillip Schofield on TV. She missed Byker Grove, Madchester and grunge. But she must have her head filled with her own junk. She must have stories. So why does she never tell them? She speaks perfect English. She isn't stupid.

When they'd come back from their first holiday together there – Jim's chance to 'to meet the parents' – they'd shown me photos of monkeys with their noses pressed up to window ledges, and lions in the wide open space behind their hotel. There was something magical in the world Kate came from. But it was like she'd left her soul behind. I always thought it must have taken such guts to get here. Such bravery. To cross the world alone and seek out something new, headhunt an Englishman, even if it was Jim.

I feel scared catching the bus. I feel paranoid getting the paper; frightened when the phone rings.

Yet I can never truly admire her. She is such an android.

When I get back from lunch The Capricorn turns to me solemnly. She points in the direction of The Martyr's empty chair.

'Signed off with stress.'

It is not even a whole sentence but it is heavy with meaning.

'She was fine earlier, plying the higher powers with biscuits.' I take my jacket off.

'She started crying just after you went out,' Jim says. 'I had to go read the newspaper in the toilet to avoid it.'

'What a Samaritan. How long will she be off?' I ask, eyeing up the Kilimanjaro of invoices on her desk.

'No one knows.'

'Fuck this,' Jim says. 'I'm not doing all her work for her.'

'We already *do* do all her work for her,' I point out.

'They said they might get a temp in.' The Capricorn divulges.

Who are 'they'? How does *she* know? It's a mystery.

'Great,' I say. 'You have to spend three days showing them how to do everything.'

'Yeah but they could be fit,' Jim points out, with a nervous glance towards Kate's desk.

'I doubt it,' I say as the fire alarm goes off like a nuclear bomb.

'Shit, it's that fucking drill,' Jim says. It's a real drill this time, not just a test. 'I'm just microwaving my lunch.'

'Regular Jamie Oliver, aren't you?' I pick up my bag. We file downstairs.

I don't get the point in a fire drill where they warn you via emails and posters everywhere of the time and date of it. Surely the test is how well we react to the surprise? Plus the fake ones lull you into a false sense of security. I imagine a future where the building burns to the ground whilst we sit at our desks saying 'It's just a test!'

I wish it was a real fire. Some pyromania would liven up the day nicely.

We congregate on the green by our office. It's almost summer but it's not been a warm spring. I pull my coat round me, stroking the synthetic fur on the sleeves for comfort. I scour the mass of faces for want of something to do and suddenly *he* is there. He is wearing a black jacket and he has on that red zip-up top underneath. He is so thin he looks like I would break him, but this is part of the appeal. He is something beautiful and delicate in this battery farm for the brain. He is sideways on to me, chatting easily with someone, smoking a cigarette. Every smoker in the office has lit up. It's an impromptu opportunity to take a lung-cancer lottery ticket, and too good to be missed.

'This is such a waste of time, it's bloody freezing out here,' The Capricorn moans over my shoulder, but I am miles away as he turns and glances up in my direction. He sees me and mouths 'hi', then takes another drag on his cigarette. I raise my hand in a half-wave, terrified it doesn't look right, terrified he can read my mind from ten feet away. Then he turns back to his conversation, and I am left stranded, totally exposed.

I'm two minutes late again and sit down with a thud. I have put on red lipstick today in an act of daring. I will probably have wiped it off by lunchtime.

'Right,' The Capricorn says. 'Lipstick.'

'Yes,' I reply. 'It is.'

Jim's computer isn't working today and he is on the floor trying to fix it. He tells me he has already spoken to the IT department who sit just across the way and they have told him that they have no one available to come and look at it. Yes, that's our IT department. They suggest checking if the power cables at the back have fallen out. Genius. Jim is *rotund* and looks pretty undignified scrabbling on the floor. Yesterday The Capricorn said to him, 'You eat a lot' which made me laugh.

It's funnier when I'm not the one on the receiving end.

Jim goes to get a sandwich and when he comes back The Capricorn says, 'Are you eating already?' She says this without any hint of a smile. I find it less funny today. It's becoming like The Toad's bullying – wearing. I can tell Jim takes offence.

Jim doesn't really know how to take The Capricorn. She never laughs at his bad jokes; she doesn't get anything. She just sits eating her soulless dried fruit and her partially-hydrated apricots. I never comment on how she reminds me of a shrivelled-up raisin. I'm too polite.

'Why don't you call Un-Handy Andy?' I

suggest. He is our crow-faced repairman who never answers his phone.

'Already tried him.' Jim says. 'Voicemail.'

Jim pleads with IT again and they tell him to swap his power cable with The Martyr's and see if that works. Unfortunately, this kills both his and The Martyr's computer. Fortunately, The Martyr is still off sick with stress.

Jim goes off in a strop, presumably to stuff his face again, in the relative privacy of the kitchen.

The envelope icon pops up at the bottom right of my screen. Normally it's bad news; complaints, queries, jobs to do. But I hate not knowing, so I have to check. It's compulsive.

It is *him*. The Fit Guy.

I look over my shoulder to check that no one is behind me. I want to savour this moment. Even if it's just a circular.

It says:

Please call Mrs Sweeney on 0207 946 0999.

PS: Did you have good weekend?
Patrick

I read it again. And again. In the distance I can hear When Animals Attack's laughter going off like a machine gun but it's not bothering me. *He* knows I exist.

Patrick.

I close my eyes. What shall I do? Shall I ring Mrs Sweeney? Shall I reply? Shall I wait? Why does he care about my weekend? How does he know who I am?

I get up and go to the toilet to try and assemble my thoughts. I stand by the sinks, looking into the mirror. My lipstick *does* look horrible. I wipe it off with a tissue, the red looking like blood next to my white skin. It reminds me of *that*, and I feel tempted, but push the thought down. This is not the right time. Besides, twice this week already. Bad.

My God, he only asked if I had a good weekend! I feel like slapping myself. I'm hysterical. I splash some water on my face. I look like I've been kissing someone because my lipstick hasn't quite come off. I rub at my mouth again. My hair is wavy and greasy and I just look hideous. How can he even care what I did at the weekend? Like he does anyway, he was just being civil...

I go into my favourite cubicle and lock the door. I stare at the green sides, the pebbledash effect of the plastic. I can't work out what colour green it is and it bothers me. It's not apple, it's not mint, it's not teal. I am thinking about it every time I come in here now. Green, green, green. It's driving me mad. I breathe in and out. In and out. Everything is OK. Everything is OK.

Someone else comes in and goes into the next cubicle, and I cough to make sure they know I'm there, so they don't start doing something disgusting and forcing me to listen. I flush the toilet even though I haven't been. I run the tap at the sink as well.

I make my way back to my desk. And suddenly *he* is there. Patrick is there, by the filing cabinets. He is a few feet away and hasn't seen me. This is sensory overload. He needs to stay up on his floor! I can't cope with this. Oh my God, why have I just wiped my lipstick off? Now I look like I've just been sucking cock or eating a burger and I don't know which is worse. I go over to the fax machine to hide. I can't face him now. Not before I've replied to the email. God, normally I'd be happy to see him down here, but now it's freaking me out.

The Capricorn comes over to the fax machine. She shakes her head at me as if she can read my mind. I try and look innocent. She can't read my mind, can she?

Patrick walks past and back up to his floor but he doesn't look my way.

I breathe out.

'There goes The Rat,' says The Capricorn.

'What?'

'Ratty. Look at him, he looks like a rat.' She scowls slightly, looking pretty rodenty herself.

'Who?' I can't compute that she is talking about Patrick.

'That fella. In the red top. Patrick is it? Ratrick, more like.'

'Ratrick' is not bad for The Capricorn, but still I'm furious. I wonder what my face must look like. I want to say, *'He looks nothing like a fucking rat, you uptight, repressed, food-obsessed curtain-rod of a human being,'* but any sign of weakness and The Capricorn will strike. If I show her that I like him, then that will be the end of my life here. I will end up hating him because she will use him as a net to catch me with. I say nothing. She puts her fax in the machine and forgets I'm there. I stalk off, a strange mixture of anger, pride and confusion inside me.

When I get back to my desk Mitesh and Clint

are having one of their bullshit conversations about 'issues'. Their tin-pot theories and tired clichés of ideas are mostly just faintly embarrassing but occasionally cringeworthy. They make the Loose Women look like intellectual heavyweights. I try and switch my brain off in the face of such crushing pointlessness.

I open Patrick's email and type in the reply:

It was OK, pretty boring. Couldn't wait to get back to work! ;-)

Are you full time or temporary, by the way?

I press send before I have time to talk myself out of it. I look at the clock. It's almost an hour since he emailed. Surely that is an acceptable amount of time to leave before replying. I re-read what I wrote with the intention of picking holes in it. I guess I did OK. Less is more. I wasn't overly flirty or friendly, no more so than he'd been? Was the wink a bad idea? Yes. God, what if he doesn't notice the wink and thinks I really couldn't wait to get back to work? Should I have said more about my weekend, and sold myself better? Almost certainly. I made myself sound like a boring hag with no friends. Which is true, but I don't want him to know that.

I close the box to stop the self-torture. Lemonade-light is pouring in through the window blinds and I could almost feel happy if I hadn't fucked up that email. I wonder if I should recall it. No, it's too late. It would look suspicious. I sit tight.

I go for lunch early as having a staring competition with my computer does not seem to encourage an envelope pop up again. I have finally used my initiative and brought some rolls from home so I just buy the newspaper and hide out in my car. Thank god it's back on the road and I am free from the horrors of lift-cadging. Sometimes I get paranoid about the battery running flat but I need music and I've forgotten my iPod. I figure the tape player must use more battery than the radio, so I listen to the radio for a while. The one DJ I like is on from 10am to 1pm on the indie station, and he has been playing my current favourite song every day this week, which is something of a miracle. He plays it again today. I take it as a good sign. I like this DJ a lot, he seems like someone I could be friends with, has the same taste in music as me. I wonder idly what he looks like, but this makes me think of The Capricorn saying Patrick looked like a rat. I feel scared again and switch the radio off.

I try and act casual as I make my way back to my desk. My screensaver has kicked in and pink letters scroll across my monitor declaring, I AM A ROBOT. I really wanted to write, FUCK OFF but it probably wouldn't go down too well. Plus it's childish.

I unlock my desktop. An envelope sits in the corner, tiny yet potentially explosive. I click.

It's a circular about petrol expenses.

The afternoon crawls. False alarm after false alarm rolls in to taunt me. I hate that envelope, but not as much as that fucking Microsoft paperclip assistant twat. No, I don't want your help, fuck off. I go to the toilet again but I'm out of razor blades and that green paint issue is still bothering me. It's an unnatural green, but it's not like a gaudy, showy green. I know I will think of the exact shade eventually, but until then it's going to ruin my life. I have a headache just thinking about it.

On the whole, though, I enjoy the anonymity of the toilet. It's easy to freak out and think everyone knows you're in there, but I remind myself you can't even see the shoes of the person in the adjoining cubicle. Sometimes I hold my breath until they go. Other times I have to get up and leave myself.

I get claustrophobic sometimes. I change my mind all the time about what's acceptable. I contradict myself and forget what I even like or don't like. I know the 'don't like' list is a lot bigger.

The toilets have a big window and I can see Wembley Stadium from beside the sinks. We are right on its doorstep. It just looked like a lot of cranes and scaffolding for so long, but now as it gets closer to being fully formed, it is still as ugly as fuck. It was truly the opposite of beautiful architecture, like a big scratch against the horizon, a giant toenail clipping.

There is a panoramic view of the sky and the sun is setting; sizzling orange light is reflected on the side of Allied Carpets. Why do humans design and create such crap? It just makes nature look even more superior. Why do we bulldoze through everything beautiful just to sell carpets or play football?

Oh, I'm like, so *profound*.

I look back at the mirror and pull a hair out of my head. It feels really, unexpectedly good. I size another one up, from the very front and pull. It hurts quite a bit but I like it. If someone comes in, I'll just pretend I'm doing my hair. See, I already have an alibi sorted. I feel in control again. I pull out another one and another one. I can see a drop of blood on my scalp at the very front. The pain is really sharp, quite out of proportion with these tiny strands of hair. I realise I should stop. I can't go over the top with this. It's just a mild diversion and besides... I need to save some for later.

I go back to my desk. Our printer has been moved 'in case it gives us cancer': no mention of all the years before when we were sitting right next to it. Why would they invent a printer that dangerous, anyway? What about printers in the 80s? If printers give you cancer, what must microwaves do? What about those house-brick size mobile phones back in the day?

Anyway, the printer is still within earshot but since it's been moved, something has obviously become jarred inside, as it's started making a noise like a hamster in a squeaky wheel every time a piece of paper goes through it. I can see the pained expressions on faces around me at the rate of about 10 pieces of paper per minute.

The afternoon slides away along with my hope. He doesn't reply.

Monday

I am running late today so I jump the fence and cut through the car park. Rats roost in the bushes at the sides. I always hope it's a bird when I hear movement but it's too loud, too clumsy, more thumping than fluttery. Plus, I've seen three of them, fat and hurried. I wonder if in twenty years time rats will roam as freely as pigeons. We are filthy fucking pigs. How could we stop them?

I can see there are men cleaning the building today, they are abseiling down the side and polishing the brown glass, which is seven floors high. The building looks very 70s from outside. It's funny how taste in architecture changes so rapidly, yet buildings can stand there indefinitely, a concrete eyesore, defying fashion.

I wonder how much you get paid to abseil down office blocks cleaning the windows. Probably not much. I wonder if the men are good-looking. The one on the far side looks about 80 from here, so I hope he's got good insurance.

I wonder about Patrick. I wonder if he will reply today.

Because I am running five minutes late and am the unluckiest girl in the world, When Animals Attack catches me at the door. He says nothing but gives me a look. No 'ahoy there' for me today – oh well, I'll get over it.

I get to my desk and take my coat off. The Martyr is not back in. I can only imagine the horror going on at her house. Probably there's nothing. She *might* just be faking it.

The Capricorn says, 'I've never seen that skirt before.' I've had this skirt around five years and probably wear it to work two days a week.

I say, 'I always wear it.'

She looks at me completely incredulous. 'No!' she says, as if I've just told her I'm breeding a superhuman race at the weekends.

Silly me to assume I know what I'm putting on in the mornings. I can't even be bothered to argue the point. I just wish she wouldn't make the point in the first place. I can feel the skin on my back crawling to get off of it. If I could just become bones in no clothes – would that suit her better?

Bowser comes over on the scrounge. I wish The Martyr wouldn't buy biscuits, it only encourages all of them, like leaving crumbs out for a mouse. However, as she's not here the tin is empty, so he lollops off, his mission thwarted.

The Toad's mobile phone rings. It makes me jump every time. It is very bizarre, like the noise of a cat meowing followed by what sounds like a trickle of water. Her ringtone sounds like a *cat being drowned*. I try and work out one single reason why anyone would want to listen to this on a regular basis. I can't. I'm baffled. It unsettles The Capricorn too, I can tell. She peers over the boards, her glasses pinched down the end of her nose. The Toad is shuffling around, looking for someone to get annoyed with. The very act of breathing ironically leaves her out of breath. Every footstep is a struggle to survive.

At lunchtime I buy a bag of chips and sit eating them in my car, my fortress against the world. I used to eat in the toilet cubicle at school;

the thought disgusts me now.

In my car I'm protected from all the rats, human and vermin. I love the silence of it and the open window letting in a breeze by my ear. It's getting warmer, but is not too hot yet. People come and go and get in their cars and drive off but they rarely see me. I shrink down in my seat just in case they think I'm weird and wonder why I'm not in the kitchen eating. No one else sits in their car to eat. No one that I've ever seen. They get things out of their car, or get in their car, and go. They don't sit waiting, like me.

I'm just a few feet away from that zoo but I could be on the moon. It's so peaceful.

I suddenly think; I need to stop cutting, I can do it, I can get a new job. But I am terrified. Drowning seems preferable to learning how to swim again.

I once knew a girl who was anorexic. Now that was real self-harm. Disappearing from view. True anonymity. It wasn't an illness – more like a design flaw. Just like alcoholism. Just like any addiction. You don't fall sick from these things, catch them like the flu, or contract them like a virus. They are just worms inside you, waiting to escape. They are just holes inside you, waiting to be filled or emptied. We don't choose them – they chose us.

No, not me.

Cutting yourself isn't really as bad as that, I swear. It's more recreational, more of a hobby. I am in control, not the wound. Not the blade.

Honestly.

Coming back from lunch I can see a new face in our department. Sitting in The Martyr's chair is the visual antithesis of our boss, a short, pretty woman of about 30 with blonde hair and enormous boobs. I don't normally notice that sort of thing, so they must be particularly noticeable. She smiles at me as I come over.

'Hello! I'm Amy.' She tips me a wink. 'I hear you're the one who does all the hard work around here.'

'Well, I'm the only one who can speak English,' I reply, putting my bag down. The Capricorn is not amused. I hold my hand out and Amy shakes it. It is probably the warmest gesture I've been on the end of in six months.

'So how do you take your tea? I hear this strapping lad likes his sugary.' She pats Jim on the back and I instinctively look up at Kate. She is glowering in our direction and my heart soars. Jim looks starry-eyed, his eye line drawn to Amy's impressive cleavage. 'And herbal for this young lady.' She gestures to a sour-faced Capricorn.

'Um, milk, one sugar for me, thanks,' I say, and she bounds off to the kitchen.

'She seems alright,' I remark.

The Capricorn shrugs. 'She's not a manager.'

'Well we don't *need* a manager.' I point out. 'We just need the pair of hands. We manage ourselves, don't we?'

'She's cute,' Jim says, very, very quietly.

Annoying The Capricorn and Kate in her first five minutes? It worked for me.

Then a dangerous thought flashes through my mind – could she be an *ally*?

Two minutes later she is back, defying nature by holding four mugs in two small hands.

47

She surveys the scene. 'So, what needs doing?'

'What doesn't?' I say.

She waves a hand. 'I've seen worse. It's cool. They called me Spongebob at my old job I was so keen.'

If she's Spongebob, does that make me Squidward? No... that would be The Capricorn, for sure. And Jim was definitely Patrick the retarded starfish. Wow, someone mentioned a TV show that I like.

I get back to work, whilst Jim turns on the charm. 'So where you from, Amy? Why are you temping?'

'Well, I grew up in England mostly, but my Dad is Australian, he's been back in Oz about ten years. So I've been saving and my boyfriend and I are going out there for a year as of next month. Until then I'm just turning tricks to pay the bills.'

Jim laughs. 'You're lucky! That's the trip of a lifetime.'

I think: somewhere now there are people in Australia sitting on a beach. Laughing. Socialising. The sun is out and they are happy. They are probably having barbecues.

This girl is everything I'm not. She's alive and doing something with her life. She has hopes and dreams and gets on with people instantly. I feel like I'm a new starter every day. Never allowing my personality to develop. This is what the life of a temp must be like all the time; this gnawing insecurity, forced politeness, feeling stupid all the time, going from place to place to place and not being a part of anything, not knowing anything.

But she is not like that.

So, how did I end up this way, I wonder, and my chest feels so fucking tight.

'Tell me about it, I can't wait. I'm going to be eating kangaroos and drinking Fosters the second I hit Melbourne, visiting the Neighbours set, all that shit.' she jokes, laughing. The Capricorn looks like she has no idea what Neighbours is.

'So how long have you guys worked here?' Amy asks innocently, and I am ashamed.

I feel ashamed I ever came back after day one.

'Three years off and on, I'm an actor,' Jim says, and then he's launching into his spiel; he's off on one, and I am saved.

<u>Tuesday</u>

I forget about Amy until I arrive at work, and then she is there again, bright-eyed and bushy-tailed, yet like Spongebob, somehow not annoying. She does not give you the standard TV-presenter smile. It is weird how with some people you just *know*, they just fit with you, they are just normal. But it happens so rarely, you forget it's even possible.

She has already made a dent in The Martyr's paperwork.

Kate comes over to do her territorial pissing. She sits on the arm of Jim's chair, stroking his hair.

'Kate, this is Amy, Amy, this is Kate, Jim's girlfriend.' I say.

Kate stops to pick her eyeballs up off the floor.

'*Wife*!' she squeals and I laugh. No kidding.

'Oh, are you guys together?' Amy says, leaning forwards. I think of the cleavage view Kate *and* Jim must be getting. 'I hadn't realised!'

Unfortunately Kate doesn't understand sarcasm. I can see a heat rash breaking out from under her M&S polo-neck. No, turtle-neck.

'Well, now you know. We're *married*.' she says, primly.

'Wow, do people still get married these days? That's cute. I'm going to Oz with the the money you spent on sausages-on-sticks.'

I imagine Amy's boyfriend as some chiselled model-type, some bronzed, long-haired cutie. Then I look at Jim, marshmallow for both body and brains. He is utterly oblivious to the verbal sparring going on around him.

Kate sidles away, fur on end.

Amy smiles at me, and something is silently exchanged. This second of clarity is swiftly ruined as The Capricorn announces she is on a diet.

'But you don't *eat* anything,' I reason with her.

'But everything I *do* eat is junk,' she says, pointedly. I look at the Tupperware tub full of an unidentifiable green mush on her desk. I decide to quit whilst I'm ahead.

An envelope pops up.

It's Patrick.

He is replying to the question I asked him last week.

I'm full time but feel very temporary. I will be searching the jobs pages tonight hoping to come across one of those fun, rewarding and fantastically well paid jobs that we know don't exist. I wish I'd done something decent for my degree. I was going to do creative writing as part of my degree but I woke up late, the course was full and I ended up studying Icelandic Myth and Saga instead – I don't regret it though since it was obviously the more practical choice! ;-)

It took him *three working days* to reply.

Well, he might have been busy. And he did do a winky face.

I read the email again. Icelandic Myth and Saga? What the fuck? It sounded so wrong yet so mysterious. No wonder he ended up working here. I feel like replying, 'no wonder you ended up working here' but I feel that won't go down too well. I have to play this from the head, but not be a smart arse, like usual. I like the email. He seems witty and clever. That's attractive. Mind you, I liked him mute, too. I like him any way, really.

I decide not to reply for now. The ball is on my side. But it makes me sweat to play such games. I probably won't hold out for long.

A new guy has started in The Toad's department filling the last empty space. I don't know what his name is. He looks like Penfold and he's wearing a tie. He says 'sweet as' a lot, which is an offence punishable by death in my book, and something no English person would say. I'm not racist, just misanthropic. I hate all citizens of all races equally.

When Animals Attack comes over to introduce himself to Amy and Penfold, and launches into another dull story about running a hundred million miles per night and not breaking into a sweat or whatever. He's so braggy, especially for an old man. I find it very childish. Oh well, running is probably my favourite subject of his to bore us with. It beats the church or the 'good old days'. He has started saying 'Ding dong!' a lot, like fucking James Hewitt, too. Argh!

'What the fuck was *that* about?' Amy asks me after he goes. I shake my head.

'Mid-life crisis.'

I have lunch in McDonald's again. I'm trying to limit it to once a week. I'm unimpressed by the supposedly 'healthy' menu and opt for a chicken sandwich and large fries. I don't need to try and look decent anyway. He's never going to fancy me.

I can't help but think, Amy will be gone soon, and The Martyr will be back and that's that.

That's that.

I am feeling quite dizzy today and my eyes are playing up. I keep thinking things are wet when they're not. I think I've taken too many of my pills; either that or not enough. They aren't working, either way.

The McDonald's probably isn't going to help matters. I look up whilst I'm eating and Ronald McDonald is laughing at me, the sinister bastard. Creepy fucking paedo. I leave soon after.

I don't feel like working in the afternoon. Depression has gripped me and won't let go. I feel like an escape artist who's fucked up, and now I'm just drowning, whilst the audience waits, clapping and whooping. There's a breezeblock pushing on my chest. Didn't Houdini die from a botched test of his strength, a failed final show off? I don't even have a trick to go wrong.

I remember my first day at work; thinking, 'well, this job won't be for long, just until I find something better.' That was *three years ago*, and I haven't even had a fucking pay rise since. It was like time stopped that day, life went on pause, but I am still ageing; the fossil fuels are still running out, bit by bit. My skin is sagging, my eggs are depleting, my arteries narrowing. The world is heating up, the sun is dying.

Amy has gone home, she's on a half-day. The life of a temp. I can only dream.

I want to do it.

Don't do it.

I want to. I want to do it so bad.

It's been a week.

I lean under my desk and rummage in my bag. I can hear the rattle of my tablets and I think of them there, safe in their little pot, orange diamonds. I'm nearly out again. But that's not what I'm looking for, that's for later, if at all. I can take them or leave them. Sometimes I do. Mostly I don't.

I find my tin in the inside pocket of my bag and open it under the desk. I slide the packet of razors up my sleeve, remembering there's only one left. No point taking the whole box.

No one is looking at me as I sneak towards the toilet.

I'm Not Being Funny, but... walks out as I walk in. She makes me jump, and I feel the razor slip out from inside my sleeve, escaping from the sanctuary of my clothes.

I have to force myself not to look. I imagine it tumbling to the ground in slow motion, elegant as a space shuttle.

5

4

3

2

1

She hasn't seen. She hasn't seen.

Please God. Don't let her see.

She walks past, nose in the air, oblivious.

I look behind me then, at the floor. My razor blade is lying in a pile of dust and fluff, unclean. I pick it up, careful not to cut myself, aware of the irony. But I'm a not a pervert, I don't get off on accidental paper cuts or accidentally banging my head. I'm not a masochist.

Then it is just me and the doors, me and the cubicles. I walk into my favourite and flick the razor into the sanitary bin because I can't use it now, it's unclean, impure.

I've failed and I'm disappointed, but I don't feel disappointment, I feel this rage building up behind my eyes; why can't I do anything right? I can't even keep a fucking razor blade up my sleeve. What if Jim had seen? What if When Animals Attack had seen? I'm a fucking idiot, a moron. I put my palms to my eyes and I can feel the back of my throat clogging up with tears, making me gag. I hate myself for being so weak. This is what they want, to destroy me.

I sink onto the floor of the cubicle, not caring now if someone comes in and sees the sole of my foot poking out. Maybe someone will come in, at last, and hear me, and care, and save me; just gather me up and make things OK.

Surely.

But they don't, and now I have no razor, and just a toilet for company. I feel along the edge of the porcelain, under the white plastic seat, gripping the coldness, hugging nothing, not caring if the porcelain is clean, or dirty. Then, without thinking, I lift up the seat and slam it down on my fingers. I almost don't feel it the first time, so I do it again, banging my other fist down on top of it to make sure.

And then – there it is – the pain. I hear myself moan but it isn't agony, it feels more like a high. I bang it down again and again and again, and it feels like euphoria, like some twisted happiness, something that alienates me from the rest of the world, but makes me never need anyone either.

It's not an accident: it's a decision.

I lift it, up and up, down and down, and under the white blur I can see my knuckles starting to bleed but I just carry on and on because feeling like this is the only time I ever feel anything.

After a while I realise I've stopped, but I also feel like I disappeared for a bit, like my head went somewhere else. The office could be in Istanbul. I could be in space. I realise I am hanging onto the toilet bowl and suddenly this seems disgusting. I try and move my hand and my fingers are stiff. There is blood running down the inside of the toilet. What the fuck have I done? The first rule of – this – is leave no trace. No trace that they can see anyway.

Only a path that I can follow.

I try and stand up, and I leave a bloody smudge on the green paint of the wall. I feel dizzy but my hand is not hurting, not yet. I pull off some toilet paper and wrap it up loosely. I flush the toilet to pretend I've been in case someone has come in and I haven't heard. I suddenly want to get out of that toilet cubicle faster than if it was a burning building.

I pull back the door and go to the sinks. I don't even look in the mirror. I hold my hand under the cold water, watching it turn pink. It is quite calming, like that stuff they make you wash your mouth out with at the dentist. Is that stuff even pink, or does the blood from your mouth make it pink? No, it's pink.

I am lost in this reverie for a moment. What the fuck *is* that stuff?

'Steph?'

Out of the green Kate is now front of me; God knows where she came from. I instinctively cover my hand, but I'm too slow. 'I didn't see you come in,' I say.

'What happened?' she asks.

I shrink away from her. She is wearing that bright blue eye-shadow again. Peacock. Sea-breeze.

'Nothing, nothing, I just banged it on the door,' I say. I feel like a battered wife with my inadequate lie.

'It looks horrible! It looks like you've just punched someone...' she looks at me uncertainly, like I might punch her next.

'I haven't, honest,' I say, 'Not today.' I attempt a laugh. I hope she'll smile. She doesn't.

'Are you alright, Stephanie?' she asks, seriously. People don't say my name that often here. Now I am worried. She never acknowledges the fact that I might have feelings or blood. Now she has no choice, as she can see it, and I am torn between wondering if she's just doing her duty, or if there is some small fibre of her that is alert to the world, alert to me, to what I really am.

'Of course,' I say, unconvincingly. 'You know me.'

But she doesn't.

Wednesday

My car has had a relapse so again I'm indebted to Kate and Jim, an unwilling hostage being wheeled to work against my will. My bashed up hand has not been mentioned, but I've wrapped it in a soft bandage.

Kate used to be too scared to drive on English roads but recently she got brave. It's fifteen minutes up the road and about five miles per hour most mornings, so it's hardly Evel Knievel time. I imagine the wilds of South Africa are infinitely scarier than a couple of North London roundabouts. Mind you, I get scared walking to the shops.

In my car at least I can kill people.

'What do you think of that new girl?' Kate asks me, holding my gaze in the rear-view mirror. She doesn't want to know what *I* think. It's a challenge.

'She's pretty cool,' I say and Kate's nose wrinkles.

'I'd swap!' Jim says, meaning Amy for The Martyr I think, but Kate seems to take it as Amy for her and turns the radio up, which is always tuned to bloody groundhog-day Virgin. Soft rock purgatory.

When we stop they have to let me out due to child locks in the door. They don't have a child. It's just to keep me prisoner until we get to work, and then I'm someone else's. At least in real custody I might get solitary confinement.

Clint isn't in today. The Capricorn says, 'Where's Clint?' and Mitesh looks nervous. He does this weird shifty eye thing. The Capricorn doesn't notice such subtleties and bulldozers on. 'He's not in today?'

'He's *gone*,' Mitesh says. I know exactly what he means. I look at the back of The Toad's head, all knotty red hair extensions. I know she is listening.

The Capricorn doesn't get it. 'Will he be in tomorrow?'

'He's gone. Forever. For good.' Mitesh says, quietly. He loves the drama. I feel a surge of hatred for him. Clint didn't deserve to be a juicy bit of gossip. He has three kids to support, for fuck's sake.

The Capricorn doesn't know when to shut up. This is a conversation for when The Toad has waddled off, not whilst she's still sitting there. I can tell Mitesh is bursting to give us all the details. I hate him for not standing up for his friend against that fucking troll. I feel glad he is trapped in this dog-shit job, it's what he deserves for being so spineless.

Clint always said 'bless you' when I sneezed. I think that tells you a lot about a person. I realise suddenly why Penfold suddenly arrived on the scene. They replaced Clint before he'd even left? Charming.

Bowser comes over and tries his Nazi-dictatorship 'all Australians together' bullshit with Amy. Unfortunately for him, she doesn't bite.

'I'm English!' she declares proudly as his eyeballs jiggle in horror. 'Oz is great, but my heart is here. My mum brought me up. This is my blood.'

'You'll want to stay,' he says, certainly.

'Nah, I don't really like the men out there,' she says, straight-faced. 'I like a bit of culture.'

Bowser huffs and puffs and retreats and I love Amy for it. She really has nothing to lose here. No gun to her head.

At lunchtime the weather looks perfectly fine until I go outside, then the clouds have a tantrum, followed by a crying fit. I don't like umbrellas and my hood does fuck all so I'm forced to retreat inside with my bacon roll.

I walk into the kitchen and see Amy is sitting by the microwave eating a greasy kebab with her fingers. She waves to me and I go sit beside her.

'What *are* you eating?' I ask.

'It's yummy! Want some?' She waves her kebab-filled mitts dangerously close to my face. I recoil.

'No!' I say, too loud, and she starts laughing.

'You're kebabist!' she declares. 'This is the best junk food on earth.'

'If you're drunk off your face, maybe.' I say. 'And even then I'd rather eat veiny chicken.'

She pulls a face. 'That is wrong. What are you looking at?'

Patrick has just walked in with a guy from his department. I nod subtly. He doesn't see me. They sit at the table by the window with a large pizza box between them.

'Who is that?' Amy asks, then catches my look. 'Oh – like that is it?'

'*Shh!*' I can feel my cheeks going red. Amy is loving it.

'He's alright. So what you going to do about it?'

'Do?' The idea hadn't even occurred to me.

Amy lifts up her kebab and gives me a pitying look. Patrick doesn't look over. I eat my roll. We go back to our desks.

After lunch someone sprays air freshener round which makes me choke. We are not meant to eat at our desks but some people do. Open-plan is driving me mental. We used to be sat in teams, in rooms of our own. We didn't know how lucky we were.

The Capricorn has brought in a little plastic tub full of pins and paperclips. They are all black and red and the push-pins keep catching my eye. I keep sliding them back over to her side of the desk when she's not looking but they keep ending up in the middle again. I keep fantasising about sticking them in my skin but I'm trying to cut down, so to speak. Resist temptation.

The pins are making me edgy so I open a new email to Patrick. I can't think of anything to write without taking the mickey out of his weird degree or mentioning pizza. Then he'll think I've been stalking him.

Someone calls and I get distracted. After that I'm expecting a fax so I wander over to the machine. I can see Bowser's shiny bald head. They have put weird burgundy screens up around the managers' desks so we can't see what they are up to. It looks claustrophobic.

The fax machine is beeping away. My fax hasn't arrived. I idly rummage through the debris to the side of it and see his name. I touch it quickly. Why has this come down here? He's two floors up. I pick it up then put it back down again. My fax is coming through now. I pull it out

61

and quickly pick up Patrick's fax. I hide it under mine and walk to my desk trying to avoid eye contact with anyone.

I sit down and open up the empty box on screen with his name on. I write,

That sounds like an interesting degree! Creative writing sounds like fun too, but it's hard to think of ideas. By the way, I have just picked up a fax for you down here, do you want to come down and get it?

Oh shit, do I *want* him to come and get it?

I jump up and run to the toilet. Amy must think I'm schizophrenic. There's that green again, I almost got it yesterday and thought it was some kind of toothpastey shade. But it's still not right. I ignore it and go to the mirror.

Oh God, it's worse than I thought. I have a spot on my chin which I keep picking and now it's at scab stage but if I pick it again it's likely to bleed and leave an unsightly red hole. I can't put any more concealer on it, it looks warty enough as it is. I have dark circles under my eyes and my mascara is flaking off. My fringe looks greasy. There's not one good thing about my face and as for my body – urgh. I try and pretend it's not there. I will have to hide it under my desk. It's my only hope.

I hurry back to my computer, concerned he might have flown down the stairs. No. No reply and the fax is still there, peeking out under mine. Everything is OK. Jim asks to borrow my newspaper and takes it to the toilet with him. I have no words for how vile I think that is, especially at work. He really couldn't care less. It all washes over him, he exists solely in Jim-world. Normal rules of polite society do not apply.

An hour passes. I try not to look over my shoulder too much.

Another envelope appears. It's Patrick.

I'm sorry, I'm really busy. Could you fax the fax to me? Is that silly?

I could go up.

But I don't want to. And *he* doesn't want me to, or he would have suggested it. Unless he thinks it's too rude to suggest. Plus, the spot. I have a feeling I may have inadvertently picked it whilst waiting for him to reply. I touch my chin. The scab is gone. Urgh!

I rummage in my bag for a small mirror. Oh yes. Now there is just an angry red patch there, twice as big as the spot was. I slam the drawer shut. Shit! Well, I'm not going up anyway. Sod it. Sod him.

Calm down. He might really be busy, I tell myself. I spontaneously draw a small dinosaur on the corner of his fax. It looks crap. I have a plastic dinosaur on my computer monitor. It mocks me by looking much better than my attempt.

'Oh fuck it,' I mutter, getting up. I fax the paper through to him, feeling like a chance has just slipped through my fingers, and nothing can be done to retrieve it.

<u>Thursday</u>

There is an eerie calm in the office today. Everyone seems very quiet and depressed. I resent Penfold for the loss of Clint, even though it's not his fault. The Toad is to blame. The Toad is wearing an ill-advised, skin-tight, long-sleeved mini-dress type thing today. She once told us quite proudly she was seventeen stone, so you can imagine what this looks like. Like too many sausages stuffed into cheap nylon bags.

I wonder where Clint is now. He's probably watching Trisha or Jeremy Kyle (the eternal dilemma of the unemployed).

At lunchtime, I eat in a cheap chicken joint, just because I'm sick of McDonald's. It's hardly a Gillian McKeith rubber-stamped alternative, but what can you do? Once Jim and I searched the net and found a website dedicated to the fake plastic chicken shops that are the scourge of London, dotted like cancer from north to south. They must have sprung up insidiously one day like dry rot, and nothing could stop them. Nothing.

My favourite cheap chicken shop is JKFC. I actually saw that one with my own eyes. Jim's was from the website: Kent's Tuck-In Fried Chick Inn. We were speechless at that one. There should be ingenuity awards for that sort of punnage.

The one I'm eating in is pretty boring. Dixy Chicken. The chicken on the menu board looks happy as Larry, whoever he is. Stupid drugged-up bird. Doesn't he know we just want to trap him in a box smaller than a sheet of A4, pump him full of drugs, then eat him?

Future generations will consider us barbaric for our treatment of animals. In the meantime, we can just trudge on blindly, with our hands over our ears, pretending chickens are just born wrapped in cling film, or covered in breadcrumbs.

I plunge my fingers into the side of my halal-slaughtered, chicken-bleached lunch, dipped in saturated fat. This is just another form of self harm, isn't it? Another way to die slowly. Another way to poison myself. Another way to make myself ugly.

I think of The Capricorn with her seeds and salads. I find that as revolting as she finds this. Our minds are just programmed differently. She was brought up, I was – something.

So, she was going to live to 100. Bully for her. She can stare sourly at people in the old folks home for thirty years after I'm dead, dribbling down her top and having someone wipe her arse for her. Lucky thing. I'd rather go of a heart attack at 60. Or 50, I don't mind.

I stare at the menu. Here under a strip of filthy neon light – under the gaze of people whose parents' parents came here for a better life, and ended up with this – I feel strangely at home.

When I get back The Capricorn is drinking Lipton Iced Tea. Why the fuck would anyone want to drink cold tea out of either a can or plastic bottle? It is lunacy. Whoever thought that up must be either pissing themselves with laughter or homeless.

I have now got to the stage where I can guess how The Capricorn is going to react to any given situation. This is a blessing and a curse. I know for a fact she will disagree with every point I make, no matter how petty or trivial. I know that she will ask me something about work, say 'Are you sure?' and then check with someone else. I know that she will state the obvious and can guess what she will state the obvious about. I know she will stare at me every time I put lip-balm or Vaseline on my lips. In fact, she stares at me a lot of the time, like I'm some strange specimen in the zoo. It makes me nervous.

I pretend I don't notice.

I have to do the monthly mail merge today which takes forever. I print all the letters off for each of us. Jim and I went on a course to learn how to mail merge because we were sick of cutting and pasting addresses on. The Capricorn has not been on the mail merge course, but still thinks she knows better.

She says,

'Can you show me where my letter template is?'

'Why?' I ask. I'm doing it, as usual, so what does she need it for?

'I want to add a field so it changes the dates that we need to hear from them by.'

'But that is going to cause a whole load of hassle. If we just say the 1st of the month, it's a lot easier.'

Especially as I'm the one bloody doing it, I don't add.

Still she doesn't get it. She looks at me like I'm the thickest form of pond life. She makes me doubt my own mind with one laser glance.

'Listen,' I say, 'We used to do it that way, and it didn't make any difference. They still don't reply on time.' I have worked here considerably longer than her. I actually taught her *her job*! And The Spanish Slug who worked here before her. But of course, she has invented a million ways to 'improve' things. She brings in her own fucking plastic folders and different coloured document wallets just to spite me. She even uses a fucking fountain pen.

She is still looking at me.

'Listen, if you want to do it that way, you can do your own,' I finally say, not nastily at all. She finally retreats back to her desk/web.

'No, it doesn't matter, it doesn't matter,' she says, as if I've just murdered her baby. Amy shoots me a look.

I get on with printing the million and two letters.

I do The Capricorn's letters first. I always do hers first, mainly because she has a lot less than me, and also for a trial run, in case I cock them up. The date is coming off too high on hers and going into the pink header bit. Oops.

I hand her the letters. 'Sorry, the date's a bit wonky.'

She scowls at me. 'Don't worry, I will do my own next time.'

What planet is she on? She is going to create more work for herself because I am not up to her high standards? That's just weird! The two people who had her job before her used to be grateful when I did the mail merge. They used to be pleased they didn't have to bother! Fucking cow. Why is she always making me feel like there's something wrong with me?

It's her. Don't worry. It's her.

I have a headache today. The lights seem ten times brighter than normal. I watch my letters print out, one after another, one after another. I remember the thing about the printer giving you cancer, and stand extra close, just in case it's true.

Back at my desk, there's that little insidious envelope again, lined up innocently enough next to other assorted icons that don't get my hopes up and then dash them again. I click.

It's him.

He says,

Thanks for the fax, by the way. That was ever such a nice pony. Four stars.

Hmm. That sounds pretty sarcastic. I reply,

It was a dinosaur! But you know that, you are just being mean.

His reply is instant.

Four stars is not mean.

I type and send,

It is if it's out of ten.

He replies straight away. He's getting good at this.

Your average star rating system tends to work on a quintoratic scale, that is to say, it is normally out of five.

That is to say...

I frown. 'Quintoratic' sounds made up. I can't work out if he is being flirtingly cheeky with me or just being a twat. It's really hard to get his tone from the email. I feel totally unnerved and exposed. I feel like things are slipping out of my control. My gaze falls to The Capricorn's drawing pins and I look away again. I type,

Nice use of the word quintoratic, although I think you made it up as this is drawing a red line under it.

He replies,

Oh, I suppose Outlook knows everything now, does it?

Well that little fucking paperclip seems to think he does, I think. And so does Patrick.

He definitely sounds shitty. Or is he? I am perturbed. Have I pissed him off? I try to make amends. I type:

I can look it up on dictionary.com?

I type the word in. It says:

'*No entry found for quintoratic. Did you mean 'quadratic'?*'

I copy and paste this into an email. There is a minute's delay before he replies.

You didn't need to look it up.

Oh dear.

I reply,

It's probably an American dictionary or something. What's the matter?

He replies,

I just think it is funny that you checked a word that I was claiming defined the 'five star' rating system. Quintoratic indeed... clearly nonsense.

What the fuck? Is he patronising me now? Because he made up some dumb word? Suddenly all my feelings for him fizzle away like a dead sparkler crushed under a heel. Glowing away one second and completely cold the next.

Extinguished.

Oh my God, I realise. He's a *knob*!

I reply,

It's not my fault the evil paperclip man drew a red line under it. Perhaps if you'd done creative writing instead of Icelandic Myth and Saga you'd have a firmer grip on the English language.

He doesn't reply. I don't want him to. I sit stunned. The chatter and phones ringing around me haven't stopped, nothing has changed, but I have.

I have changed.

He called my dinosaur a fucking *pony*!

On the way home Kate starts to invite me round to dinner, and somehow this is worse than nothing, this seems like real potential horror. I'll have to feign death. Luckily Jim is going to band practice and he starts strumming his guitar loudly in the passenger seat so Kate and I can't talk. He plays The Smiths badly and Kate doesn't know who they are, but Kate doesn't know anything, so what's new?

'And when you want to live, how'd you start, where d'you go, who d'you need to know?' Jim sings, and it is less singing and more of a wail, but I can still mouth the words along, and it still hurts. So I press my face against the glass so they can't see me, and I can't see them.

<u>Friday</u>

I think about Patrick, but not too much. I preferred him more when he was mute after all. Ah well. Over before it even began. As usual. I don't feel disappointed because I expected him to disappoint.

Ok maybe I'm lying. But I just don't want to think about it right now. And you can't make me.

Amy is off making tea and The Capricorn grabs me to bear the bad news. The Martyr is better and coming back on Monday. Amy is out.

I knew it was coming but it still feels like a slap. A week has passed without The Martyr. Could anyone be less missed? Her desk is like a Mr Muscle advert. Everyone feels calmer, happier. Probably even the birds are singing happier songs in the trees nearby.

'Hey!' Amy greets me when she gets back. 'So it's my last day. You wanna go out for lunch?' She is asking me, not The Capricorn.

I am caught unaware. She wants to go to lunch with me? And I'm not immediately trying to think of an excuse... I feel a bit frightened, but mostly just... curious.

At lunchtime I suggest McDonald's because I'm broke and nutritionally sub-normal. Amy doesn't bat an eyelid, doesn't turn her nose up. She orders a large double quarter-pounder-with-cheese meal with a chocolate milkshake.

'KFC's my favourite shit joint.' she says as we sit. 'I heard the chemicals they pump the chickens with make your boobs bigger. I think the Colonel owes me a new bra.'

I laugh and we talk easily about music and TV and films. Culture is a subject firmly off the menu with the rest of the drones. She has actually heard of the bands and TV I like. She talks easily about her friends, and the places she goes out.

'I will really miss England,' she confides. 'But it's only a year. It will all still be waiting when I get back. All the dirt and shit weather and pasty indie boys and Coronation Street and fucking Ant and Dec and that Big Brother shit. None of it will miss me.' She pours a sachet of salt onto her tray and dips her chips in it. I do that too, but not in public, because I think people might think it's weird. Amy doesn't seem to care.

Already I don't want her to leave. But The Martyr must return. She hadn't died from stress. More's the pity.

Even if she had, Amy is a temp, and she is going to go to Australia to meet her long-lost dad, with her chiselled boyfriend.

And I am going nowhere.

Best not to think about it.

'So what do you think of everyone?' I ask her, as she sucks on her chocolate milkshake. 'You've done a full week. Dish the dirt.'

'Well, Kate's introduction was hilarious...' she says. 'I knew the second I clocked her she was with Jim and she's hanging onto him like a fucking boa constrictor.'

'She really sucks the life out of me,' I admit. 'Jim's pretty funny. I don't know what he sees in her.'

'She's a ball-breaker, he has no choice in the matter, mate. Trouble is, if you hang on that tight, they eventually choke.'

It is such a relief to hear my own feelings about someone reflected back. To know I'm not going mad. That it isn't just me. It's *them*. I can feel myself pushing upwards, out of the mire.

'As for Ms Green Tea with her fucking locust stuck to her monitor. Shit. She is *seriously* uptight. A week of that is one thing. You're stuck with it! That mail merge thing was a joke.'

Another surge of joy. And I want to tell Amy all about my name for her; 'The Capricorn', but I'm still too scared. I'm scared she will laugh, that I don't know her well enough, that she will let me down like everyone else.

'Please tell me your boss isn't that bad.'

'I can't.' I say. 'She is. She's a hundred times worse.'

Amy leans back in her chair. 'I knew it from her desk. Complete schizo, right?'

I nod.

'You need to get out of that place, mate.'

'I know.' I agree.

And I do know.

'I feel fucking sick, now.' Amy says, pushing her tray away. 'Let's go have a fag.'

So we do.

'It's still pretty cold,' I say as we walk back towards the office, taking the path behind the retail park.

'Hey, look at that,' Amy says, pointing. Behind Asda they are throwing out a bunch of old junk, and what looks like about eight wooden chairs piled up. 'Let's nick two.'

The gate is open, but it still seems a bit dodgy.

'They're probably broken or something...' I say.

'Nah, look, there must be two that are OK. Come on!' she says, grabbing my arm and pulling me through the gate. And I realise that if she had dared me to rob a bank right now, I probably would go along with it, just for the ride, just to be part of something for a minute.

'Look,' she sits on one, rocking back and forth. 'This one's fine. What about that one?'

I pull one from the stack. It's a bit manky but not broken. 'Yep. Seems sturdy enough.'

She picks up hers and I pick up mine and we walk towards the gate, happy with our find.

'HEY!'

Oh shit.

I knew it.

I turn and see a red-faced man running out of Asda. 'Come back here!'

Amy turns and laughs. 'Come catch us, then!'

'You... you...!' he says, and I start laughing so hard I can't run properly. I am pulling the chair along and it is bouncing along the ground. Then he pushes some magic button and the gate starts to close us in. It's like some no-budget Indiana Jones.

'Chuck it!' Amy shouts, a step ahead, and I throw the chair as hard as I can into the street behind her. The gate virtually shuts on my arse.

My chair goes clattering into the road and nearly hits a Jeep. The guy in it starts beeping and hollering. I feel like I'm in Eastenders.

Behind us the red-faced man comes puffing up to the gate, locked in by his own metal trap.

'I know where you work!' he lies, trying to

shake his fist, but he's too out of breath.

'I know where you work too, what do you want, a prize?' Amy shouts. She can't stop laughing, and I can hardly walk. The Jeep guy has pulled over and gets out and starts shouting at me. I am trying to pick up my chair in between being out of breath and hysterics.

'I'm so sorry,' I am trying to say, and Amy rolls her eyes.

'It didn't even hit you! No one cares about your dumb Jeep. Have you heard of climate change? Don't you care about polar bears?' she demands.

He literally starts spluttering, and then it is too late. My feet are working again and we are running away. We get to the patch of grass beside the office and dump the chairs next to the hedge. My make-up is streaming down my face.

'You won't forget me now!' Amy laughs, sitting on her chair. It is a right battered old thing anyway, and they were obviously going to be scrapped. What was the big deal?

You're right, I won't forget her. But I don't say it.

I sit down, breathing hard.

'That was so funny. That guy's face!'

'Which one?' Amy laughs, her face glowing. Her cheeks are flushed. She lights up a fag. 'Want one?'

'Nah, I don't.' I say.

'Wise move.' she says. 'These chairs are our thrones. This is our Narnia. When you sit here, the office doesn't exist.' She looks at me. 'Even when I'm gone, you can have a place to yourself out here.'

And I am torn between being touched that she has realised I need a place for myself, and gripped with fear at the thought of her going.

'I'll hide them in the hedge. I'll just get them out when I want.' I say.

'You could invite that guy down here...' Amy says, cheekily, winking.

'Nah – I'm over him.' I say. 'He *corrected my spelling* in an email.' I pull a face.

'Oh my God! What a wanker! You could do better than that anyway. He right fancies himself.'

I smile. I can reassure myself with those words later when the panic kicks in.

The sun comes out from behind the building as we sit quietly, getting our breath back. Amy blows three perfect smoke rings as I watch, enamoured.

I realise everyone I've ever liked has been a smoker.

<u>Monday</u>

Penfold comes in late, but he gets none of the grief that Bowser gave to Clint. I can see him at Bowser's desk, chatting easily. It's amazing what supporting the same rugby or football team can do for your chances of promotion around here. That, and having a penis.

The Martyr tells me she has had 300 emails since she's been gone. None of us ask about her breakdown. She looks neither better nor worse. She is just her, eternally.

Her being back makes Amy being gone seem a thousand times harder.

But also easier. As if she was never here.

Once someone leaves work they are forgotten about so quickly. Even if you liked them. They are dead within a week.

It's true.

The Martyr is back with a vengeance. Her desk already looks like scenes in soaps when someone acting really badly (Phil Mitchell, usually) runs their hand along every table and mantelpiece and wrecks the joint. And she's only been in an hour.

Another new guy has started, down at the call centre end, by Bowser. I can tell he's new as he's wearing a tie; he's got the Penfold disease. But this is no Penfold. He is skinny, with dark hair, and he has an unusual handsomeness. Others might notice. If they do, I will be at the back of the non-existent queue again.

Still, I watch him. He is about three rows of desks down from me. Mitesh and The Toad are both right in the way of my view. But I can see him when he stands up to make a cup of tea. That'll do.

A hubbub has started around The Toad. What's this? She's smiling! I pretend not to listen as Mitesh pats her on the back. The Toad almost looks demure as she soaks up... congratulations?

'... picked me from nine candidates... using my holiday days so I can start in two weeks time...'

Oh my God! I look at The Capricorn to see if she has heard, too. I can tell she has, of course she has, with the size of her ears. The Toad is leaving!

This is confusing. How come *she* can get out of here but I can't? Why her and not me? But at the same time I feel secretly pleased for her. I imagine how she must feel inside, looking at us. Old news. Not even a whole month's notice to work off. Annoyances would suddenly be currency for future happiness. *I won't have to put up with you much longer*. She must feel ten foot high instead of ten foot wide for once. Now I feel jealous. I want that power, that glimmer of hope instead of this void.

Oh my God, what about Clint though? That was so mean sacking him when she knew there was a chance she was leaving. If only he'd hung on an extra week... but he's better off out of it.

The Martyr asks Jim to come into 'the cupboard'. She actually means the shredding room, I have no idea why she calls it 'the cupboard'. This can only mean one thing, he's been up to something and she's caught him out, or someone's just ratted on him in her absence. I have been in 'the cupboard' twice, once for hanging up on someone and the other time for swearing too loudly. I have fantasies about being fired. It never seems to happen.

They come back two minutes later laughing. The Martyr isn't exactly the most terrifying boss. Jim probably sweet-talked her. I email him.

What did you get told off about?

He replies,

I put down a whole day when I was half an hour late last week. I've been 20 mins early every day this week though, and didn't put it down so it was a load of balls, really.

Typical Jim. He's always on the make. I doubt very much if he was in early every day. Still, bless him for lying.

Rain is pouring down outside. It batters against the window and makes a horrible noise like blinds rattling in a storm. Some people find the sound of rain outside comforting, but I've always found it frightening, like it's trying to get in. Like it's trying to get to me. Incidentally, I also hate the sound of birdsong. What do they know that we don't? Fair enough, talk amongst yourselves, but keep it at a reasonable level, OK?

I want to go to the kitchen and the First Aid Kit, but Un-Handy Andy has put a vending machine in there now. It has ruined everything. The zombified masses are so desperate for their Diet Coke and fucking Kit Kats that my peace has been destroyed. Still, I will go. I just have to pick my time.

The rain turns into a massive thunderstorm. Hailstones like little white bullets batter against the windows, despite the fact it's June. The sky spasms thunderclaps like first-day menstrual cramps. Everyone gets excited and goes to peer out the window like children. The cute new guy looks out almost nonchalantly, a mug of unidentifiable drink in his hand. After a minute he sits back down again. Whilst everyone's attention is diverted, I go to the kitchen.

I have no scars to patch up, or to create, I just want a bit of peace and maybe to touch the green plastic, or unclip the white catches. Just to reassure myself it's there.

The offending vending (ovending?) machine hums and glowers at me.

Oh, it does Smarties.

I make a mental note of this but I will not give it any more of my attention. There's a temptation that's a lot more irresistible to me. I approach the First Aid Kit. It opens up like a treasure chest. But wait, what's that? Something golden glimmers inside. This is an unexpected and unwelcome surprise, a new item upsetting the status quo. I feel for the Airstrips, but the packet is empty.

They never fucking restock. My attention turns back to the new thing, a bright yellow package. I turn it over in my hand, perturbed. The packet contains a Face Shield. What the fuck is that when it's at home? I read on – 'for protected mouth-to-mouth resuscitation'. Protected mouth-to-mouth resuscitation? Is that so you don't get pregnant? I am slightly alarmed at the image of someone lying choking to death on the floor whilst someone swathes their face in plastic to avoid making skin contact with their fellow – dying – man or woman. What next? Firemen moaning about fire being a teeny bit too hot?

I slam the First Aid Kit in disgust, and head for the toilet. I can't cope with the office yet, everyone oohing and aahing at a perfectly natural weather phenomenon. I go to my cubicle and lock the door, just to breathe and be me. The lid is up on the toilet and it says 'if anything but unscented bleach is used, it may result in chemical attack'. I would like to see this. It sounds fun. I can't see a bit of pine-forest scent eating the toilet seat like acid though, but maybe I'm just incredibly uninformed and ignorant of chemical cleaning procedure.

It's possible.

I slam down the loo seat and look up.

Oh my God. They've fixed the ceiling. It looks so weird, all those colours and all those wires plastered over, like a bandage on a wound. The tiles are white, clean and sealed. Shut tight. No one could come out and kill me now if they tried. It should make me happy, but instead I feel even more claustrophobic. I breathe in and out, in and out, waiting for the storm to pass.

<u>Tuesday</u>

The Toad is off 'sick' today – coming so soon on the heels of her new job I expect she's just lying in bed eating chocolate. This has given me a great vantage point, though. As Mitesh is so small, I can basically see right over to the new guy. Well, I can see the top of his head and his ear most of the time but occasionally more. I try not to look too much. He definitely looked at me once but it was probably an accident. I can hear his voice now and then, he is quite well-spoken. He is elfin-looking, slight and a bit jug-eared. I haven't got close enough to tell the colour of his eyes. But he looks intelligent. He looks sexy.

Mitesh tells me one of his stories with no point or punch-line to it. He rambles on incomprehensibly about any given subject, spouting things he's read in the paper as if he wrote them. I think he thinks I'm eyeing *him* up today instead of the new guy. It's a concern.

The Capricorn and Jim start having a conversation about film. The Capricorn is discussing the pros of French men and French cinema.

'Well if you compare Trainspotting to a French movie then the Brits probably don't hold up as well as sexual icons,' Jim concedes. 'But in reality, I'm better in bed.'

I snigger, and they ignore me.

'But English men are not as attractive as the French,' The Capricorn insists.

She's right; there are some sexy French men out there. I don't want to back her up, though.

Also, where did she miss the bus? Normally French women were classy and well- groomed. The Capricorn's dress sense made bland look hot. She looked like she dressed out of Bonmarché, and that isn't even really French, I think, it just has ideas above its station.

'But French men stink, don't they?' Jim declares. Both The Capricorn and I look at him, horrified.

'OK maybe that's not fair then...' he backtracks.

'It's actually racist.' I point out.

'OK then, I'll comment on my own culture as well!' Jim says very loudly, 'I mean, if you take this office as a cross-section of society, looks-wise it's pretty dismal, really.'

A silence descends. Way to insult everyone all at once; I couldn't have done better myself.

'No offence,' he adds, laughing, and I laugh too. Even The Capricorn seems perky.

Two minutes later the phone rings. I pick up. 'Hello?'

It's Thyroid, of course, who never says 'hi' or raises a smile when I walk past her. She is best buddies with The Toad, could pass for her twin-sister, and she also happens to be one of those still blocking the mildly-improved view of the new guy, so I doubly dislike her.

She says, 'Do you think you could keep it down up that end, please, I can't hear myself think.'

'What?' I reply, slightly stunned.

'Your laugh,' she says. 'It goes right through me.'

'Oh... OK.' I say, and hang up. Oh, OK? What

am I talking about? I'm only laughing! I can feel my cheeks turning red. I can't look up in case she is staring at me. She is literally close enough to have shouted over rather than called.

It's not like I'm *always* laughing! It's not like I'm *ever* laughing!

I can feel myself falling into a black hole. Everything around me seems to have vanished. I can't hear anything. I can't speak. I suddenly realise.

This is it for me.

This is it for me forever.

I have to get out. I walk, not looking at the left-hand side of the room. I want to set fire to that cunt, I really do. Halfway out the building I realise I made a packed lunch today but left it at home. Could anything be more painful than getting up *early* to make sandwiches, and then forgetting them? I suspect not. It's not like you ever eat them later. I have no money to buy something else. What's the opposite of a cash flow? I normally look forward to lunch, the sting of salt on my lips. The foodless hour stretches out before me with nothing to fill it. But I'm not hungry now, anyway. I'm just mad.

I go and sit in my car. It is safe in my car, Afro Ken hangs serenely from the mirror, my iPod plugs happily into the tape-deck, because tapes went out of fashion over a decade ago. Everything has its place.

My stomach rumbles so I close my eyes and look at the sun, then I close my eyes and look at the sun in negative. I listen to Bright Eyes.

A couple of people walk past but they don't see me. I'm a crash test dummy. A beaded car-seat cover.

I push in the cigarette lighter. I like the red ring that lights up around it. I like the click it makes when it's ready.

I rummage in the glove box for anything; sweets, gum. I only want something because there's nothing. There is nothing. I never eat in my car, or on the computer. I could read and eat forever though. It's funny the habits you cultivate. And the habits you look down on.

Click. The glow fades. I push the cigarette lighter in again.

A song comes on I don't like. Even on **all songs>shuffle** it picks the same fifty first every time. It's not random. It's quite predictable.

Click.

I push the lighter in again.

I wind down my window for some air. It is not raining today. I can see Kate and Jim's car, their South Africa bumper sticker. I can see The Martyr's car next to mine, an explosion of CD cases filling the foot-well and strewn over the passenger seat. She doesn't take care of anything, does she?

I lick my lips, bite my nails. I change songs. The lighter clicks, stops glowing. I push it in again.

My battery will survive. I'll go back soon. Before…

I look at the red ring, lit up. I look at my white wrist, blinking. I can see the imprint of the light on my arm, like an optical illusion, like I've stared at the sun too long. Which I did. But this isn't that.

No. Not the wrist. Don't you dare do the

wrist.

I'm not doing anything!

Click.

I stare at the lighter, its wavy little symbol.
How quickly does it cool? It is like playing
chicken, waiting those few seconds extra. Just
waiting for it to cool a little.

No, that's cheating.

I push it in again. I know I won't look next
time. Won't give myself the chance to back out.

I'll just draw my gun and shoot.

I look at The Martyr's shipwreck of CDs.
Daniel O' Donnell, James Morrison, Russell
Watson. All that middle of the road shit never
gave her any peace of mind, did it?

At least my music speaks the truth.

We are all fucked.

Click.

I grab the lighter fast and push it against the
inside of my forearm. Not the wrist, but five
inches up, towards the elbow. I don't just touch it
there, I *push*, and I can feel the hot metal searing
into my flesh like a branding iron. No, not *like* a
branding iron, this *is* a branding iron. It hisses
like an old-fashioned kettle and my skin screams
underneath it, but I still *push* until I can't
anymore, and then the lighter drops to the floor,
between my feet.

I think I black out. No, I *white* out. I am just
gone.

There is nothing but pain.

Nothing but white-hot pain.

I can almost *see* the pain soaring past me, so
unfathomably far away, yet everywhere. I try and
attach myself to it, feel the rush, feel the rush,

just feel the rush, I tell myself.

But nothing has been excreted like when I cut. I don't feel purged. My skin is on *fire*.

Inside my mind my arm goes black, white, red, like a sick traffic light, a gloating disco ball.

Then the smell hits me. How did I not smell that sooner?

Then fear hits me. Oh, God, what have I done?

I open my eyes.

I am frightened of what I might see.

I look.

I *peek*.

A perfect circle of mottled brown flesh. The edges are vivid red, deep and weeping. I can see the pattern of the filament in the middle, a maniac squiggle. The detail is surprisingly clear.

Something like steam is coming off the wound. My skin is crackling and dotted with black flakes, like barbequed steak.

I am *insane*.

I look out the window and realise anyone could have walked past whilst I was futilely chasing the pain, like a surfer chasing a lazy wave.

Anyone could have seen.

I don't care, I think. I needed to get out. I needed this.

I look at my arm again. It is pulsing and shaking like a dog that's just been run over by a lorry, but hasn't decided whether or not to die yet. But it will in a minute, because it's easier than suffering this. You'd beg for death to be away from pain like this.

I might need a skin graft.

No. I'll TCP it later, wrap it up snug. It will settle. They settle. The thought of the TCP, the smell of it, makes me gag. Just the memory of it brings tears to my eyes.

I gently roll my sleeve down. My arm is still twitching, still not-quite-road-kill.

My sleeve goes over it somehow. There. It's disappeared. It never happened.

I bend down to look for the lighter. My fingers connect with metal. It is cool now. Safe. I hold it up to the light. Oh my God. Bits of my flesh are melted around the edge of it, like wax or plastic.

It is unreal.

'*Urgh!*' I throw the lighter out of the open window and it skitters away, far away under a car.

I don't smoke anyway. It's bad for you.

<u>Wednesday</u>

I am driving to work and singing along to the radio. My arm is swaddled in Savlon (I couldn't bear the TCP) and more soft, stretchy bandage. Last night when I'd tried to take my cardigan off, the fabric had stuck to my arm, and ripping it off was like having my legs waxed.

I try not to think about the pain but it's difficult as my arm is throbbing in time to the music. It hurts most when I change gear but it's bearable. I sing louder. I don't tend to care if people are looking because I rarely look at them and they will never see me again. My car is my castle. I am waiting for a gap at the roundabout. It's always gridlock at this time. Something catches my eye on the left hand side. It is a guy on a motorbike and he is looking at me.

Oh my God, it's him! It's the jug-eared mug boy! On a motorbike! He has a yellow leather jacket on! That sounds horrible, but actually it looks cool on him. I realise I have stared for too long and someone beeps behind me.

Motorbike Boy pulls off with a roar and I pull out behind him, but I can't catch up. Oh God, he must have seen me singing! How embarrassing.

I can't believe he rides a motorbike. It is quite a contrast to his usual shirt and trousers look. His shirt looked too big for him yesterday. I'm not into guys with motorbikes, but he definitely wears it well. I picture myself sitting on the back, riding pillion.

OK, maybe that's a step too far.

By the time I get to work his motorbike is

already parked. I hurry inside and just pretend to work for the first half an hour, as is my tradition every day.

I think Motorbike Boy catches my eye a couple of times. I regret singing. At least you couldn't hear through windows, I console myself.

I get up to make tea. I have bought new shoes and they are rubbing. I never wear heels, despite being short. I don't do pain.

Not in that way.

But even these new flat shoes are hungry for my foot-flesh.

I can hear the First Aid Kit calling me. So I go.

No one is in the kitchen and there is a fresh pack of Airstrips, cushioned and plump, ready to protect me from the tiny teeth biting the backs of my feet. I put one each on the back of my heels and make my tea.

I am satisfied.

Ten minutes later I notice the shoes are digging into the skin just below my ankles. Fix one bit of pain and another pops up. And another.

I know all about that.

Rambo, the IT dude, comes around with a pot for the Grand National. Sometimes Rambo, me and this other guy race our cars on the way home. It's a subtle race, but it's a race nonetheless. They tend to win as it becomes about male pride and then the rules of stopping distance and speed limits become dangerously flaunted. I will do 40 in a 30 zone, if safe to, but on the whole, I value my life over my dick. Especially as I don't have a dick.

'Put a pound in, pick a ticket and the winner takes all.' Rambo says, smugly. He does everything smugly.

'OK then,' I volunteer. I pick out a horse that is 40/1. My ticket says, 'Pink Biscuit was looking strong a couple of years back but an operation for breathing difficulties have put pay to his chances in recent times'.

'Great,' I say, 'Trust me to pick the fucking asthmatic.'

'Ha ha, you picked a donkey.' Rambo gloats. 'Don't worry, I picked a donkey too. 100/1.'

The Capricorn picks out one that is 100/1, too. Jim is too tight to fork out a pound for a ticket. He pretends he has no change, in the hope one of us might sub him, but we don't fall for it.

I go back to my work, one eye firmly on Motorbike Boy.

Penfold seems to be having a competition with himself to see how many clichés he can fit into one sentence. He has taken to calling Mitesh 'Mr Mitesh' which is pissing me off no end. I can see The Toad quietly simmering at his chirpy demeanour, so at odds with her own. She is back from her sickbed and looking remarkably well, apart from the chronic obesity, which will no doubt be followed by early-onset diabetes.

'No rest for the wicked, hey, Mr Mitesh,' Penfold says. Mitesh is happy for anyone to talk to him and not bully him, so he seems quite happy with Penfold's banality.

I wonder who will come in when The Toad leaves.

I wonder if I will ever get out.

Frustrated at nothing, I take the mail up. I'm

Not Being Funny, but... eyeballs me as I put the mail in to be franked. She counts every pen, pencil and ruler safely in as if they are her own children. She'd cut your throat rather than give you an extra paperclip.

She has already criticised my placement of addresses on envelopes for being too central. I put them in the plastic box fast, but not fast enough.

'Have you got any letterheads in your department, Stephanie?'

For some reason 'letterheads' as a phrase really bugs me. 'Headed paper' seems more sensible.

'Yeah... about half a packet,' I venture.

'Could you do me a favour?'

'What?'

'Could you diarise the usage in your department for the week for me? I want to get a rough idea on how many reams we can cut back on.'

'Diarise?'

'Yes... diarise. Write down. In a diary.' She speaks slowly.

My god, I'm being patronised by someone who's chief joy in life is making people acquire a licence for every Blu-Tack dog they make! She's making up words and then explaining them to *me* like I'm a particularly slow child.

'Diarise... is that a word?' I'm definitely not happy about it.

She looks at me as if I've missed the point. To her, I have missed the point.

'Of course it is. Could you do it for me?'

'Diarise? Are you sure?' I'd never heard

anyone say it before. It sounds like some word people make from mushed-up words and speak as if it's gospel on afternoon talk shows. Like 'volumptuous' instead of voluptuous. I know who could solve this one – fucking Patrick.

'I'm certain,' she says, and goes back to franking the mail.

It is still troubling me as I walk down the stairs. I say nothing and unlock my computer.

I look up 'diarise' on the internet. I can't find it on dictionary.com. I Google, and it comes up, but mainly as 'diarize'. That doesn't surprise me. Bloody yanks and their fucking zees everywhere. I'm still annoyed that it even half exists, though. That she was half right.

The Martyr is at her desk for once and the reality of the situation is obviously proving too much. Amy's Mr Muscle spring-clean has been unceremoniously decimated. The Martyr is on one of her 'for fuck's sake' rolls. I count them sometimes. Sometimes I count the theatrical sighs. I feel like my stomach is eating itself up when she really gets going, she makes me so nervous. It's only a matter of time before her *next* nervous breakdown. Or my first.

She turns round to me. 'Stephanie, have you heard back from head office yet?'

God, what is it with everyone at the moment? I minimise eBay in under half a second, but she's oblivious anyway.

'No, I haven't heard. I left a message.'

'It's quite urgent. Can you liase with them?'

Liase! A crime worse than diarise. Who invented these fucking terms? Was there some jargon-spewing monster out there, sucking out normal people's vocabulary and turning them into robots? Whitewashing their individuality, suffocating their imaginations?

'No I can't liase with them. I can just call them up and speak to them, like they are our fellow human beings.'

'What?' The Martyr says. She's got the phone glued to one ear.

'Yes...' I say, quietly. 'I'll call them.'

Thursday

Something is going on between The Martyr and one of the reps, Santana Man. Me and Jim always do the Santana music when he walks into the room. He once told us a tale of a star-studded barbeque at his place, apron on, Santana on the stereo, and the star guest, Robbie Williams' dad. Every time I hear that awful song I picture Santana Man in one of those aprons with a naked woman on. It just has to be one of those.

The Capricorn and I have both noticed a change in The Martyr recently. She has started wearing more make-up, nicer clothes and dangly earrings. Jim and Kate went for a drink with a few of the others after work (I know, how horrific) and apparently The Martyr and Santana Man were *kissing*. Kissing in the pub! How low can she stoop? She's 50. Did I mention the guy is married?

Santana Man has brought in a box of cakes. On the other side of the office I hear I'm Not Being Funny, but... say 'No thank you! I'm sweet enough!' and giggle. I beg to differ.

Our reps keep bringing cakes into the office. It feels like they are having a competition to see who can butter us up the best. Every day they up the ante: a seemingly unlimited box of pastries and other sticky delights to tempt and bribe us. Cakes or lollies or muffins or cookies, fucking giant great crater-sized cookies at 10am! Krispy Kreme doughnuts that seem to have been cooked at the bottom of a deep fat fryer, they are so greasy and no doubt stuffed with MSG and trans fats. I don't need the temptation, thanks. I eat enough calories at lunch.

I watch everyone stuffing their faces in disgust and feel like The Capricorn. I try and estimate what percentage of the office are overweight (me included). Probably 50% at least. That percentage can only rise if people keep eating sugar-coated, cream-filled radioactive filth for breakfast. They will have to get special chairs made for us because we will become health and safety hazards. We will all die young.

It's not all bad, then.

My head is pounding today. Trails are coming off the computer screen and my scalp feels like it's shrinking on my skull. I always thought a migraine was just a bad headache that people wanted a fancier name for. But this is one of those headaches, one so bad I feel like I need to lie down to get rid of it. The pills I've taken don't ease the pain, just dress it in a fog, like a transparent outfit failing to hide the jutting bones of an emaciated supermodel.

I can't look at the screen anymore, it seems as unnatural as staring at the sun. I stagger to the toilets, avoiding eye contact.

Safe inside I put the toilet seat lid down and sit, leaning my head against cold tile. I would do anything to just curl up on the floor right now, but instead of a pillow I have the choice between a toilet roll dispenser or a *something*-green MDF partition.

I close my eyes. I couldn't even cut at this moment if I wanted to. The pain is so bad.

What if I have a brain tumour?

So what if I do? I'll be signed off work. I can

hang out with the cat and read magazines all day. Someone will come round occasionally. It'll be something different.

All my life I feel like I've been waiting for that moment, *that* conversation with a doctor, or *that* knock on the door. I feel permanently tense with the expectation of it – the knowledge that some unidentified yet horrific thing is going to happen.

Just let it happen.

Let it happen and then maybe I can move on.

But what if something else happened after that? Then something else?

My mind strings out the various possibilities, none of them good.

I wonder how anyone can ever have a baby. How can they knowingly pass on this legacy of dread? How can they put that on someone, someone they profess to love?

Because not everyone is like me.

But how can that be?

I cannot comprehend how it must feel to be different. Not even a little.

What made me this way, I start to think, and then stuff it back down. I don't have some dark secret, some cliché fuck-up excuse. Yeah I have family... things, but who doesn't? I'm not using that as an excuse.

I think I was born this way. I honestly do.

I do.

I open my eyes and the light above the toilet is startling. I feel like an alien waking up in Roswell. The back of my head is cold from leaning on the mortuary-slab of the tile.

I close my eyes again and try to let the drowsy pill-fog take over. Just five minutes of unconsciousness would get rid of this ache.

Please.

I try and picture the pain like someone told me to once, make it real like a cancer, then shrink it. Take it downstairs. Put it in a bag. Put it in the bin and take it outside. Shut the lid. Lock it up.

But I have no patience or imagination for that kind of bullshit. If that sort of bollocks worked then we wouldn't need prescriptions. Or operations.

Nothing works.

I open my eyes.

I can't feel my arm, the nagging pain that's been with me since Tuesday. The throb where the metal sank into my arm earlier this week.

Why can't I feel it?

I roll my sleeve up and pull it back, slowly, slowly. My skin underneath is completely smooth. No scratches, no scars. No burnt circle of fire.

My arms look as white and unspoilt as uncooked chicken breast.

How has this happened?

A feeling that I realise can only be joy starts to crawl up from my belly.

I roll up my other sleeve, more frantic this time. It is the same. The criss-cross of scars tattooed on me like crazy-paving are gone. Years of work. Years of abuse. Different sessions ran through my head – it hadn't all started and ended in the fucking toilet cubicles. I remembered so many times; so many bedrooms, bathrooms, kitchens. The first time; sitting with my back to my unlocked bedroom door so no one could walk in. Most teenagers were trying to hide their boyfriends from their parents. I was hiding my blades.

But no. I must have got it wrong. My arm is as unspoilt as the skin of a new baby. I run my finger against the flesh. It is soft, springy, smooth.

I can start again.

No, not start cutting again, start *life* again.

I am a blank canvas. I was free.

I am free.

I hear the bang of a cubicle door and I jump. My eyes open again. The pain in my head has dulled, and I still can't feel my arm, but it is a cruel consolation.

The lie crumbles around me. I don't need to roll my sleeves up this time.

I am still me: scarred for life.

I've had that dream a thousand times.

Every time it fools me.

Every time.

I get up from the hard toilet seat and flush the loo for show. My eyes are stinging, but I won't cry, I'm not weak, I'm not a baby.

I go back.

Half an hour later Jim sends me an email of a slideshow of young foreign boy with a dirty face smoking a cigarette. He looks about four years old. I wonder who put this slide show together. It's not meant to be funny. What is it meant to be? I don't know how to do slide shows, work PowerPoint. I said in my CV I could but it was a lie. I did work out how to scan my signature so I don't have to sign my name on letters anymore, though. Except now people can send letters and pretend they're from me, should they want to. Someone could write poison pen letters threatening unpleasant deaths to one and all, and cut and paste my signature onto it. I could do it and claim it couldn't be me, because that would be stupid; a cunning double bluff. I quite like that idea.

Mentally I feel like I have taken a turn for the worst this week. Motorbike Boy is sitting across the room, but he might as well not exist. I can't feel for him today. Depression has turned to fear and I feel threatened by each approaching day. Each Monday feels like a stalker, a molester, just waiting for me, but the weekends offer no comfort, just a wait, wait, wait. Rage seems to be struggling to get out of me at every turn. I try hard to keep a lid on these feelings. Sometimes I can push them down for a while, but they are always *there*, like a tapeworm or an unwanted pregnancy. My inner-self is no more than a parasite.

I wonder what it must be like to be happy. To feel real joy like I felt in that dream. Or to even just be normal. I can't even imagine it.

Friday

The Martyr is driving me mad. There's like this constant external dialogue. 'One... two... three... four, that's that done. I'll just put that there. Right! What's next? Oh yes...' I want to tell her to shut up, just shut the fuck up, but I can't. I doubt if she even knows she's doing it. Any of it.

I imagine her with a plaque above her desk saying 'you don't have to be mad to work here, but it helps!' I would bet any money she would think that was hilarious. Every tired cliché reeled out was revered in this place as if it had fallen from the lips of Oscar Wilde. What was the fucking point, of any of this? We were just kissing our life goodbye, every day, over and over and over. No one would give a fuck about this in 50 years, let alone 500. This isn't a legacy. It isn't even a footnote.

No.

Stop thinking.

I know it's not safe to get into this spiral of thinking.

I get up and go into the kitchen. I make tea, the routine saving me from panic. I have one eye on the First Aid Kit, but only one. I still remember the betrayal of the Face Shield. As I stir the tea, I notice my hands are trembling more these days. Maybe I've got Huntingdon's. I like watching documentaries on these horrific long-term diseases people get, or worse, are born with. I like looking the true brutality of life in the eye. It makes me feel marginally better by comparison. I might be fucked, but I haven't got progeria. I haven't got multiple sclerosis.

I can't concentrate on the computer today but I have some things to post to people which need photocopying. I have been wary of the photocopier since they replaced it and I am right to be. It starts biting chunks out of my original.

'Argh!' I try and pull it out, and my fingers get sucked round with the wheel, and the fucking thing *bites* me. I kick it in return.

Motorbike Boy taps me on the shoulder. 'You want a hand?'

Oh my God! I feel embarrassed I was making such a fuss. I stare at him. I don't normally like brown eyes, but his are massive and beautiful. They actually are. Fucking hell, stop staring! I look at the photocopier, instead of him, which is like looking at a fucking tower block instead of the Taj Mahal.

The screen flashes: PAPER JAM. Then I notice my finger is cut.

'It just bit me, I swear.' I say. I want him to suck it, to kiss it and make it better. This feeling rises up in me before I can even stop it.

He looks and nods, almost touching it. 'You should sue.'

'I wish it had my arm off, then I could get a few weeks off work.' I say, slightly hyperbolically.

'You masochist.' He pulls out trays 2 and 3 and starts feeling around. 'They should really replace this thing.'

'They replaced it like a fortnight ago. The old one was crap but at least it wasn't blood-thirsty.'

'Does it still say jammed?' Motorbike Boy is on his knees in front of me. I can see his arse.

'Yep. Hey, don't worry about it.' I say. 'I'll call

Un-Handy Andy. I'm sure he'll get round to it at some point before the Olympics.'

Motorbike Boy laughs, standing again.

'Think I saw you driving to work yesterday? You must live in my direction.' He did see me! I dart between happy and embarrassed, ashamed and elated.

'Yeah, I saw your bike.' I say. 'It looks good. I live by the station.'

'Oh, me too,' he says. 'I live like, five minutes up from there.'

'Whereabouts?' I go to ask, but am rudely interrupted by The Martyr yelling at me that I've got a phone call.

'Sorry,' I say, and hurry back to my desk. He watches me as I go and I feel frustrated that our conversation was cut short. Five minutes from me? I can feel a stalking coming on. What if we were neighbours?

After I get off the phone I log a call with Un-Handy Andy and surprisingly, he comes down quite fast, beckoning me over and breathing on me too much. He has a pen on a bit of string round his neck. It's not exactly haute couture.

He clearly has no idea what he's doing. Maybe that stupid blonde woman will come out again. Well Jim can be the designated person this time. I'm done with it. I make my excuses and leave him to it.

Motorbike Boy is not at his desk when I walk by. However, Thyroid barks at me as I go past. Thyroid — the laughter police. She says my name twice. I stop. Four of them are sitting round.

'What have you done to your hair?' Thyroid demands. I had been to the hairdressers last weekend.

'She's had streaks put in,' one of her lackeys points out helpfully. *Streaks*? It was lighter, but not with... streaks. Just the word 'streaks' makes me blanch. We're not in the 80s anymore, despite your outfit. Naturally I don't say this.

'I had it like... highlighted and some lowlights to cover the red,' I over-explain.

'What colour *is* your hair naturally?' Thyroid asks without any warmth. I am reminded of being at school, confronted by a gang of girls in the changing rooms, any change seen as a threat.

'Um... kind of mousy brown,' I volunteer. Four pairs of eyes on me.

'So you weren't naturally ginger, then?' she says, with a smirk. I wasn't *un*-naturally ginger, either. I had been a cherry-red, however.

'No, not ginger. I dyed it red but it was hard to keep up.' I say, defeatedly.

'Oh yeah, I can see your eyebrows now.' Thyroid comments. She says nothing more.

I walk off, aware of them whispering after me.

Ok that's done it. I need to get away. I really want to go and cut but I know it's not a good idea. Besides, the burn counts for several cuts. The burn is weeping and weeping and pounding at night time, keeping me up like a good book or a bad dream. The Savlon has done fuck all. I had reverted to TCP, and my whole body screamed. I want to die just thinking about it. I just want it to scab up now. Don't make me go to the bloody hospital with that. I don't think 'I tripped, fell, landed on the car lighter' is going to wash. I'd be like one of those blokes who pretends he's fallen backwards onto a cucumber that just happened to be wearing a condom.

I go to the kitchen and look in the First Aid Kit to see if there is anything useful in there, some magical cure to fix self-mutilation, some potion to heal third-degree burns without proper medical help. Instead, I see a box of safety pins in the corner. I suppose they are for fastening bandages, which seems archaic. I use stretchy ones at home. They are tight, like a corset.

Safety pins seem wrong in the First Aid Kit. Everything should be soft, spongy, sterile and sealed. The safety pins rattle in a small cardboard box, pointed and sharp.

I remember having safety pins hanging off my bag or holding my fishnet tights together when I was at school and trying to be cool. I want to line them up like that now, but pierce them through my skin, in and out, down my forearm (the *other* one), totally symmetrical. I would make a good punk rocker. I knew how to pierce and tattoo. I knew how one could lead to another. And another.

I shut the box and sit at a table, pretending to stare at the street. For some reason I think of the people who are the opposite of me, the people who sew people like us up. I had been sewn up but only once.

Don't think about it.

I remember the blood pouring from me, all over the bathroom floor and I had to let them in, I had no choice. I remember their faces. I remember them picking me up and I just pretended to pass out because I was so humiliated.

And the nurse, she had held my hand and

looked at me pityingly. But the doctor who had treated me was angry. He looked at the leaflets the nurse had handed me with disgust, like I was a heroin addict, or a pregnant twelve-year-old. And who's to say I was any better than them? Or the guy with the cucumber?

I was just wasting their time. A thrill-seeker. A home-medicator.

But I never went back.

I never bothered that doctor again.

I never went back to either place, actually. Home, or the hospital.

Monday

I hate people who reverse into parking spaces. I have never reversed into a parking space in my whole life. Why would I? These people seem to be a certain breed; vindictive, spiteful, *forward-planning* wankers who put their reverse lights on when you least expect it and force you to back up. I hate them. I'm sure they hate me for all the reverse reasons.

It is windy this morning and a carrier bag follows me almost all the way across the car park like a needy pet. I feel irrationally touched, yet embarrassed at the same time. Then it gets caught behind a wheel and it is gone.

Motorbike Boy's bike is not in the car park. It is nearly five to nine so I am surprised as he normally comes a little earlier so he can take his leathers off. I can only imagine that scene.

I'll have to try and find out where he lives when I next see him so I can casually drive by his house. OK, that sounds bad. I wouldn't necessarily do that. It would be nice to know where he lives, though.

I make my way upstairs. I can't find my ID card to get into our office so I have to stand like a lemon waiting for someone else to come by. As usual it's bloody When Animals Attack. I am certain he wants rid of me. It's not a paranoid fantasy. I am not one of his good robots. My hair is a scouring pad and my mouth doesn't defer like it's meant to. I don't simper, scrape and curtsey like I'm supposed to. Because I don't bow down to him, I can see he's planning my disposal.

Well I'm onto him, too. I know he's just bluffing his way through. This is a man who thought The Martyr and The Toad were suitable people to be put in charge of others, when I doubt they could work a TV between them.

When Animals Attack is a religious maniac. A dominating father. He is probably a wife-beater too, why not. He thinks he knows it all. Well, I know his sort.

By the time I get in, it's five past nine. I look at Motorbike Boy's desk. Empty.

Perturbed, I sit down. Jim sounds like he's on the phone to his agent. He is a jobbing actor, but he doesn't get much work. Sometimes he leaves for a few weeks to go on a poorly-paid tour but like a boomerang, he always comes back. Oh, and Kate likes him where she can see him. You think she'd want him to go and pursue his dream and make it big. It seems like she wants him to become something else instead.

He is making excuses the second he puts the phone down.

'Well it's Shakespeare but it's only £300 a week and Kate's parents are coming over at around that time...'

So what if her parents are coming over? What if he was filming a big blockbuster in Hollywood or something? Unlikely, yes, but they wouldn't be complaining then. His spinelessness bothers me. She is a lot to blame, but the buck ultimately sits with him.

'So you want to work here for the rest of your life?' The Capricorn asks him, rather facetiously. I feel almost proud at her daring. He has already burnt most of his bridges with his agent by greedily planning to get married *twice*. When will he wake up?

'Well, I'll go to the audition then,' he says. We all know by tomorrow that Kate will have put her kitten-heel in and the audition will be cancelled.

Ten o' clock comes and still no Motorbike Boy. I stare at the empty space. Mr Happy and Mitesh are sharing a joke by his desk. Nothing else happens.

I'm Not Being Funny, but... comes over to talk to The Capricorn and I pretend to type but I can't stop looking at the skin tag she has on her face, just below her eye. I fantasise about cutting it off. How can people live with that? Like The Capricorn she is one of those women who doesn't put on weight ever. Also like The Capricorn, she is strangely sexless. I imagine someone trying to have sex with her would be about as sexy as someone struggling to carry a wardrobe up a staircase. You might sweat a little, and something would poke against your ribs now and then, but that would be about it.

The Martyr is talking on the phone to someone with a foreign name and keeps repeating it, as if to prove she can pronounce it. She once went into an ill-advised spiel about Muslims and I nearly had a heart attack waiting for her to shut up before anyone heard. She was oblivious.

I go to the toilet, just because I need the toilet. It does happen sometimes. The green is as vulgar and taunting as ever. I block it out. After I wash my hands I catch sight of my face in the mirror. Sometimes the urge to cut my *face* is so strong I have to fight it off. I fantasise about it, slashing my cheeks, cutting myself some new cheekbones.

I will never do it.

There are boundaries.

Boundaries imposed by society, not me.

I read once about Ian Curtis from Joy Division. That when he hung himself he sliced his mouth at the sides so it would look like he was smiling to the person who found him hanging. It was so grotesque and beautiful an image I wondered if it could be true. I searched and searched for information about it but Google was unyielding. It was probably common knowledge a generation before. I still wonder. Is it an urban myth? I thought it was an act of sickening heroism.

I wonder about things in people's heads. In my head.

We have our own suicides of course, my generation, whatever the hell that is, but it is too easy just to shoot yourself. Lazy. Gives you time to write stupid suicide notes blaming mummy and daddy and quoting rubbish songs.

Hanging yourself requires commitment. Time to think.

Extra details were something to ponder. Things to leave behind, in the absence of a note.

I roll back my sleeve to look at my burn mark. It has finally started scabbing up now, thick and brown. I can't wait to pick it in a couple of days. I know you're not meant to pick them. I know that, of course.

But I'll still do it.

I do a lot of stuff I shouldn't, have you

noticed?

I go to the kitchen to make a cuppa, reasoning it will kill five minutes. My mum used to call tea 'mind-sellotape' at home because it always sorted you out if you were in a mess. My mum used to call water 'council-pop'. She had a nice line in beverage-based nicknames but not much else going for her.

But I still call tea that in my head.

Bowser is sitting in the kitchen alone, looking pensive. He doesn't say much to me normally, so I just ignore him and make my tea as fast as humanly possible.

I am nearly out the door when he speaks.

'Steph?' It seems strangely casual.

'Yes?' I say, turning.

'How long have you worked here?' he asks. Great, *now* he wants a conversation, now I have burning hot tea balancing between my hand and an open door. The question sounds like a trick.

'Three years.'

'Don't stay here much longer,' he says, and he reminds me of an old soothsayer, a wise man up a mountain. I'm not sure if it's a threat, or friendly advice, or something else.

He leans back and the speckles on his bald head seem to twinkle in the light from the window.

'There's a big world out there.'

And I'm left with a slow-burning hand and a massive sense of creepiness.

I sit back at my desk, and look over to his chair. Nothing.

Where is he? Probably ill. Possibly dead. I imagine his motorbike wrapped round a lamp

111

post, a tree, a lorry. I imagine him decapitated. *Now you see him.*

Stop it! What the fuck is wrong with me? He's probably got a day off. He's probably a temp. He's probably just on a half-day.

Still, fear lodges in my stomach. Because you never know.

You just never know.

Tuesday

Something even worse has occurred than the previous empty desk of Motorbike Boy. This morning *someone else* is sitting in his seat, a fat new bloke with a nu-mullet who looks like a Gary or a Barry. I just want to go over and physically remove him. I dare to risk embarrassment by asking The Martyr about Motorbike Boy. The Capricorn has gone to make a herbal tea so the coast is clear.

'What happened to that guy who was sat down there last week?' I ask, casually. Despite her neuroses, The Martyr knows most things, and what she doesn't know can be discovered pretty sharpish.

'I'll find out,' she says conspiratorially, and disappears off to talk to Bowser. Two minutes later she's back.

'He wanted this week off, but he's only a temp so they fired him,' she says, matter-of-factly.

'Oh,' I reply, and my heart pulls down the shades and folds in on itself. I feel like I'm getting a repeated kicking from some imaginary God I've annoyed. Two men in less than a month have evaporated; one revealed as a prick, the other dispensed with. I can foresee an incredible drought ahead (and possibly a plague of locusts... one is stuck to The Capricorn's computer already). But I don't give a fuck about Ratrick. I actually *like* Motorbike Boy.

If only I'd found out where he lived. If only that phone hadn't rung.

Then – what?

On dictionary.com the word of the day is **antipathy**: *A strong feeling of aversion or repugnance*. I wonder if you can be antipathetic. I type it in. Yes, you can. Good.

Jim is flicking through yesterday's paper. 'What was your horse called again?' he asks me.

'Um... Pink Wafer or something.'

'Mine should have been called Limp Biscuit.' The Capricorn cracks. A witticism! I'm shocked.

'*Pink* Biscuit! That was yours, wasn't it?' Jim says to me.

'Yeah, why?' I ask. 'Did it die going over a fence?'

'You came second!'

'Cool. So much for my donkey, hey?'

'Hey, I wonder who came first? If no one picked the winner then you've won.' Jim says.

'It's worth asking,' The Capricorn agrees. I shrug and go over to Rambo's desk, expectations fairly low. He sits prone behind it, reminiscent of Jabba The Hutt receiving his courtiers. I don't feel much like Princess Leia.

'Hey, guess I didn't pick a donkey after all, Rambo,' I say, cheerfully.

'Why, what did you come?' he asks. He has a picture of his baby as a mouse mat. There's nothing worse than people acting like they are the first people on earth to have a baby. Any pea-brain could procreate, as Rambo had proved quite adequately.

'Second place.' I reply. 'So who won, then?'

'Ah well,' he says, twirling his pen round his disgusting trotters. 'That's the thing. I did.'

I frown. '*You* did? I thought you picked a donkey.'

People start to look.

'I did, but I also picked the winner.'

'I didn't know we could pick two.' I say.

He shrugs.

'So who saw you pick your tickets?' I am half-joking around, but I can tell I've got his back up.

'These girls,' he says, gesturing vaguely to some of his team.

'Who saw him, then?' I ask. They all kind of shrug or look at their feet. I am only teasing, really; mostly, but he is riled.

'What are you saying?' he snaps. The pen has stopped twirling.

'I'm just saying, if I was running the sweepstake, I'd make damn sure someone saw me pick out the winning ticket. Out of fairness.'

Which is true.

'So you're calling me a cheat?' he asks, getting all puffed up. I can't believe how quickly this has all run away from me. Now *I'm* annoyed. I would fully expect questions to be asked if the tables were turned – it doesn't seem unreasonable to me at all. Plus I'm still pissed off about Motorbike Boy and maybe I want to hurt someone. But that's another story.

'You're the one with £40 in your back pocket,' I point out. I am aware that 'the girls' are looking at me with a kind of abject horror.

'Well no one else has complained,' he says.

'That's because no one else came *second*,' I point out. 'Oh forget it,' I say and walk back over to my desk.

'That sounded like it went well,' The Capricorn says.

'No kidding,' I reply. 'How dare I have an

opinion or a horse in remission?'

Later I pass Rambo as I go to the toilet. He blanks me. I realise that this is no bad thing; it will actually make a nice change from having to smile and say hello to the fat fucker in future. I wonder who else I can annoy. I might actually get some peace around here.

I push open the toilet door. They have changed the perfume in the air freshener and now it's like a really strong wicker-basket full of granny-scented pot-pourri. It makes me choke. I look at myself in the mirror and see I'm quite flushed. My skin is crap. My body is always letting me down. I put some water on my cheeks and look back at the mirror. Something catches my eye.

Oh my God, what is that?

Something is glimmering at the top of my scalp. I lift up a section of my fringe. Is that a *grey* hair? I can feel my heart pounding as I weed out the culprit. I had only just had my hair done. Did they miss a bit? I yank it out. This isn't as fun as last time when I was yanking normal hair. I hold the follicle up to the light. It's worse that I imagined. The root looks pure *white*! Oh my God, how can I go white, I haven't even lived yet. The humanity!

I turn from the mirror and go into my favourite cubicle. Everything is fucked up. Motorbike Boy is gone, everyone hates me, and now I am officially over the hill. Motorbike Boy would never have fancied some old, *white*-haired fat girl anyway.

I bang my head against the cubicle wall but it wobbles. It's not solid enough to really help. I try again but it makes a funny noise and I think I'd better stop in case it breaks. I'd have trouble explaining that one. Sorry, When Animals Attack, I fell through the toilet wall. Can I go home now?

That old granny smell is too overpowering, anyway. I go back to my desk, and look through my inbox. And it occurs to me that everything is a battle of wills, a battle of personality; even the blandest work email is fighting to be heard.

I reach under the desk and into my bag for my tablets, doing it underneath, so The Capricorn can't see. But the bottle doesn't rattle in my hand.

I'm out.

<u>Wednesday</u>

A temp has started work, a pretty student, with iridescent blonde hair and red glittery shoes. The Martyr admires them, coveting the 'ruby slippers'. I wonder if they remind her of something in her past, some missed opportunity, some lost hope. I am envious of them, too. I wouldn't have the courage to wear them, to make myself stand out. The ruby-slippered girl has been employed to print off very skinny yellow labels and stick them onto every single one of the hundreds of hanging files that line the office walls. It looks mind-numbing in the extreme. I'm surprised they didn't ask me to do it.

Because she doesn't have a desk, no one really talks to her. She just prints labels, and sticks them on, a ghost between the walls. I am envious of that, too. But still, I suppose my desk gives me some false notion of status.

Some people are so obsessed with status, the fact they are one step up the ladder to you. It never occurs to them you don't even want to be on the fucking ladder in the first place.

Some people get off on telling people what to do, demanding respect.

But no one really tells me what to do. And I respect no one.

Especially not myself.

Work really reminds me of school; these people all look like kids in their suits. It's virtually school uniform. Dressing up. Faking it. Except at school you are rewarded for intelligence, whereas here it's stamped upon.

Initiative terrifies these incompetent buffoons, scared for their 32-grand-a-year team-leader roles. Like I want that. Like that would ever be my ambition. So I play dumb. No one knows what I'm plotting, their demise. Or my escape. Whichever comes first.

An email announces itself. They have redone the telephone list. I put it up, pushing a drawing pin into the partition that divides Mitesh and I. I am jealous of the feeling of it going in, the satisfying way it pushes through the dark blue fabric, into the board beneath, making a perfect hole. I fantasise about doing it to my arm, right here, so everyone can see.

I can't stop thinking about it.

Holes and holes and holes.

The Martyr is lurking and is talking on the phone very loudly. She is telling someone a postcode and she says 'Zee for Zeebra'. I feel like saying, 'It's not fucking *Zee* for *Zee*bra, it's fucking *Zed* for Zebra.' But I don't. Fucking Americanisations. She'd probably spell that 'Americanizations'. I feel furious about it. Furious at her for existing.

After her phone call is finished The Martyr turns round and tells me that Thyroid complained about *my laugh* in a meeting. Yes that's right, that's my fellow colleague complaining about someone *being happy*. I would almost be speechless at this if I hadn't already had a hint of it with her phone call. How does one control their laughter? Laughing is an instinct, it comes from the heart and the gut. Basically she is saying she wants me dead rather than laughing. That is the only conclusion I can reach.

The very premise of business seems to be about crushing people. It's frightening. I want to stick a pair of scissors in Thyroid's throat. Every time *she* laughs (extremely loudly, I might add) I glare in her direction. She doesn't see me. She only notices me when I dare raise my voice over the required level.

I hate The Martyr too for mentioning it, for feeling she needs to. It is another jab in the ribs.

The Martyr's friend Rita comes over to look for her but she's buggered off. Rita is about The Martyr's age, around 50, that age where you seem to start losing your marbles, especially if you're a woman. The age where you get your hair cut short.

Rita once commented that Patrick 'seemed to glide like a vampire'. I think of it every time I see her now. Every day lately her and The Martyr seem to be involved in a kind of dance back and forth, one trying to find the other. There is something very Benny Hill about it. And like Benny Hill, it's chronically unfunny and repetitive.

I escape to the kitchen. Jim is the only person in there. He looks morose.

'Hey Jim, what's up?' I ask, pulling out the seat beside him. It scrapes backwards with a guttural yelp.

'Oh, nothing. You know.'

Jim is not usually down. Lazy, yes. Ignorant? Certainly. Obnoxious? Always. But down? It doesn't seem right.

'This place can really hurt.' I say. I had meant to say 'suck', but hurt just seemed to fall out of my mouth. Jim doesn't correct me.

'It's not that.' He says, rubbing his eyes, and he still looks young to me, like a boy, even though he is over ten years older than Kate and five years older than me. He looks like he should still be behind the bike sheds. 'Well, it *is* that. I'm just wondering when I'm going to get a break. I'm not young anymore, Steph. I pictured my twenties playing a leading man. Bang, I turn around and they've gone.'

Yeah, like five years ago, I think.

'I hate to tell you this but you're no Josh Hartnett, Jim.' I say, and he laughs. 'Not even in your heyday.'

'He's a shit actor, anyway. No, but now I'm just a character actor. Worse, I'm an unemployed character actor. I'm a character actor without a character.' He presses his palm against the table. 'When I think of all the things I could have done.'

That was Kate talking, not him.

'But you *couldn't* have done those things.' I say, honestly. 'Because you were compelled to be an actor.' I don't know how I know this is true when nothing has ever compelled me except an irresistible urge to butcher myself. But I do.

'You're right.' He agrees. 'But where has that got me?'

'Listen,' I say. 'You have to look at it like an episode of Deal or No Deal.' He raises an eyebrow. Even I don't know what the fuck I'm saying.

'No, really. Is it worse to take the gamble and lose everything, than to take the money and have regrets? You might wish you'd taken the money now, but you'd hate yourself if you had.'

He nods. 'I know.'

I know Kate never says things like this to him. I know she says the opposite. She had said some shocking things in front of me about acting, about how it is a selfish, silly profession, so God only knows how she browbeats him behind closed doors.

I think of the entertainment industry. I think of all the contestants who try out for things like X Factor and all the other talent shows. On top of that, I think of all the brilliant singers who wouldn't be seen *dead* trying out for X Factor. Add to this the writers, artists, and everyone else creative. I think of how many make it. Less than a fraction. I think of all those broken dreams laid out end to end, back to back, an infinite spiral, an endless road. Most of them end up in a place like this. If they are lucky, they keep their dream as a hobby. If they're unlucky, their partner tells them to grow up, pack it in. Or they just pretend it doesn't matter anymore.

'You look sad, too, Steph,' Jim says, and I'm aware I'm staring at nothing, staring at air.

'Some days just seem worse.' I say. 'But nothing really changes.' These words sounded more comforting in my own head.

Jim leans back in his chair like we used to at school, at a 45 degree angle, fingertips balancing against the table.

'So when are *you* going to get out of here?' Jim asks me.

'I'm...' I start to say and then the door bangs. The Capricorn appears in the doorway with a felt-tip frown; an angry centipede.

'Oh, *here* you are!' She says. 'Fancy doing any

work today? *Both* your phones are ringing off the hook. Am I your servant, now?'

Neither of us answer, but we both stand up and follow her out. Jim catches my arm as we walk out the door.

'It'll be alright, Steph.' he says, and I'm not sure if he's telling me or himself.

The phones are not ringing off the hook. An email pops up in my inbox called **Hello, friend**. It is from J.D. Piggles.

The body of the texts reads:

What else should you do to make her happy?

self-policy licking stone charity work cluster bean pile-woven hair washer all-eyed sugar-chopper sickly-looking smoke-paint gutta sundik sheep bell full-freight pulse-time modulation flag officer

pia-arachnitis sizer tap multiple-die uniform-proof squeeze-up coffee break mis-seek pine-tree flag sock lamb

'Multiple die' catches the eye. Strangely so does 'pine tree flag sock lamb'. I stare at this random mixture of words. There is no link, just a colourful use of language to fool the spambots. I wonder if they've given me a virus. I wouldn't mind. I'd just accept it, along with everything else.

<u>Thursday</u>

I am beginning to feel a pathological hatred for Thyroid. I don't even want to sit on the toilet seat anymore in case her fat arse has sat on it. I go two floors up to make sure. There's no way she would haul her heavy load up this many stairs. I feel powerful, I am going somewhere they don't go.

This toilet is virtually identical. I expected some minor differences, like when you go into different chain restaurants and they alter the colour-scheme to try and hide the fact that they are homogenising the world, bit by bit.

The only big difference is the view, which is more panoramic here. I feel slight vertigo. I can see the roof-tops of the superstores. This must be how God feels. Permanently disappointed.

The cubicles look the same although the toilet seat is slightly less comfortable than the downstairs one. Maybe these toilets are slightly dirtier than ours. Probably the cleaner is tired by the time he or she gets to these ones.

I feel like I'm having my period every two weeks these days. That is how fast time is flying. It is terrifying. What if years pass and I don't notice? I'll just keep counting the days, ripping them off my desktop calendar with soul-destroying quotes such as 'a life without cause is a life without effect' or 'The most important trip you make in life is meeting people halfway.'

I don't want to meet people halfway. I just want to feel something other than this.

I can't help thinking about Motorbike Boy

again. How he could have saved me. Then I hate myself for being so stupid, as if life is that simple, as if women are still that backwards. Yet the fairytales were so fucking potent weren't they; all that Rapunzel-shit got buried deep inside and nothing can root it out.

We were so lied to.

I think about when I was a child, how self-assured I was, certain that I could do this, this and this, and that everything would fall into place.

I was certain one day I would magically turn into an adult.

And why not?

That was what we were promised.

It just never happened.

And the grief seems so strong, to be this child, in this adult body, and none of the bullshit was the slightest bit true.

Work hard at school and you'll get a good job. False.

Every girl wants a white wedding. False.

Every girl wants a baby. False.

If you wish hard enough, or work hard enough, or just believe, or pray, or fucking dream it you can do anything. False, false, false.

And the worst part of it is, all those fucking adults who told you those lies, or who read you those lies, knew it was a fucking lie, too.

They brought you into this world knowing full well.

The pain of this disintegration of trust just seems too much to bear.

I remember believing that adults knew better, or at least knew *something*. The shock when you realise – it's all just a game, they're just acting as well – it's devastating.

Oh, just fucking grow up, Steph.

Get over it.

Get on with it.

So I will.

I have a razor blade in my sock today. I know I shouldn't keep them there, I could easily slice off a toe, or into a vein, but sometimes it seems too frightening not to have... things to hand. Everything is in one box or another, the First Aid Kit, my tin, me. I want to be a maverick, shake things up a little. I don't want to wait.

I hold out my wrist and roll up my sleeve. I'm not doing the arm I burnt. I don't even want to look at that right now.

This arm is better. My skin is so white. I'll just do three.

I pounce.

One, two, three. Familiarity doesn't breed contempt, so there it is again. Freedom. I lean back against the cistern. This must be how junkies feel. And am I any better or worse?

I feel it.

I feel it.

I feel it.

My head is so clear, like water pouring from a spring. Like the view of the green belt from a hot-air balloon.

This is love.

But it's fleeting.

It won't hurt for a little while but then sometimes it will itch all night. I love the scabs apart from the itch; I love picking them off. It's comforting.

I haven't done the burn one yet. I'm saving it up for when I've forgotten it better.

I loosely pull my sleeve down. It's not bleeding much, water will wash it away. A plaster will cover it.

I walk downstairs and go into the kitchen. Empty – it's my lucky day. The First Aid Kit sits on the wall as proud as a stuffed deer's head. It calls to me. I walk towards it, checking over my shoulder.

I unclip it, rummaging inside. I wonder who restocks it, and if they care about it as much as me. I think of the Airstrips. I think of white bandages, rolling out like streamers, stretching out, curved, a pathway out of this place.

What's this?

The Airstrips have been replaced with a different make of plaster. Gone is the white packaging, and the lettering in a safe navy blue. Instead, in gaudy red lettering I read 'Europlast'.

Europlast? Urgh. I hate to think of Europe encroaching into my space. I imagine opening the packet and seeing Tony Blair or Jacques Chirac embossed on the plasters, fucking ruining everything. Even imagining my blood seeping over their faces doesn't help. 'Stephanie?'

I turn round too late. I was too involved in my fantasy and now I'm exposed. The First Aid Kit lolls open like a retarded mouth. I have a box of Europlast in my hand and a bleeding wrist. I've been caught with my pants down.

The Capricorn is looking at me. She's got me sussed. I just know it. I'm praying blood isn't crawling out from my sleeve, dripping on the floor. I imagine great pools of the stuff, like stigmata.

I am Jesus.

Probably there's nothing.

'Looking for something?' she says.

I want to say '*fuck off*'. I want to say, '*yes, duct tape for your fucking mouth, you nosy bitch.*' I want to say, '*yes, your personality.*'

Instead I sneak a look at my arm. It's OK. Everything's OK. Keep calm. Keep breathing.

'I've cut myself,' I say.

'Stop doing it then.' She looks right at me.

Time stops. I know it's a cliché, but the kitchen is now on pause, like a Sky box or a DVD.

'No, no... it was an accident.' I try to explain.

'It's not an accident, Stephanie,' she says, and my stomach feels like it's having a punch up with my liver and losing.

This is not meant to happen. She is not meant to know. How the fuck does she *know*? I feel like I just went over a big dip on a rollercoaster and the ride may not be over yet.

'I...I...' I'm stuttering. I'm agog. I didn't even know it was possible to be agog in real life, only in books.

She says, 'If you will keep picking at your fingers, they will bleed, won't they? It's inevitable.' She has the tone of a prim mother.

But still, I am saved.

I suddenly realise we're talking about a severe form of nail-biting, and not self-mutilation. My stomach lies back down like a good dog.

I put the Europlast back and push the First Aid Kit shut. It clicks satisfyingly. 'Thanks for the advice,' I say, sarcastically, and walk past her, relief mingling with the afterglow of cutting.

Everything is right with the world.

I live to fight another day. I feel the damp stain under the cotton of my sleeve and know that only I know.

Nothing can hurt me.

Friday

Fridays child is loving and giving.

Allegedly.

The Toxic Racist is pushing Mitesh around in the middle distance, joking that he stinks of curry. I use the word 'joking' extremely loosely. The comments he makes are so predictable yet vile it makes my blood simmer. I just don't understand how it can even be happening these days; is this office in a time warp? Do we not have human rights here?

I turn to Jim. 'I find that guy's casual racism completely offensive.'

'Tell me about it. He's scum.'

I realise I love Jim (sometimes).

The Capricorn interjects. 'Why don't you take Mitesh aside and ask if it bothers him?'

'I don't give a shit if it bothers him, it bothers me.' I snap. Mitesh would sell out his grandma if it got him in with the 'cool kids', it didn't mean I had to listen to it. It wasn't the point.

The Toxic Racist is an outside contractor of ours. He is disgustingly ugly with a glass eye and a menacing leer. He swans in like he owns the place and The Martyr seems to love him nearly as much as she loves Santana Man. In fact she seems to have a pretty faulty cunt-dar. Which is probably why she has nervous breakdowns like I have trips to the toilet.

At lunchtime I dive out to get some air and some food. Sometimes I think it's good to be unattractive walking down the street. It must be horrible to be beautiful and ogled, beautiful yet objectified. I like my anonymity. My obscurity.

How can people desire to be famous? I couldn't think of anything worse. People following you with cameras. Chasing you. Coming up to you when you were shopping, or eating, talking to you, thinking they knew you. I'd snap. I'd kill someone, really I would. How can people stand it? How can people desire it? Am I an alien for not understanding? So many people want that. Why?

I feel disconnected from the world. Puzzled by it.

But at least it doesn't notice me.

I wonder how many times I've written down my address, or read out my phone number. How many times I've signed my own name. How many times I've written my address. How many times I've said 'hello' or 'thanks'. All the signatures and hellos and thanks in the future seem so endless and frightening. I want to cut them off, throttle them. The weight of things to do cripples me. But it's not major things that scare me. It's the minor ones that taunt me; the thought of 50 years of electricity bills, 50 years of shopping bags, trips to the doctor, trips to the toilet – trips to the First Aid Kit.

And 35 more years of work. Elasticated waists. More make-up. Questions as to why you aren't married, why don't you have a family, what are you going to do with your life?

Except no one cares enough to ask.

Parts of my past seem so distant and far away. Memories seem so tainted by age that it is hard to believe it was me as that little girl, or that teenager. Me that had been to that place, said that, seen that, or done that thing.

I feel disconnected from myself as well as everything else. Like a spectator.

Or a spectre.

Back at work, I notice people gathering at the bottom of the office. Jim and The Capricorn go to have a nose, so reluctantly I peer over my monitor to see what is going on.

Of course, The Toad is leaving today. She's done her time. Jammy cow. A gift is being presented to her. No one asked me to contribute, I have no idea why. Bowser makes a stirring speech about her having 'a hard exterior but a heart of gold'.

Translation: she's a bitch.

The Toad is giggling like a little girl. She says amongst other banalities, 'I've met loads of nice people and progressed in many different ways.'

Mainly in her jeans sizes increasing, I suspect. This public display of love and affection makes me want to hurl. No one bats an eyelid at each other usually and then when someone leaves it's like they're being knighted. Some vile red punch is handed out that tastes like cough medicine. She's probably poisoning us as a stylish, final goodbye. Now that would impress me.

Being forced to look at The Toad for this long (something I normally avoid) it occurs to me that she actually has nail *flab*. Her nails curl dangerously under the pressure of her fingers expanding. I wonder idly if anyone has ever got so fat their nails have pinged off. That would be a big hit on You've Been Framed.

She finishes, 'I've really enjoyed working here

and will miss you all very much.' I can't work out which of the two is the bigger lie. It's a mind-boggler right up there with the colour of the paint in the toilets.

Thyroid gets up and gives her a big jiggly hug. I can't count the rolls of flesh on display but they make me look positively anorexic. Never mind booty, they've got the whole fucking car and a bike rack twice over. Thyroid doesn't have nail flab, because her nails are stuck on. She does, however, have trotters.

Thyroid says, 'We've had our good times and bad...'

Translation: we're both a pair of bitches.

I switch off for the rest. It is actually getting painful standing here and witnessing this, but I risk further alienation if I return to my desk. I swig on the putrid punch and bide my time. Obviously I'm the first to run away when the cloying speeches are over. I go to the kitchen and pour my punch down the sink. It trickles away like blood.

'Not keen?'

I turn around.

Oh fuck. It's *him*.

'No, not really.'

'Nah,' he continues. 'I'm not too into this exotic stuff myself.' I don't want to look at him or his dead, glass eye. Yet disturbingly, he is advancing towards me. His other eye seems similarly dead; cold and fish-like.

The Toxic Racist.

He leans his arm against mine as he stands at the sink. I step back but he is still so close I can almost taste what brand of cigarettes he smokes.

I can see his stubble like cinders, his fingers like stubs.

'You've got a nice rack on you.' he says, and smiles, but it's not really a smile. It's like someone has cut his face open and yanked his lips apart, and his little teeth are all red from the punch.

'You can't say that!' I say, pathetically.

He just has.

He's a moronic, slobbering vampire. I think of litigation. But he's not even a real employee.

But now his look changes. 'What's up? I'm doing you a favour. You're not the skinniest bird in this place.'

I wonder if anything has ever felt *less* like a favour in my entire life.

'I still have full use of my eyes,' I say, not really meaning to insult *his* eye impediment, but that's clearly how he takes it. His real eye narrows, and he grabs my wrist.

'You should watch yourself,' he says. 'You're not quite as smart as you think you are.'

Is this really happening? This is like something out of a nightmare. Wake me the fuck up already! I look up at the First Aid Kit. Help me! But it does nothing.

The door bangs open behind us and he lets go, but his fingers still feel there to me. He touched me! The Toxic Racist touched me, and practically threatened me. For no reason!

His touch is made more horrible by the fact no one has touched me in... in... I slam the door on that thought.

He is walking out, he is leaving the kitchen, and I'm doing nothing. I want to shout at him, call him out. But I don't.

You're not as smart as you think you are.

Well that was true.

But I was smart enough to know that much, at least.

Part 2.... Onwards and Upwards

Monday

As if by magic, summer comes. It is like someone has turned on a gas fire in the sky and suddenly it is warm, a muggy city warmth. How long will it last though? Probably not until the weekend.

There is a dead rat in the car park today, as big as a puppy.

I walk around it.

The tyranny is over. The Toad is a distant dream. Still there are so many obstacles in my path. Bowser. When Animals Attack. The Martyr. I imagine picking them off with a sniper rifle. I point it at Bowser's head and fire. It explodes like a melon, spewing out juices. I will stalk When Animals Attack longer, he will cry and beg under my command. The Martyr I will let live. She is not intentionally cruel. She is not like them; predators.

But she does have her down side. Her son has just started working here for the holidays, just back from university and thinks he knows it all. He's studying rocket science, of all things. I want to imagine scientists as mysterious and sexy, not acne-covered little runts with no off-switch. He just talks and talks at you. I can't be bothered to even pretend to listen.

'And then me and my uni mates took all these people back to our digs...'

I wonder what his home life must be like, what relaxation time with The Martyr felt like. But I knew it didn't exist. I knew she'd fly from one crisis to the other even at home. Even if it was just burnt toast, chipped crockery or dirty

139

washing. She'd ham it up. She'd make them pay.

'... won six games of pool, *in a row*! They couldn't get me off the table...'

Please shut up.

A card comes round. Patrick is leaving. This once would have caused me something like pain but I can't be arsed to care now. Motorbike Boy hurt way more, because there had been a glimmer of something between us, at the roundabout and the photocopier. There had been something. He lived five minutes from the station but it could have been five hundred miles, Proclaimers-stylee, because I didn't know where, did I?

Apparently Patrick is going to another office just like ours, for a couple of grand more. What's the point? If you're going to get out, *really* get out. That's what I'll do.

One day.

I put 50p in the collection money envelope and write in the card, 'hope your spelling improves in your new job'. I don't sign it.

Jim sends me an email.

It says;

All the boys over there dream of having you in a gang bang.

I look at Credit Control – Penfold and Mitesh, nobody's dream dates. They don't even have a leader now. That would be just my luck, sex symbol to the geek contingent. It was just horrible enough to be true.

In between the filing cabinets I can see Rocket Science Bore chatting up Ruby Slippers. Poor her. No desk and now she'd caught the eye of the Mini-Martyr. Unlucky.

I get up and go to the toilet, whacking Jim lightly round the head on the way. The green isn't bothering me today, I feel strangely calm. I am wearing a crochet cardigan that wraps round, and the tie at the back keeps dangling down the loo so I keep having to remember to rescue it. As I do, an orange Post-it note flutters down to the floor. I pick it up.

Frigid

Hmm, I wonder who could have put that on my back?

I say nothing and write one of my own back at the desk. Except I use printer labels instead of post its. Post-its were clearly not up to the adhesive requirements of this particular job.

Alcoholic

I also get wise, and stick it to the back of Jim's jacket. Then he can be laughed at for being an alkie all the way around Tescos or the pub, or wherever he ends up later, instead of solely at work.

Rocket Science Bore and Ruby Slippers carry boxes up and down the office. The hired help. I watch them go backwards and forwards, backwards and forwards like robots. At least they had a university to escape back to one day. And Rocket Science Bore had the cosmos to comfort him.

The Martyr calls me into the 'cupboard' for my one-to-one. We are meant to have them each month. This is my first in a year and it's only because it's any-excuse-to-not-give-us-a-pay-rise time and she has to have something in black and white.

We sit in that cramped little room together,

the shredder in between us. She takes out a wire-bound notepad.

'So how are you getting on?' she asks me. Her expression is blank.

'Fine.' I stare at the boxes, all piled up. I stare at the filing cabinets.

'What do you think you've achieved this year?'

Not committing suicide. Not killing everyone in sight. Not severing a vein in the toilets.

'I have no idea.' I say.

The notepad remains blank.

I rest my hand against my own notepad and push a biro against the webbing between my fingers. I push and push until I leave tiny circles between each finger because the nib isn't pushed up. It pleases me, the pattern on my skin. She doesn't notice.

'Do you think you've met your objectives from last year?' The Martyr says, and I'm back in the room.

'I have no idea what they were.'

She rummages through her papers. It is futile. She doesn't know where last *week's* work is, let alone last year's.

She stops. 'Nor do I.'

'Shall we just not bother with this?' I say. 'My timekeeping is good... I turn up every day. Just tick yes for everything.'

So she does.

When we get back Kate is sitting on Jim's desk chatting. She holds her hand up and I see the **Alcoholic** sticker clinging jauntily to her index finger, which she points at me accusingly.

'Naughty Stephanie!'

God, she was such a spoilsport.

'I'll get you next time, Gadget,' I say to Jim.

'Sure you will, Steph, sure you will.'

I hear a cry and look up. I notice a woman I've never seen before carrying a baby over by Kate's desk.

Kate squeals and excitedly orders Jim over, a maniacal look on her face. I watch as Rambo stands, his arm encircling this perfectly normal and sane-looking woman. Oh my God, it's the mousemat sprog.

Jim is pulled into the circle, cooing over the Junior Rambo. Kate couldn't have looked happier if it was her own. Of course, this was the Holy Grail of all her scheming, the gold at the end of the rainbow. If she could just get knocked up that would put paid to Jim's silly dreams for good. It would be B&Q, MFI and IKEA forever and ever, amen.

Why is she allowed to bring a baby in here anyway? It's a security risk, a health hazard. Rambo's wife is small, slim and pretty; what's she doing with him?

Somehow The Martyr has got hold of the baby, and she and it loom up at me. She looks satisfied by its existence, not stupefied, as I am. Had she forgotten how marriage and babies were the sticks invented to beat her with?

'I bet you can't wait to have one of your own,' she says, and I can barely contain myself. I look at it, squirming, its hands grabbing at the air. It lolls in The Martyr's embrace, gawping gormlessly at nothing in particular. I think of the selfishness of Rambo, forcing another person to live this life, to have no choice but to live with him, to take on his ideology, to be born into a future of prospects that were raised no higher than working in another shithole like this – probably something worse as the planet was slowly dying on its arse. The audacity of Rambo to pass on that legacy, like it was something worth celebrating, and then pointing it at me like I was supposed to be impressed. How fucked up can you get?

And why can't they see it?

Later Jim sends me an email called Bad Day at the Office. It has an animation of a little stick man tapping away at his keyboard. He starts tapping faster and faster until his little stick arms turn to bloody stumps. After this he starts banging his head on the keyboard over and over again and red blood and his cartoon brains spatter everywhere. It is hypnotic in its rhythmic speed, like a flick-book from childhood. The little stick man's eyeball flies off and his face turns to red mush, but still he keeps banging his head. Finally he lays still, his face buried in his bloody keyboard.

Well. That pretty much sums things up.

Tuesday

Today the dead rat has started decomposing. I catch it from the corner of my eye across the car park and change my route. I avoid it by walking around two cars instead of one. I don't need bitten-out eyes staring at me at this time of the morning. There were quite enough walking corpses inside the office.

A new guy has started in the section next to ours, sitting opposite The Capricorn. I know it seems improbable that staff-turnover would be at such a high rate, but perhaps that tells you all you need to know about this place. The new person is actually quite good-looking, but not my type. Too generic. Too blonde. He speaks in a mumbling not-quite-identifiable Antipodean accent. I look down the staff list online for a new name but can't find him.

I am printing and Jim points out a name on his screen to me. One of our customers is called 'Billy Wiz.'

'That's the best yet,' I reckon.

'Nah, I still like Miss Shitta,' he muses. Miss Shitta actually works for us. Two of our customers are Sultana Banjo, and Elizabeth Hurley. I like it when she writes to me. The Capricorn once wrote a letter to a Mrs Wanka and didn't bother to even tell us until we saw the letter had been printed out. What a killjoy!

'Remember Jeffery Dahmer?' I say, and we both fall about laughing. A guy called Jeffery Dahmer applied for a job in our department once. The Martyr just ripped up his CV without even reading it. Poor bastard. What kind of discrimination was that? Serial killer name discrimination? Later, I reasoned he should have simply put 'Jeff'. That might have been enough to get his CV read, at least.

The new boy's eyes seem to be following me round today. Maybe he is thinking how fat I am or wondering what on earth I'm wearing? It doesn't look like that, though, it feels like… something else. I am not used to it. It makes me think of Motorbike Boy and his quirky beauty. I miss him.

I can hear Mitesh, Penfold and the new guy playing on an anagram site. They obviously have no work to do. They put their names in. The new guy's anagram for his name is 'Smooth Dragon.' I still don't know what his real name is.

Mitesh sends me the link and I put my name in. It comes up with 'Smothery Pisser.' I'm not best pleased. It could be worse, The Martyr's full name comes up with 'Climax Nasal all-rounder.' Quite a mouthful.

Just as I am searching Jim's name my computer completely dies and the lights all go off. The whole office makes a sighing noise as all the electricity cuts out. It isn't dark as there is natural daylight, but it seems kind of spooky when everything is abruptly unwired.

The Martyr jumps up and goes to talk to Bowser. Everyone is talking at once.

'This is exciting.'

'Not if you have work to do.' The Capricorn says.

'No, I just come here for a giggle.'

'Do you think they'll let us go home?' Jim

asks, hopefully.

'Good point.' I say. 'They'll have to, I reckon. Health and safety.'

When Animals Attack swoops in and gives orders to the other stooges. The Martyr comes back over.

'We've got to evacuate. It's not safe with no power, the fire alarms don't work.'

'Told you.'

'Can we go home?' Jim asks.

'No, we're just going to the emergency meeting point.'

What a crock.

Everyone starts to file out. I walk behind the new guy, Smooth Dragon.

'Bit of excitement for your first day?' I venture, which is brave beyond belief for me.

'I know, can't be bad.' He says. 'Hi, I'm Sam.' He smiles at me.

'Steph.' I reply, shyly.

Just as we get to the bottom of the stairs all the lights come back on.

'Goddamit, I was going to have a fag!' Jim complains.

'You *are* a fag,' I say, and The Capricorn does not look amused. I wouldn't say that to anyone but Jim, though.

I walk behind the new boy, noticing his trousers. He has on trousers that are flirting with the casual side of smart. I realise I'm looking at his arse. I didn't mean to, it's just *there*.

An hour later I get an email.

It's from Smooth Dragon. His full name is Sam Goodthorn. It's a sturdy name and it suits him.

Why is he emailing me? My chest feels tight.
He says,

**It's me, Sam. Opposite your mate with
the glasses. I'm bored! Bored, bored,
bored.**

I relax. I can't see him from here as he sits
diagonally opposite me and our computers are in
the way. The Capricorn gets the good spot.
Actually, that's not a good spot. I'd die if I had to
face him all day long.

I look at his email. I realise I don't want to
make the same mistakes I did with Patrick. I
want to seem cool, confident, and funny. I don't
need to run off to the loo and hyperventilate. All
I need to do is reply.

I peek over and see the top of his head but
he's not looking up. He has bleach blonde surfer
hair. *Definitely* not my type.

I reply,

That was a very boring email! ;)

He replies,

**Oh, like that is it? I'm not allowed to
speak to you unless my material is pure
gold. I can't handle that kind of pressure!**

I smile and type back:

**I'm sure you can handle it. Ps. She's
not my mate.**

A few seconds later he replies,

**She keeps giving me evils! I'm tempted
to start smoking again just so I can go
outside for ten minutes. Are you with me?**

I look over my shoulder to check no one is
watching me. The Capricorn and Jim are
engrossed in work and football results
respectively. The Martyr is off somewhere.

I reply,

I think we should start shooting up heroin on a daily basis, it might make everything more fluffy. So anyway, is Mitesh the most boring person on earth? Discuss.

He responds a minute later,

Well, to be honest at first I really didn't get him but strangely enough he's actually growing on me! It's a disturbing, warped little growth but it's growth all the same. Isn't growth an odd word when you look at it? Growth, growth, growth.

Words! He likes words. 'Growth' does seem strangely peculiar, suddenly.

I reply,

He is harmless, he just talks complete and utter rubbish. He's a bit pervy, too. Growth *is* a strange word. But any word is strange if you say it enough.

He types back,

I'm going for a cuppa, you coming?
Then he gets up and walks off to the kitchen. He doesn't look at me as he walks past.

Fear grips me like hands around my neck. This is something, this is like a chance. Go, go, *go*!

But I can't. I can't move.

I can't get up. I can't go to the kitchen with him and have him look at me. Words are one thing, words I can do, this is something else.

I should email him back, make an excuse. But what excuse is there?

I'm too scared to go for a cup of tea?

He'd think I was deranged.

I feel like my chair is a magnet and my body is iron. I'm the iron lady.

I stare at the screen, stare at the word 'growth', that weird little word that brought us together for a second in cyberspace, in Outlook.

Five minutes later he comes back. He doesn't look at me. I think of the animated guy bashing his head against his computer. I think of me.

<u>Wednesday</u>

Today the rat looks like someone has run over it. It's completely decomposed except for the tail, which is almost perfectly intact. It is as thick as rope. It is boiling today, the sky is a fierce blue, unrelenting, like a television screen. It doesn't take long to obliterate a rat corpse in the summer time. In a week it will be like it never existed.

I'm envious.

This thought bounces round my head as I catch the lift to the inside of the volcano.

No emails for me today. Well not from Sam, just from people improbably called Quintupled H. Removals and Nudism D. Pork trying to lure me into visiting their online pharmacies. I marvel at the literary creativeness of these internet highwaymen. I think Mike F. Expropriating is a step too far and redistribute him to junk.

They always come back with a new name though.

Maybe I should try it.

I think of Sam and the cup of tea that never was, how we could have sat easily in the kitchen as friends, discussing the day's headlines or gently complaining about our colleagues. It would have been civilised. Normality.

If I wasn't such a fucknut.

My diary flashes and I see I'm Not Being Funny, but... has scheduled a meeting for next week. I feel immediately wary as she favours the more... *experiential* approach to these things. If we have to do a fucking ice-breaker where we throw bean bags around and 'get to know' people whom we've worked with for three endless years I'll seriously break that bitches' neck. Hers or my own.

I bend a paperclip into an ugly sculpture, and push the pointy end under my cuticles. The Capricorn shoots me a laser-beam glare.

I look back at the meeting invite. I don't like anything that draws attention to myself, anything that involves speaking, sitting in a circle, standing up in front of people, being nice, or networking. Even this word forming in my own head fills me with unimaginable panic. The screen demands, Are you able to attend this meeting? I put down my mangled paperclip and hover my arrow over 'No'.

I type, 'I am unable to attend due to a brain haemorrhage/ family funeral/ chronic inability to look keen about *anything* for two whole hours, especially if you are running it, you squid-faced ring-licker. My apologies.'

I delete this.

I click 'Yes.'

It occurs to me that the definition of an outsider is knowing that nothing you like appeals to others, yet having to tolerate others not knowing this about themselves.

This thought depresses me, and I lift my bag onto my lap. My fingers connect with a tin of lipbalm, my keys, the newspaper. Finally, they hit their target. My little coffin. My little empire.

What can't be cured must be endured.

I wheel back my chair and head for the toilet.

I haven't cut for a week. One week. Seven days. It's not like cigarettes or heroin, where it eats away at you at all time, where it dictates your actions and mood. This creates its own mood, but it doesn't control me.

I control it.

You can't pin it on me any more than that.

But I do try and... cut down.

The bad joke filter in my head lets those pass, but I know I don't want to analyse it anymore. I just want to act. I deserve it. I earned it.

Inside the cubicle, I take off my cardigan. I want to do my upper arm because my lower arm is getting crowded and hasn't been healing as well. Certain cuts are weeping, whilst others are scabbing together in clumps. When I touch certain parts of my skin, I can't feel them anymore. Nerve-endings severed. Half my arm looks like cheap, veiny own-brand ham.

I still like peeling the scabs off, of course, who wouldn't? I like seeing the pink new skin underneath. I'd done the car lighter one now, it had felt simultaneously orgasmic and horrific ripping it off. I'll probably pick it once more before I let it heal for good. One more turn. One more go on the ride, get your money's worth, right?

Sometimes I swear I can smell my skin rotting.

Don't think about that.

Luckily, there is still some territory left unspoilt. I want a smooth surface to work on, to design, to sculpt. Plus, my upper arm is fleshy. There is something appealing about that, like roast chicken, plump and waiting to be carved. I lick my lips, imagining how it will feel, sliding through. I imagine the blood, the bite.

I'm a magician, and the razor blade is in my palm. Derren Brown's got nothing on me, I can do sleight of hand any time I want to. I can even do that thing where he sticks pins through people's skin and they can't feel a thing. I can detach my mind from it if I have to, like Houdini, and just *draw*.

But most times I want to feel it.

That's the whole point.

I twirl the razor blade in my bitten fingers, realising I'm teasing myself, that this is some sort of foreplay. The anticipation is like getting off a plane in a hot country. You're ready to see it, to experience. That feeling like you could be anywhere and no one knows you.

I feel ballsy. I feel like saying, *bring it on*.

I slash myself about four inches across. It smarts like a shot of neat vodka, tart yet warming. Bits of my brain that normally lie dormant suddenly fuse together, crackling like Rice Krispies. The skin parts easily and blood drizzles out like paint. I want to do another, but the canvas is smudged, and I don't want to do one higher. I want to take it all in.

My first drink of the day. My first hit. I think of the junkie on the stairwell waiting. It was all about the wait – then the hit. Then the circle began again, sooner... or later.

No, I can control this. Seven days I'd waited.

I never do both arms at once. I'm not greedy, not in this respect. I need to conserve space. My body is more inner-city London than the countryside, especially these days. Parking is at a premium.

No. I won't do another. It will just lead to

another. I feel strong today. I'm not reacting to something, this is my choice.

My skin feels tender, and I feel sorry for its trauma, yet elated at the release. It is a million times sexier than the burn in the car. It feels righter. That was a mistake, in retrospect. This is the good stuff – the escape, the elimination.

The artistry.

I push on the flesh of the gashed skin to test the damage and blood trickles down my arm. It's quite deep.

I'm torturing myself, a quiet part of me admits.

If I was doing it to someone else, that's what this would be classed as. I'd be locked up.

It feels terrifying and fascinating, horrific and beautiful, that I am causing this decay, that I am destroying myself from the outside, in such a laborious way, dragging out my death, teasing it out.

But it doesn't feel like torture. It feels like a reward.

I hold toilet paper on my arm, watching the blood butterfly under the tissue. Now it's stinging, and I'm glad I stopped when I did.

Just stop forever.

I can't, I wish I could.

No, I don't, I *can* control it.

I'm on top of things.

I ease my cardigan back on, checking the blood isn't creeping out.

No, everything is OK.

I walk back to my desk and Sam is just standing up with his mug in his hand. He flashes me a white-toothed smile that seems genuinely warm, and I smile back, shy. I watch him as he walks past, the brightness of his plaid shirt making his skin look more tanned. He has a natural glow that no English boy could carry off.

Maybe that tea might be on the cards.

Maybe tomorrow.

I can just pretend I am normal, for a bit.

I might not get found out, not straight away.

I can do it.

I sit down at my desk and turn to The Capricorn. 'So, are you going to this meeting next week?'

<u>Thursday</u>

Today the rat has gone completely. It is the fourth day of unbroken sunshine. I remembered the parking space the rat was on like a grid reference on an Ordnance Survey map. Not even a speck of dust remains. He just disappeared as if he was never there.

I am trying not to look up today. I see him arrive from a distance but I avoid eye contact.

The cutting I did yesterday is hurting under my clothes. It's too warm to wear long sleeves, but I've got no choice, and not just for today, either. Forever sweating, forever entombed underneath layers, long sleeves for the summer, autumn, winter, spring. I can feel my skin itching, crawling. I feel angry because I don't even want to do it again when I feel like this, but looking forward to doing it is the only thing that gets me through.

So where am I left in the meantime?

An email pops up.

It's him.

Even after I snubbed him two days ago.

His email is called **Psst... over here.**

It says,

Hey, how are you today?

My arm forgotten, I reply,

I'm cool, how are you?

He replies,

I'm OK but it's less than a month to my birthday. 26 beckons... I'm a Leo... grr!

I reply,

Everyone's a Leo around here. You're

meant to be self-obsessed. I nearly wrote 'elf-obsessed' there. Which would have been quite wrong.

A few seconds later he replies,

I wouldn't describe myself as elf-obsessed, do I come across like that?

I like the way he has left it as 'elf'. I open up Google and image search 'elves'. I reply,

No, not at all. But on the whole Leo's are a bit 'me, me, me'. I don't believe in all that, anyway. I just tried to look up a picture of an elf for you but all these naked women elves came up!

He replies,

Well forward them on, then! About that self obsession thing: I think I have a tendency to show very little interest in other peoples business at times which could be interpreted as being a bit self involved.

Well he seems to be showing interest in *my* business... I forward him a cartoon drawing of a Manga-style half-naked elf-woman.

You can't get sacked for circulating elf porn, can you?

Well 95% of people you work with (actually, scrap that, make that 98%) are complete wankers, so why would you be interested anyway? I was thinking I could write a story about this place. But the readers would kill themselves it's so painful.

He replies,

I know what you mean and I've not even been here a week! Nice pic of a naked

elf by the way. She's hot.

So this story of yours, how would you have written it? Would it be funny? Tragic? Dark? Uplifting? Soul-destroying? Hmmm? Would there be any steamy office affairs?

I reply,

I guess it's would be a black comedy. You want a cameo role?

I have to send a fax. Sam is at his desk, but I can feel his eyes on me. And the office affair thing, I might be out of practice, but I'm not dumb. He was flirting with me, right? I doubt myself even as I think it.

I push an invoice into the fax's waiting mouth. The number I need to send it to is upside-down and backwards. It's tricky to read. The fax starts bleeping and then I hear a disembodied voice coming out of it going 'Hello? Hello?'

Urgh, I'd dialled the phone number instead. I press several buttons, all of which do nothing. Why could there never be a simple fucking 'cancel' key with CANCEL written on it? A STOP or START button? It was all like some secret bloody code, hieroglyphics instead of plain English.

The fax continues to say '*Hello*?' in a woman's voice. I want to smother it, or kick it across the office, to murder her. Who uses fax machines anymore these days? It's like using a VCR or an iron maiden.

Sam strolls over. 'Sounds like someone's stuck in there!'

'That's where I keep all my captives,' I reply.

I wonder if I have lipgloss on my teeth.

'I like your badges,' he says. I look down at my cardigan. I am wearing one badge saying 'Stop looking at my badge' and another one saying 'I hate work'. Suddenly I feel about 16.

'Thanks,' I say. 'I have a badge making machine...' Jesus Christ, why the fuck did I tell him that? Now I sound about 12.

'Wow, really? That's cool.' He thinks for a moment and then said, 'Is the stuff for it expensive? I'm in a band and we wanted to get some badges made up, but I didn't really know how to go about it...'

'Oh it's pretty easy...' and I'm stalling because I'm thinking, God, he *is* gorgeous, after all. His eyes are bathroom-tile blue, and he has a Disney-hero jaw. I hadn't even liked him at first and now he was getting under my skin, and I fucking hated it. 'Its pretty cheap. I've got a lot of refills for it, I can bring in the template if you want, then you can just design it on the computer or draw it...' I'm talking too much but I can't seem to stop. 'Then I just bung in the machine and voila... badges galore.'

'*Hello? Hello?*'

Hadn't the disembodied voice got the message yet? We were busy here!

'Wow, would you do that for me?' he says. 'Yours are really good. It would be so cool if you could design one for me.... I know it's cheeky to ask. Just tell me to fuck off.'

Yeah, right.

'Nah it isn't hard... I'll do it this week. I'll just do one first though in case it makes you puke. I might need to know what kind of band it is, and

160

the colours you want... and the band name...!'

I'm such a fucking geek. I hate myself.

'I'll email you the link for our website...you can check us out... is that cool? That would be so decent of you to do that. I realise you're probably really busy in the evenings.'

'Not really. I mean... I can make the time.' I try to sound casual and fail.

I am a loser.

He touches my arm, I can feel the tips of his fingers grazing one of my scars through my top. I know where each and every one is.

'*Hello? Is anyone there?*'

I am holding my breath without realising.

'I owe you one, Stephanie,' he says, looking straight at me.

I want him to owe me one. I want to owe him one. I just want us indebted one way or the other, so I can end up fucking him if I can, and maybe somehow I could make him fall for me, if I lied somehow, kept my clothes on, or became someone else.

I realise I am just dumbly staring at him, and he looks down at the fax.

'You cancel it with this button,' he shows me, and the ghost in the machine is silenced.

<u>Friday</u>

I am on time. It is a small victory. On everyone's desk has been placed a white sheet of A4 paper, like a napkin. I hang my coat up and pick up the memo, turning my computer on with my spare hand.

Dear All,

Please be aware of company policy regarding the answering of phones. Our recent mystery shopping results are attached, and show that some staff are not answering the phone in the correct manner. We expect a 10% increase in satisfactory- to-excellent customer service by next month.

Please find the correct procedure below:

Good morning/ afternoon, Sir/ Madam, ... department, ... speaking. I apologise if you have been kept waiting, as we value your custom. How can I help you today?

I turn to Jim. 'This is a joke right?'

Jim is staring gormlessly at the Sky Sports webpage. 'I haven't read it, what does it say?'

'You're fired?' I reply. He doesn't even respond. I give up. There is about as much chance of me reading out said-speech as getting a gold medal in pointless-and-soul-destroying-time-wasting at the 2012 Olympics. If I was a customer on the other end of that speech I'd hang up. Oh, maybe that's the idea...

Something hits me gently in the head. It is Sam's memo, folded expertly into a paper aeroplane. He smiles at me over the top of his computer.

'What's up with you? Just read the speech!' he jokes. 'If you don't, you'll be replaced by a robot, missy.'

'They can replace Jim with a Furby in that case,' I reply. 'No, that's too advanced. A Tamagotchi.'

'You're showing your age there,' Sam replies, winking at me. I would normally find winking abhorrent. Instead, I feel mildly aroused.

Jim is oblivious to this gentle abuse, safe in his little football-results cosseted man-web.

I sit down and read several dull emails and attempt to work out some formulas in Excel. Half an hour crawls by. Then one pops up from Sam.

Did the sandwich lady just come and ring her bell or did I just hallucinate that?

Normally you'd see Thyroid *et al* dash for it at the sound of the bell so I suspect not. Before I can reply, Sam stands up and makes a break for the door. He comes back two minutes later, empty-handed.

She was here but she didn't save me any savoury pasty treats, damn her eyes.

I don't know how he could eat that anyway. Saturated-fat in the form of calorific sausage rolls was just asking for trouble at this time of the morning.

At any time.

You shouldn't eat that crap anyway. You will die! I warned.

Yes but I will die happy with little pastry crumbs all over my shirt!

It was a fair point. I wasn't exactly Gillian McKeith. Suddenly Jim snaps out of his reverie. 'Did I just miss the sandwich woman?' A look of

163

panic crosses his face.

'A fucking Furby, I'm serious! It'd get a pay rise, wouldn't it, Jim?'

'What the fuck are you talking about?' he asks, frantically picking change out of his desk drawer. I can hear Sam laughing from his desk, and for a fleeting second, I am happy.

Two seconds later, The Toxic Racist appears behind Sam. I haven't seen him since he assaulted me in the kitchen last week. The thought of it makes my scabs itch.

He is walking in circles, talking into his mobile phone like it's a walkie-talkie. A tinny voice drifts out from the loudspeaker. Wanker. Why do people do that? Just hold it to your ear and have a private conversation like a civilised human-being, for God's sake. I bet he uses a fucking hands-free, too. He is just the type to wander through the town centre, looking like he's burbling to himself like a madman.

He comes over to Mitesh and makes a crack I can't quite hear. I feel myself curling up like a hedgehog, but it just gets worse. He puts on a poor Indian accent and cackles away, his wonky glass eye bobbing like an abandoned beach ball at sea. Mitesh just laughs.

He's about as Indian as I am.

I want to smash the Toxic Racist's teeth in and I hate myself for not saying anything, I hate him for ruining my happy feeling.

I make a promise to myself that if he does it tomorrow, I'll call him out on it, I'll expose him. But I don't know if I will. I let him grab my arm and did fuck all.

I did fuck all.

I walk out to the kitchen to breathe for a second. Think of Sam. Just think of Sam. I feel a strange streak of excitement along with the usual rage and despondency. I look out the window so I look slightly less self-conscious as I wait for the kettle to boil. A kid walks past outside and spots a set of car keys on the ground. He picks them up and looks around. He can't see me as I'm a floor above him. There is a fob on the keys and he points it at the cars parked in the bay alongside him. None beep. He looks disappointed and skulks off. I laugh.

'What are you laughing at?' comes a voice from behind me and it is him, not the Toxic Racist, but Sam. I explain the little scene to him as he makes himself a cup of tea. I pass him the milk and the sugar. It is pleasant, normal. I sit down at a smooth beech table. He stands by the counter top.

Rambo comes in and gets a cup of water from the dispenser. He is still ignoring me. He has his shirt collar turned up for some reason, and it makes him look an utter prick.

I roll my eyes as he leaves.

'What's the deal with you two?' Sam asks.

'He robbed me, so now I'm the one in the wrong.' I explain about the horse debacle. I feel embarrassed telling the story, like it's too petty for his ears.

'He's a smuggard, anyway,' Sam says, stirring in his sugar. He has three spoonfuls.

'Bless him, he tried to palm me off, but I just wasn't having it. It was quite funny really, in retrospect.' I say. Sam looks puzzled.

'Palm you off?' he says.

165

'Yeah. You know, give me the brush off.' I say. Then it dawns. 'What did *you* think that meant?'

He can't stop laughing. 'That means something *completely* different in New Zealand!' he says. 'I thought he wanted to...'

'Oh my God! What a thought! You've just got a dirty mind!'

He laughs, and then just looks at me. He can't take his eyes off me. There is space between us, but there is something filling the space, like a craving or a need. My fingers feel shaky as I watch him. He leans on the vending machine, just looking at me. There is silence.

I glance at the First Aid Kit for reassurance. Then Mr Happy walks in, teeth gleaming, and the atmosphere dissipates.

I am aware of a missed opportunity and an endless weekend awaiting me, like a gaping hole. But on top of that, a new feeling.

Something like hope.

<u>Monday</u>

The Capricorn looks up as fast as if a gun had gone off down the other end of the office.

'Do you have *lipstick* on?'

'No!' Too defensive. Not this again. Is lipstick a crime?

Jim swings round on his chair. 'She does! Who you trying to impress, Steph? Your mouth looks like a baboon's arse!'

'Jim!' I shout, sinking into my chair. I go red too easily. I pray Sam is at the fax, in the loo, anywhere but listening to my humiliation by these two jokers. I can't even think of a good comeback.

Jim's phone rings. I can tell it's his agent. I imagine him free, creative, happy, on a stage, admiring eyes upon him. Him in his rightful place.

Maybe in the next world.

'Job?' I say, as he comes off the phone.

'Possibly, they're looking for a camp Northerner.' he says, enthusiastically. 'He gets hung pretty early on. Sounds alright.'

'Sounds delightful.'

Sam sends me an email.

Maybe they're casting for the Wizard of Oz?

Underneath is a picture of the cowardly lion. I laugh before I can stop myself. It looks exactly like Jim. It's uncanny.

Jim turns around and catches sight of my screen. 'What's that?'

'Nothing!' I say, desperately clicking to shut

it. 'Jim, what does the cowardly lion say in the Wizard of Oz?'

He stops to think. Then inspiration strikes.

'Put 'em up! Put 'em up!' He punches the air. I laugh so hard I almost start crying.

'What!' Jim laughs. I show him the email.

'No way...'

'You so do, mate,' Sam says from behind the wall of his computer. 'They must be doing a West End show of it eventually... just bide your time!'

'Fuck off! Hey, she can be in it with me,' Jim says, pointing at Ruby Slippers amongst the filing cabinets. She has been lumbered with Rocket Science Bore again and he is droning on. Trying to get him to stop would be as pointless as telling a joke to a dog.

Sam gazes in her direction. 'Her shoes are pretty cool.'

'I know.'

'And you can be one of the Munchkins, Steph.' Jim says, smugly.

'Fuck off!' I reply.

And we all know who the Wicked Witch is... Jim emails on the sly. I think he's quite enjoying the attention.

The Martyr comes back from a meeting. She is oblivious to every atmosphere, be it one of jollity or despair. She carries her own mood round like an accessory, her own cartoon cut-out black cloud, and makes you breathe it, whether you want to or not.

'How did the meeting go?' I ask, trying to act like I care. I am double-bluffing myself though as no one expects me to. The Capricorn folds her hands and peers over her glasses, awaiting the response.

'They've said you can only have four glasses of water per day,' The Martyr says. It is such a bizarre statement, I think I've misheard.

'What?'

Jim has already turned back to his computer. He's not interested.

'From the machine. Apparently we're all drinking too much. We're only allowed four from now on.'

'Jesus! Who's going to keep count?' I am joking of course, but I look anxiously at The Capricorn as soon as it leaves my mouth. She'll probably have an Excel spreadsheet knocked up by the day's end.

'I don't know,' The Martyr says, back under her rock. Has she ever laughed at a joke? Been in love? Had a dream?

I eat alone, buying myself a chicken nugget Happy Meal (I'm broke), and sitting on a wall opposite McDonald's. It's fairly unglamorous. The toy isn't great, either.

After I've eaten I peel off a plaster that I put on my finger at home the day before. I picked too much skin off round the nail with a pin. I'd done five fingers yesterday. It's an obsession; as soon as they scab up, I lever off the scabs with any given sharp implement. My teeth are too clumsy sometimes to slice thinly or precisely enough. I prefer pins or a tiny screwdriver. I don't feel the sting anymore. When there isn't a pin or some tweezers close to hand I get anxious. I hate it when they start to heal up. It is hard to find a good starting point again.

Underneath the plaster the skin is wet and

169

white, wrinkled like after a bath. The exposed flesh round my nails is an angry red. I look at the jagged, pulped edges and want to peel off another layer, I want to tidy it up.

But it never ends.

I drop the plaster in a bin nearby and walk back to work. Sam and Mitesh start giggling uncontrollably as I walk back to my desk.

'What's going on?'

'He's a genius.' Mitesh says. 'We love this boy!'

'What is it?' I say, sitting at my desk.

'I'll email you.'

Sam copies in me and Jim, but not The Capricorn.

POYF

You've got unpaid invoices? Do you think we care?

We hear you cry 'this is so unfair!'

We won't answer your calls cos we're too busy laughing

We won't pay your bills cause we're too busy crafting

New ways to insult your family and friends,

Cos it makes us feel good to know you're at the end

Of your wits,

Fuck you twits,

You make us sick

With your shit

(Chorus)

And if you even think of bringing them to

this place,
You best be prepared for us to piss on your
face!
Piss on your face!
Piss on your face!
Come near this place, we're gonna piss on
your face!

And before you think about crying to the
boss man upstairs,
With all of your petty complaints and fears
You'd better know this man, yeah we're all in
on it,
Who the fuck do you think encourages this
shit?
Missed calls,
No replies,
Lost letters,
Faked sighs!

(Chorus)
And if you even think of bringing them to
this place,
You best be prepared for us to piss on your
face!
Piss on your face!
Piss on your face!
Come near this place we're gonna piss on
your face!

We will scour the globe looking for vermin,
To put in your house, we know just how you
like them,
To shit on your floors, to burn down your
doors,

To rip out the sink, you'll be on the brink,
Of total mental collapse, then we might just
relax
And say, 'we've decided to refund
Your money's here, come get it, yeah!'

And when you show up at our place,
WE'RE GONNA PISS ON YOUR FACE!

Jim and I both start laughing in at a volume and in a manner that is entirely inappropriate for the workplace. Especially after my prior laughter ban! If Thyroid hears she's going to go loco. The Capricorn looks disgustedly at me as if we're taking the mickey out of her. The Martyr doesn't bat an eyelid.

Jim stands and gives Sam a high five.

'You are the man. Fair play. Nice work.'

'You should release that with your band,' I say. 'That's a number one right there.'

Sam shakes his head, laughing. 'Just a little ditty I knocked up...' but I can tell he's enjoying the praise.

And I start to think, oh God, I really like this guy. He's smart, funny, handsome. And it makes me panic. It really does.

It makes me scared to death.

Tuesday

Hi Stephanie, it's Sam from the Payments section, I have the details of a gentleman who left a message on my phone over lunch, I believe he might have been trying to contact your department judging by the nature of his message, could you possibly contact him to assist him further?

He says you have his number.
The property in question is:
198b Church Road, London, NW10 3DT
Thank you for your help on this matter.
Regards,
Sam Goodthorn
Credit Control
PS. Let's go to lunch together.

A rush not unlike the feeling of cutting envelops me. Only this time there is no guilt attached. There is only the freedom.

I type:

Hi, Mr. Credit Control. I'd be happy to help with all of your demands.

But only the PS part.
I don't do scary landlords.
Many thanks,
Stephanie Morrissey
Princess of Refunds

I wait.

That's a real message by the way!

I respond,

That's a real answer! I'm hungry.

I can see When Animals Attack milling

around so I have to keep minimising my emails. I wish he'd piss off and let me have my moment.

Sam replies and I furtively peek at the email.

I'm hungry too, I want a saveloy.

I pull a face.

Urgh, they are weird.

When Animals Attack flounces out of the room and the walls exhale with relief.

Yeah, apparently the red skin is cancerous too, but what isn't, huh? All the best things in life kill you.

Well that much is true. Or at the least, hurt you.

I wait for lunchtime like it's Christmas morning.

We go to a café opposite McDonald's. I have never dared go in there on my own. It is a greasy spoon owned by someone scarily devoted to Freddie Mercury. On the grubby-looking walls there are drawings his kids have done of Freddie. Signed records. Framed concert tickets and photographs. The owner of the café is even wearing the famous yellow Wembley outfit. Ok, I'm lying about that one.

Sam sits down under a signed picture of Brian May. I wonder how Brian May has pretty much looked the same for 20 years, except the grey cloud hair, obviously, yet still manages to look so incredibly old. Thoughts of Brian May inevitably lead to thoughts of Anita Dobson, so I try and look at something else.

I am sitting opposite Sam. We both study the menu intently.

'What you having?' he asks. I want chips, but don't want to appear fat. My second choice would be a sausage sandwich. Also not sexy. I had to be careful here.

'Maybe a baguette?' I venture. I imagine trying to stuff it in my mouth with any semblance of dignity. 'No... a chicken sandwich.' I correct myself. I look over my shoulder. 'I'm not that hungry. I don't think you're gonna get a saveloy in here.'

'Is that all you're having? No, no cancer for Sam today, dammit. I'm gonna have an omelette, I think. Follow your healthy lead, Stephsy.'

Freddie Mercury Man comes over and we order. Disappointingly, he doesn't have a moustache. On the plus side, he's probably not been dead from AIDS since the last Millennium either.

'So how's your book coming along?' Sam asks. 'Am I in it?'

'I'm not writing it, it was just an idea,' I say, embarrassed.

'You *should* write it!' he says. 'Give it a nice happy ending. Girl meets boy. Boy teaches girl how to love again.' He winks. Most people can't get away with winking but he does. I feel like he could get away with almost anything.

'I'm not very good at happy endings.' I confess.

'We can but hope.' I feel his foot touch mine under the table. So lightly you almost wouldn't notice.

'I made your badge, then,' I say shyly. I can hardly look at him.

'Oh wow, you're amazing,' he says, rather hyperbolically. I've never met anyone so positive (except maybe Amy). You can tell he's not

175

English.

'You haven't seen it yet,' I warn, rummaging in my bag. My fingers touch the metal. 'I really liked your band. I listened to the tracks on the site.' I had listened to them over and over. There had been photos of him, playing guitar and singing. It was a tantalising glimpse behind the curtain. I had imagined watching them live. Being out for the night. 'The site looks really slick, too.'

'I'm glad you liked it. It's cool you like your indie stuff. Are you on MySpace?' he asks.

I think of pouting teenagers with 13,000 friends.

'No.'

'You should join. It's pretty good. We've had 4,000 listens of our top track.'

Maybe he would invite me to come see his band. Maybe I could be a groupie. No, groupiness didn't suit me. I could be Yoko Ono, though. I could live with that hate quite comfortably.

I hold my hand out with the badge, and he touches my fingers as he takes it from me.

I study him whilst he studies it. His hair is slightly too long to be spiked up and is falling to the side a little. I can see little freckles on his tanned skin, and a scar under his eye. His eyes are that pale, pale blue that only some people achieve, and his hair so blonde it looked like it should have sand in it. He is a prototype surfer boy who just happened to end up in grubby Wembley. Just like Freddie did once.

I can feel my breathing in my rib cage and through my nose.

It all fits.

He looks up at me. 'I love it. I love the colours and the design.'

'It's black and white...'

'It's just right,' he takes my hand and looks right into me. 'Thank you.'

I can feel myself blushing, and pull my hand back. 'It's cool.'

'Hey,' he says, 'What's that on your arm?'

He touches it. I haven't been touched in... I can't remember.

Since the Toxic Racist.

I snap my hand back. My sleeve has rolled up and an angry red mark is peeking out, betraying me. I pull it down, feeling my face redden.

'It's just a scratch... my cat...' I begin, flustered.

'It looks pretty nasty... cats can be right little buggers, can't they?' he sympathises. 'I hate the way they look at you too, like you're their intellectual inferior. You feed the little bastards then they use you as a scratch post! I'm a dog man myself...'

Jammy, my cat, doesn't scratch me. She loves me. I'm such an old fucking spinster. I hate myself suddenly. I feel like my face is next to the grill, along with my sandwich.

But he doesn't notice. I can tell he hasn't. Then I am saved as our food arrives. Sam pulls out his Metro. 'Do you mind if I read the sport?' and I don't. The sexual tension I may have simply invented evaporates and I am left feeling comforted by his ease around me. I take out my own newspaper, luckily not the Mail today, and we both sit there reading quietly. There is a strange apartness and closeness. We could be an old married couple. We are enjoying a silence. He is not forcing me to talk, and make a fool of myself.

I feel safe, here with Sam, under the watchful eye of Freddie.

Wednesday

Lately I've started to notice The Capricorn's stuff creeping onto my desk. Our desks are attached but there is a fine grey line clearly marking out the enemy territory. Yet more of her things are casually crossing the boundary. I gently push them back when she's not looking. She's not noticed yet.

The Martyr's phone has broken and she has been given a temporary replacement. It is the kind that has a ringtone that gets louder and louder if you don't answer it. My nerves feel like the only part of me with a blood supply as it gets louder and louder and LOUDER as if saying 'Please answer me! PLEASE answer me! PLEASE FUCKING ANSWER ME!' except more whiny. She is not at her desk, and it's not in our caller group, so I'd actually have to *move* to answer it. Not going to happen.

To distract myself I open an email to Sam. I can see Mitesh is bending Sam's ear about music and I feel like saving him. I feel braver since our lunch. I wonder if luck changing is inevitable or still just a dangerous dream.

I write,

Doing any work today?

He replies five minutes later:

I will do as much or as little as I normally do, I'm very consistent like that. I'm such a stupid-head, I was bored last night so I tried to download a new ringtone for my phone, the BBC cricket tune, I paid 5 pounds to do it and it

sounds nothing like it! I got burned.

I laugh almost under my breath and get a look off The Capricorn. I don't think she's used to me showing emotion.

That is such a sad story. Why don't I feel sorry for you?

I can hear Mitesh saying, '…and the lead singer used to get so drunk we'd have to carry him into the van…' and Sam making perfunctory yet not entirely convincing 'I'm listening' noises. I can hear him tapping keys to reply to me already, and it feels good, that his attention is already with me, not Mitesh.

Aw, you're a meanie! Mitesh is being so annoying, his stories about his band days are so lame! Help!

I reply,

He thinks he's found a kindred spirit, a fellow muso! Don't send him over here or I'll kill him. He stands too close to me. What sort of band was he in anyway?!

The phone goes again.

'Jim can you pick that phone up, please?' He's sitting right next to it. 'Jim!'

No response.

Sam's reply pops up.

Weddings and birthdays! Hardcore!

I laugh and type,

It doesn't bear thinking about.

After a promising minute of silence, I hear Mitesh say, 'And I remember this other time we went to this place in Birmingham…' and I can picture Sam's face and every bit of me empathises. I feel his pain. But I'm so glad he's here. I needed something to change so badly before.

At lunchtime it's raining so I can't face going out. I sit in the smooth, beech kitchen and read the paper, eating a packet of crisps, listening to the buzz of activity around me. Rambo is sitting with Thyroid, a hotbed of poison. Sam comes in and sits down next to me. He has heated up a Tupperware box full of pasta. I didn't even see him come in.

'Hey,' he says. 'We don't see you that often in here. Slumming it in cattle class. I know you're normally into fine dining.'

'I can't afford the luxury of the Freddie Mercury café every day, you know,' I smile.

'Well of course not!' he says. 'The Freddie Mercury café is for *dates* only.'

'Was that a date?' I laugh. 'That was the best date I've ever had.'

Which was true.

He nods. 'I bet. Is that all you've had?' He points to my origamied crisp packet.

'Yeah – I'm alright, though.' I say.

Cool people don't eat. Just look at them – skinny and stuff in magazines. Stupid but skinny. I'd swap. It would be easier to not think so much, to just think about calories and clothes, and not my internal apocalypse every day.

Rocket Science Bore comes over. 'Hey you two. Do you want to come to my party?' he asks.

Oh my God, jelly and ice-cream at The Martyr's! No thanks. I try not to physically back away.

'What's the occasion?' Sam asks, humouring him.

'My 21st. It's going to be amazing. It will

181

mostly be my uni mates but there's room for a few oldies,' he says, generously.

I think: I would, but I don't want to.

Sam says, 'Maybe. Let us know when it is, yeah?'

'Cool!' He looks chuffed. 'I'll send you the deats!' Then he runs out of the kitchen, banging the door behind him.

'Did he just say 'I'll send you the deats?'' I ask Sam.

'I think so. I think we'll be passing on that one, don't you?'

'Yeah, I don't think it's my thing, somehow.'

'You should go, in fact, you'd probably be the only girl there...' Sam points out.

'I'd rather go to one of Mitesh's wedding discos. So what did you get up to last night?'

'Nothing – the highlight of my night was watching Jackass 2.' He cracks open a can of Pepsi.

'Are you into that twaddle?' I tease.

He laughs at the word twaddle. 'I know. Boys like twaddle, though. Especially stupid or dangerous twaddle. Ha, yeah, like when I was at uni, do you know what two of my friends did?'

'What?'

'They were doing chemistry and they filled a fire extinguisher up with petrol for a prank.'

'That can't be true.' I say.

'I swear!'

'It sounds like an urban myth.'

'It wasn't. I knew them. They got caught and chucked out.'

'Before or after it set the place on fire?' I ask.

'Before, luckily.'

182

'Well, that's taking the Jackass thing a *bit* far. Ha ha, you got your face burnt off. That's not a prank, that's manslaughter.'

Sam laughs. 'You Brits have no sense of humour.'

'Your mates have no sense...'

'True. But then nor do I. You haven't figured that out yet though, so that's OK.' There is a twinkle in his eye, like in books, as he jabs me in the ribs.

And I think; suddenly it doesn't hurt so bad anymore; the pain of being here, because there is someone human to diffuse the soporific hum.

I haven't cut all week.

And I'm not going to.

<u>Thursday</u>

How many more mornings will I come here? I wonder who invented the five-day working week and two days off. It's sadistic. I want to go back in time and kill that man, because of course it would have been a man. Women didn't work in those days. Not being allowed to work sounded quite good. Anti-feminist, but good. All the housework, cooking, lying back and thinking of England stuff – not so good.

I'm not listening to The Martyr's and Santana Man's conversation until their voices drop, then immediately my ears prick up. Why do people do that? If you want a private conversation, try email, or a meeting room, not an open-plan office.

I focus back on the whisperers to take my mind off it. My bat-hearing picks up something about a restructure. Great. Move me to another department. Give me another name. Maybe something will change.

Please, let something change.

At lunchtime I am walking out alone, when I hear someone running up behind me. Sam taps me on the shoulder.

'Wow, you fucking move it at twelve! You hungry or what?'

'No, just keen to get out of there,' I say, pointing backwards at our offending building.

'I can see why,' he says, lighting up a cigarette. 'It's my third day and I already feel like I've worked here twenty-five years. And I'm smoking again.'

184

'Blink and it will happen,' I warn him. 'I'm not joking. As for the smoking, I don't blame you.'

'If you're not hungry, do you want to grab a drink? There's a pub over there, isn't there?' He points across the street. There is a sports bar about three buildings up from the Freddie Mercury café.

'Sure,' I say, crossing the road after him. My stomach is spinning. We are going for a *drink*! He'd spent almost every lunchtime with me this week.

Do I have a friend at last?

Do I have something more?

'Mind if I finish this?' he asks, and I don't. I am jealous of the cigarette hitting his lips. I am happy to be his passive smoker. I watch.

Sam chucks the butt and holds the door for me and we enter the Sports Bar. I've never really understood sports as a theme for pubs; sport and booze didn't seem like natural bedfellows. Except for darts.

The place is so sporty it's disgusting. I'm probably the first person with a vagina to ever set foot in here. There are framed football shirts lining the walls. Memorabilia in glass cases. I half expect to see a taxidermied George Best propped up in the corner. The place smells of BO and regret.

They are showing American Football on ten different TVs. Unsurprisingly, no one is in here.

'Quick, save us a seat!' Sam jokes. 'What do you want?'

'I'll have a vodka and lime, please.' I sit down at the table furthest from any TVs, by the pool table.

Sam comes over with the drinks and a gigantic packet of crisps.

'Thanks,' I say, as he rips open the packet to share. 'I can't believe you're drinking Magners, though.'

'Why! I thought it was quite hip now. Am I not hip?' He pouts.

'You've fallen for the advertising! For the ice! In my day cider was drunk by the litre by teenagers and tramps.' I nick a crisp.

'In your day? When was that, grandma, 1950?' Sam glugs on his drink. 'Damn, it tastes good!'

We both stare at the TVs despite the poor output. It's a compulsion.

'You wanna play pool?' Sam asks.

'No, I'm crap.' I say. I've never played it.

'I bet you're not. What *are* we going to do with you, Stephanie Morrissey?'

'Pump me full of Prozac?'

I stir my drink with a straw. I wish I'd got something in a bottle so I could peel the label off. Peeling was calming. Ripping and tearing. Strips and strips. That sounded like a bit of me.

The door opens and we can't help but look in an empty bar.

When Animals Attack walks in. He sees us, looks sheepish for one second, then looks straight through us.

'Drinking alone at lunch!' Sam whispers.

'Maybe he's meeting someone...' I suggest. But he isn't. He sits alone, his back to us, but far enough away. Still, it makes me nervous.

'So, how long have you lived over here?' I ask

Sam.

'About a year. My grandparents are English so I can stay as long as I want. But I'll probably go back in about a year unless something major happens. I love London but I miss home. In New Zealand you can just get in a car and drive to a beach or a lake. I miss that part. The open space.'

'You can do that here, but our beaches are shit, it would take you two hours, and it would be raining.' I say. 'It sounds amazing there. I don't know why people come to London, it's rubbish.'

'You're not a Londoner, though, are you?' Sam says. 'You must have come to London. So why did *you* come here?'

Because I never went home again.

'How do you know I'm not a Londoner?' I say, deflecting the question.

'Because you say 'month' funny.' He does an impression to demonstrate and I laugh too loud. I see When Animals Attacks' feathers ruffle across the bar.

'I do *not!*' I say, poking him gently. He has got a really great smile. I hate my smile. I want to put my hand over my mouth and hide it. 'London is OK in some ways. No small town mentality, fewer plebs. Less prejudices. And at least you're invisible here.'

'Do you like being invisible?' Sam asks, very directly. Our fingers accidentally brush in the crisp packet, vying for crumbs.

'Sometimes.' I say, quietly. 'Sometimes not.'

'Well, we hoovered them up pretty quickly.' Sam says, looking at the remnants of the crisps. 'Another?'

'Cool.' And we drink and eat and talk easily

against the glare of the screens. It is perfect.

Walking back to the office we pass DFS and Sam grabs my arm.

'Let's go jump on the beds.'

I look at my watch. We've got ten minutes.

'Let's do it.'

I follow him in, marvelling at how dated everything looks. In a world homogenised by a single Ikea lamp these frumpy recliner chairs and three-piece suites looked straight out of the 80s.

Sam bypasses the recliners and heads straight for the bedroom section. He throws himself on the nearest bed and calls my name.

I tentatively lie down next to him. We stare at the ceiling.

'I *knew* I'd get you into bed eventually,' he laughs.

'It was so easy, as well,' I agree.

A nervous-looking teenager approaches us. 'Can I help you, Sir, Madam?' He peers over us. We stay lying down.

'Which is the best bed?' Sam asks.

'It depends what you're looking for.'

'Which is the most expensive?' The Man/Boy leads us to the corner of the shop floor. Sam takes my hand, and bits of my brain that I thought were long dead start kicking in merrily. We stand staring at a king-sized, wrought-iron monstrosity. With Memory-Foam™.

We lie down on it together, our heads touching. I wish we *were* in a bedroom, with covers, and a locked door, and a week off work, and no Man/Boy staring at us.

'So what do you think, Joanne?' Sam asks me.

'I don't know... Nick,' I reply. 'It's a bit... tacky.'

Man/Boy's jaw hits the deck. He can't help himself. 'This bed costs *seven thousand pounds*. I doubt you could afford it.'

Sam sits up. 'Wanna bet? You want to show a bit of respect, laddie. My *wife* and I have just won the lottery.'

His wife! I jump for joy inside. I die inside of happiness at a charade, a silly game.

'Oh, really?' Man/Boy says. Then how come I saw the pair of you coming out of that dingy little office block 45 minutes ago? It's not exactly Wall Street, is it?' He turns to me. 'And I've seen that piece of shit *she* drives.'

Sam and I burst out laughing. Man/Boy starts herding us towards the door and Sam catches my hand again.

'Fine! We'll take our money elsewhere!' He shouts, as we fall out the double doors together, still laughing. We stand together on the concrete.

'All this could be yours if you marry me, Steph.' He says, pushing my fringe out of my eyes. 'Disgusting beds and McDonald's and Freddie Mercury-obsessed greasy-spoon men and bottles of Magners.'

'Are you proposing?' I ask.

'Only if you win the lottery,' he says, 'Come on!' And he leads me back towards our building. And I can still feel how his hand felt in mine. How it felt to lay beside him.

Even if it was a lie.

It was the best lie I knew.

<u>Friday</u>

I still dread work. But maybe I dread myself less? I can't decide.

As I arrive at my desk I see something rectangular on my chair, encased in black plastic.

'What's this?'

I pull back the catches on the case. It is an old-fashioned typewriter, slightly rusting, but still elegantly glamorous. It is the opposite of homogenised. It has a character, a story to tell.

Jim is paying attention for once and nods to Sam, who's heading back from the printer.

'Sam?' My heart wobbles a little.

'For your black comedy,' he says. 'My mate works at the tip and brings stuff home to sell on eBay. He owed me, so I grabbed it for you.'

'Wow...' I am speechless. I doubted if it worked, but it was still enthralling, a romantic notion, some poetry in this artless office. I am stunned that he would even think of me outside these four walls.

'It's nothing,' he assures me.

But he's wrong.

I email him.

Hello, Mr Dragon. Thank you so much. It's really wonderful. How are you?

I can feel The Capricorn's eyes boring into me. I swear she can tell when I'm not working. The typewriter has piqued her interest too, but strangely I don't feel scared anymore. So what if she knows? There's nothing she can do to sabotage it. Only I can do that.

Hey Stephsy. You remember the

dragon thing! That's going to haunt me. Anyway, I'm good, can't complain. Well, actually, I do have one complaint. My massive novelty-sized sausage roll is undercooked! It's all doughy.

The typewriter is on my lap. I stroke the plastic case.

Oh dear. Are you going to eat it anyway?

He replies,

I've eaten half but I don't think I can eat any more, it's just not tasting like it should. I don't want to end up feeling crook. It just goes to show, looks can be deceiving. I was hailing it as the king of all sausage rolls but it turns out to be a phoney, a pretender, a faker, a con artist...

Feeling crook! You had to laugh. He was straight out of Yabbie Creek. Except not from Australia.

I reply,

Beware of false idols, cobber.

Something inside me just feels warm. It's this unexpected feeling, teetering on the edge of a crack, but staying safe, staying balanced. I don't even know where to put a feeling like this. It is completely alien to me.

I glance at The Capricorn. She has bought stationery from *home* again! She spreads out her brightly coloured pens like trophies next to me. I suddenly think of my compass at school, digging up my skin all those years ago.

Urgh... stop. Not today. Maybe not ever?

Avoid the cracks.

Anyway, moving on from breakfast, we can both wallow in self pity on our lunch break if you like...?

I realise it's still there, that thing rising inside of me, some yellow bird of hope. I try not to push it back down, like every part of me would normally.

Just go with it! Enjoy it, for fuck's sake, Stephanie.

You making me an offer?

He replies,

I have an expired quiche in the fridge which I could happily walk away from. That and the sausage roll might just tip me over the edge into food poisoning territory...

I smile.

Well, if I'm doing you a favour...

But I can still see the compass in my mind, I can imagine it sticking out of the yellow bird's neck. What the fuck is wrong with me? Just let me have one *second* of happiness.

 I think I need to take my tablets.

I put the typewriter on the floor. My palms are sweating. I peek in my tin; just an empty tobacco tin, decorated with a silly monkey-rainbow sticker. The Anti-First Aid Kit. two razors, a couple of sewing needles on and some old steri-strips. I haven't used those in a year, but you never know, you just never know. It comforts me like the First Aid Kit, but it haunts me, too. It's always there, right inside my bag, just in case.

Just in case what?

I notice I still have those stupid kitten

matches in my bag, too. Maybe I should start smoking.

The morning drags, but at 12.00pm exactly Sam and I walk out together. He is so good-looking. I feel shallow for thinking it, but it is just strikingly obvious. Thoughts of how good-looking he is crowd around my head every time he catches my eye. I swear he is getting better looking by the hour. It's fucked up.

I wonder what he is doing hanging round with me. I feel like a lump. I imagine the prettier girls in the office thinking all sorts as we walk through the office together. The walkway feels as unsteady as a rope bridge sometimes. Why can't I work down the other end, and just slip out, unannounced...

Ruby Slippers waves her tape gun at us as we go through the double doors. I can see she is looking at Sam, too. 'Have a nice lunch...'

'Thanks,' I call back.

Sam turns to me. 'Hey, shall we just get a sarnie and sit on the grass? It's sunny out.'

'Yeah, good plan,' I agree. 'I've got chicken rolls anyway.'

We wander to the shop then stroll back to the grass outside the office.

'You wanna sit on my paper?'

'Nah, not at all. There's chairs in the hedge but it's nice enough to sit on the grass today.'

He frowns. 'You have chairs in the hedge?'

'Don't ask!' I say. I think of thrones, Narnia and Amy. I wonder where she is now. Happy. Somewhere happy and suntanned, and I am glad, not envious.

I sit down in the shade of a tree. Sam sits

beside me, stretching his legs. He peels back the cellophane on his sandwich. I unwrap the foil from my brown rolls.

'You're not regretting passing on your quiche, then?'

He smiles. 'It's two days past the expiry. I'll bin it when we get back.'

'I would.'

We are silent again for a bit. 'Oh, my iPod's got a little speaker on it, I'll put some music on.' I say.

'Cool, do it.'

I pick something summery, something meaningless yet pretty. I lie down, looking up at the smattering of clouds. The sky is glimmering blue, a lake above our heads.

After a while, Sam lies down next to me, eating his sandwich upside down. 'You've got your long sleeves on again, it's hot today. Is that cat still attacking you?'

He meets my eye, and I wonder... does he know?

Does he?

'I'm not flashing my flesh at work, Mr,' I reply, hoping it sounds casual, and I don't sound like some stuck-up, prim virgin. 'I don't want Mitesh getting excited.'

I sit up, brushing grass and helicopter leaves from my clothes.

'What about *not* at work?' He meets my gaze. I look away.

'Er... probably not then either.' I reply.

Oh my God – did I just say that?

Sam looks up at the building, hands laced behind his head, at the looming brown windows above us – seven floors of steel. Wembley Stadium peers beneath the trees like a spaceship, imposing but unspectacular when you've seen it for the three-hundredth or three-thousandth time. Will they ever finish that fucking thing?

'You drive, don't you? We should go for a drive one lunchtime. Too many eyes here...'

I nod, frightened and excited at once. I wish he'd ask me out in the evening, give me a thread of hope to cling to. Maybe I'm being too greedy...? I'm lucky to get this much. Lucky to get anything.

I kick my shoes off and feel embarrassed of my bare feet. Yet they are unspoilt, and I can reveal them. Prove one part of me is OK, normal.

He touches my leg, very lightly.

'Do you know what the first thing I noticed about working in this place was?' he asks me. I can feel my cheeks reddening. I think I might have hayfever or a brain tumour.

'What?'

'Oh no, hold on,' he corrects himself, putting his crusts into the empty plastic triangle of his sandwich packet. 'The first thing I noticed was your bloody boss – her voice raking inside my head, over and over, like a fucking banshee...'

I laugh. 'I know! She has no volume control. I want to kill her quite a lot.' I pick a fly from off my top. Then I feel brave. 'So the first thing you noticed wasn't me?'

He sits up, shaking his head, but smiling. 'Well, I didn't want to look in your direction because that's where all the horrible noise was coming from! But... then I heard you laugh. You looked pretty depressed 90% of the time... but when you laughed you seemed like a different person.'

This compliment makes me feel both happy and sad, empty inside, but hungry, too. I kick him gently. 'Well, I am pretty depressed 90% of the time, I'm at work, aren't I...'

'True, true. I'm glad you're here, though.'

'I'm glad you're here.' I say, too fast. I look at him for a second too long, and then I get out my book to hide behind. Sam flicks through the Metro and does the Sudoku puzzle in about three minutes.

'I don't know how to do that,' I confess. 'It looks complicated. Any tips?'

'I'll give you a hint...' he says, conspiratorially. 'Just fill it in. Any numbers. No one checks it. Makes you look smart.'

'Oh my God!' I laugh, shocked. 'Is that what you do!?'

He shrugs. 'Maybe I do, maybe I don't.' There is a glint in his eye and I just can't read him.

'We should do this more often, Stephsy,' he says. It should really annoy me that 'Stephsy', so clunky, so not me. But it doesn't.

He reads the paper. I pretend to read my book.

I am happy.

'Hmm... come on you,' I say eventually, checking the time on my mobile phone. 'Time to pretend to work again.' He follows me down the path, back into the office.

We are at our desks about ten minutes when Jim pipes up. I am enjoying the air conditioning after sitting in the sun.

'Who was that cartoon character that lived in

the filing cabinet?'

'Uh?'

'The filing cabinet! The dog.' Jim clarifies.

'Top Cat lived in the bin.' I suggest.

Jim looks at me like I'm thick. 'Not the bin, the filing cabinet.'

'What are you two talking about?' The Capricorn asks, more to try and shut us up than to help us discover the answer.

'I have no idea what you are talking about, Jim...'

'Hong Kong Phooey!' Sam shouts over partition.

'Oh, yeah!' I say, remembering. 'I hated Hong Kong Phooey. That must be why I wiped it from my brain.'

Jim's face lights up. 'Hong Kong Phooey! That's what we have to call filing cabinet girl.'

I look across the office and see her in her twinkling shoes, her Ruby Slippers. She is making skinny yellow labels, leaning on the metal cabinets. She is still deskless, still at the mercy of Rocket Science Bore.

'OK,' I reply. I forgot she even exists at times, and now we have a nickname for her. Well, I already had a nickname for her, but that was private. 'Let's print out a picture of Hong Kong Phooey and stick it on the inside of the filing cabinets.'

'Yeah, cool!' Me and Jim race to Google Image Search. He finds the best picture, damn him, of Hong Kong Phooey springing out of the cabinets. Jim sneaks round the corner and affectionately sticky tapes the print-out to the inside of the end cupboard.

Sam emails me.

I'm surprised I got the Hong Kong Phooey thing, I have the memory of a tropical fish.

I reply,

Do tropical fish have worse memories than say, goldfish? PS. I think this might be a rhetorical question.

Ruby Slippers/Hong Kong Phooey walks back up towards our desks. I peer between the cabinets. I can see Jim doing the same.

'Oh my God!' she shrieks. She looks so young. She has perfect teeth, magnolia skin and wide eyes, like a best-in-show dog. She probably doesn't even *remember* Hong Kong Phooey. 'Hahaha, is that me?!'

She peers between the metal cupboards at Jim.

He nods sheepishly. I can see her smiling, the yellow labels clenched in her hand like straws. And I can tell she is just pleased we have noticed her. She is just pleased to be acknowledged. And I understand. And then I can feel that yellow bird inside me again, and the First Aid Kit and my tin seem a long, long way away.

Monday

The air conditioning is broken. The air feels like someone with giant man-hands (i.e. Thyroid) is crushing my skull very, very slowly. I look over at the inch of Sam I can see from here and worry about sweat patches. I swear I can feel a drop of sweat trickling down my leg. This isn't the English way. I pray for rain.

The Martyr says 'Can I borrow you for a minute?' to Jim, which makes me cringe. She calls him 'into the cupboard'. What's he done this time? I look over at Kate to see if she's noticed. Of course she has. She watches her man like a police helicopter watches a flailing criminal trying to throw off a heat-seeking camera. Seemingly stealthy, but you can still hear the clatter of her a mile off. She catches my eye. I shrug and frown. She shrugs and frowns.

The Capricorn is eating from her tub of green slush. Her plastic stick insect looks at me. She looks at me. Another imaginary trickle of sweat runs down my leg.

I hope it's imaginary.

'They need to supply us with fans,' she comments, as if she felt it, too. 'It's a health and safety issue.'

'Like they give a shit about our health or safety.' I reply.

She nods. 'I'll bring my own in tomorrow.'

I bet she will. I can picture it already, solely pointing towards her, labelled lovingly with her name. They'll probably bill her for the electricity in this place.

I stare at my screen. I can't bring myself to work. I go onto dictionary.com. Word of the day is **apotheosis**. The meaning is: *An exalted or glorified example; a model of excellence or perfection of a kind.* Hmm. No wonder I didn't know what it meant.

Suddenly Jim is behind me. 'I'm leaving, I'm leaving,' he says. His tone is serious.

'What?' I spin round in my chair. 'What's happened?'

He pulls his name badge over his head. The chain glints in the sunshine. He meets my eyes. 'They've fucking sacked me, Steph.'

'What? They can't do that! You've been here *forever...*'

This can't be happening. Not Jim. Please, take The Capricorn instead. Take me. Actually, that sounds appealing. I look over at Kate, but she's trapped on the phone – bad timing or what? Still, the helicopter eyes are upon us, more frantic. The Martyr is nowhere to be seen.

'Four years.' he says. Four years is like life without parole in this place. He looks like he's put on four *stone* since I started. A pound of flesh nearly every month?

Was it possible?

He begins emptying his drawer. It doesn't take long, it only contains sweet wrappers, loose change and timesheets. Then he pulls out something that looks like a scalpel.

'Here, Steph,' he says. 'You like pointy things.'

I take it from him, too shocked to speak. How did he know... shit, how much *do* they know? I feel see-through.

Jim looks like he's going to do an Incredible

Hulk. And who can blame him?

Maybe it's time for the Kalashnikov.

No. Shut up. I could accidentally hit Sam. Plus, it's a cliché.

Still, I want to see it. I want to see heads explode. This is as good an excuse as any.

OK, I don't have a Kalashnikov.

My mind is running away. Focus. What does this mean for *me*? What can I *do* about it?

Nothing.

I'm impotent as usual.

Kate is virtually standing now, virtually dragging her phone cable towards us. But she's still metres away. Metres that could be continents.

'What explanation did they give you? They can't just sack you.' I am still trying to make sense of it in my head. The Capricorn has stopped eating, at least.

'I'm just a temp, Steph. It doesn't matter how long I've been here, they can get rid of me like *that*.' He bangs his hand on the desk.

Of course, Jim is an actor, on a temporary contract, despite the years he's put in. Dispensable. But he seemed untouchable, the golden boy of our department. The only boy, but still.

'What reason did they give?' I don't get it. The Martyr loves Jim. He does half her job for her, for starters.

Jim's eyes are blazing, and he seems genuinely hurt, as well as angry. 'It's *him*.' He points down in the direction of Bowser. 'He says I've been fiddling my timesheets.'

I follow his gaze down to the offending

Australian. Jim blatantly does fiddle his timesheets, but The Martyr lets it slide, as Jim is... sorry, *was* – her right-hand man. Even if you took off all the time he spent online, eating, or reading the paper in the toilet, he was still here more than her. He still did more than her.

I am in a state of shock. I'm still waiting for him to turn round and tell us it's a joke.

'What the fuck has it got to do with him? He's nothing to do with our department.' I am angry now, too. It's bleeding into me.

Kate is still trying to get off the phone. I can see her foot tapping desperately. It will kill her that we knew about this before her.

'It's done, Steph. I have to leave *now*.' He closes down his computer.

The Capricorn finally speaks. 'Surely you have to work some notice.'

Well, that was sympathy personified. I am standing now and Sam catches my eye over his monitor. He looks genuinely concerned. I'm still sweating. Maybe more so, now.

'She said I could leave now if I wanted.' Jim says, picking up his rucksack. 'I'm not hanging round here longer than I have to.'

'Oh Jim, this is so shit...' I say. How can they do this to him? Jim is well-loved here. Even I *quite* like him. 'I seriously can't believe it. You're part of the furniture. In a good way. Like a cool retro chair or something.' He smiles a little.

'I'm more like a fucking lilac bath suite at the moment, Steph. My era is over and I'm getting ripped out to make way for a square sink or some bullshit. A walk-in fucking shower. I'll tell you something else as well,' Jim says, turning to me.

'Remember we had to rush to get all the figures done last week? That was because she *knew*. She wanted me to do them before they gave me the chop. What hope is she going to have next month? I virtually have to wipe her arse for her.'

He's right. She *used* him.

I can't speak. I am scared of what I might say.

'Bye Steph.' Jim puts his work phone and name badge down softly on The Martyr's desk. 'I feel like a sacked Deputy handing in his gun and badge to the Sheriff.'

I laugh and he gives me a sad hug. 'Look after yourself Steph. I mean it.' He turns to The Capricorn and waves. 'See ya.'

'Good luck, Jim,' she says, and even she looks a bit upset; a crack in the concrete. Jim walks over to Kate who has just come off the phone and looks like she's doing a dance of anticipation.

I sit back in my chair, watching Kate and Jim talk like shadow-puppets in the distance. I can't hear what they're saying from here. Kate starts crying. Her perfect world shattered – the Master Plan. If only Jim hadn't wanted to be an actor; he could have knuckled down here, could have been a manager by now. If only he had wanted to sell his soul, like she did, so freely, to these fucking bastards, for no thanks whatsoever.

But she never had a dream. Not like him.

Not like me.

But then what was *my* dream? I was a dreamer without a dream.

'I can't believe that,' The Capricorn says. 'So suddenly.'

'I can... in this fucking place, I can believe anything.' I realise I still have the scalpel in my hand and stab it into my desk, where it goes boiiiiing! The Capricorn looks disturbed.

The lack of loyalty on The Martyr's part floors me. The lack of respect or care for people's feelings. I can feel rage building up inside me, the only decent person in this place, my best friend really; and they fucking sack him.

An email pops up from Sam.

Are you alright?

No, I am not. I watch Jim leave, and Kate walks out with him, but she'll be back, kissing arse, cosying up to the very people who sacked her own husband. I'd bet everything I owned on it. Which was pretty much a cat and a typewriter that didn't work, but I liked both.

Then as if she has been hiding round the corner waiting, The Martyr reappears, looking sheepish. I hope I look as livid as I feel.

'What the hell was that all about?' I demand. I'm not scared of her. Let her sack me too.

It might save my life.

The Capricorn gives me a 'shut up' look.

'Listen,' she begins. 'It was out of my hands...'

'How can it be? You're the manager of the department!' I am pleased I have found my voice. I couldn't *not* say it.

I can see she's annoyed with me for making a scene, but also that she's on the back foot. She talks quietly.

'I'm not the *only* manager, Stephanie, I have to answer to *my* manager.'

I get it. And he has to answer to his. That's how it goes isn't it, in business, a chain of arseholes, each one blaming the other, so no one ever has to take the rap. Well, fuck that.

Of course When Animals Attack would have had a hand in this, too. But I knew the initial push had come from Bowser. He'd been gunning for Jim from way back. Still, we were *her* staff. She called us her babies. She had the final say.

'After all Jim has done for you...' I say, looking her right in the eye. But her eyes are so dull, boredom brown, there's no life in them, no fight in her, no spark of morality, or passion. She knows I could expose her in a second. But would any of them listen? Anyone with an eighth of a brain could see she can't cope and hasn't been able to for months, and no one has stepped in to save her. Except Amy.

'Stephanie, come and talk to me in the cupboard – calmly.' she says.

'No...' I say. I look around. The Capricorn is staring, they are both staring at me, expecting me to back down, expecting me to give in. And then I'm gripped by this bravery.

'Just... no.' I repeat.

And then I'm walking out. I'm walking out, and I'm not looking back.

<u>Tuesday</u>

Well, this is it.

I sit in my car, staring at the ugly brown building that I'm contracted to tread water in for the next 40 years. If I look in my rear-view mirror I can see Wembley Stadium, bulging behind me, monstrous. I hope for a terrorist attack.

I'm kidding myself that I'm just waiting for the song to finish before I go inside. Or am I kidding myself that I'm going to go inside?

This decision is important, I know that much.

But isn't it already made by the fact that I've driven here?

No. No it's not.

I watch people get out of their cars. I watch people slam doors, join up with other people like magnets, drawn to mediocrity and the banal. How many more times will I have to talk about the weather with people I don't give a fuck about? Hours and days stretch out before me like lines of dominoes; once collapsed pointless, just flattened and finished. I just can't stand it; the thought of it cripples me.

I don't want to do it. I feel like I can't breathe and it actually feels wonderful, like a choice, like an unmade choice, not like this one.

I imagine how men must feel, lonely men, driven to suicide, men who take their families to cliff-tops and make them breathe carbon monoxide until they all sleep together. Not the angry ones, who spitefully text ex-wives, not the sick fucks who slit their kids' throats, but the calm ones, the certain ones, who just slip away together. The people who just want to fade, and go somewhere else, or even take a chance to *not* go somewhere else, because that seems better. I think about them, and their urge to just to be away from that moment – maybe just one particular predicament, or a lifetime of bad choices – and I feel for them, I really do.

Those monsters.

The song ends and another starts. So that's that excuse gone.

Still, I am early.

I catch my face in the rear-view mirror and try not to meet my own gutless eyes. Why did I come here? Why didn't I stay in bed, give myself to the covers, hide inside a lair of quilts? Lose myself in sleep, to dreams, where I could be a spaceman, a chicken, or a fucking library book if that's what my mind decided.

The mirror stalks me.

Why do eyebrows always look so bushy in natural daylight? I look; pores like full stops on my skin, lines around my mouth. I imagine getting older, and older, and older, and more and more things going wrong, just a gradual rotting, like the rat I'd seen, except I could be alive. I could be alive to see it.

I want to cry but I don't know how. I want to walk away, to drive away, but I don't. I can't believe I've come back.

But still. There's *Sam*.

Sam and the fear, Sam and the hope.

'Steph!'

Oh my God! Kate is tapping on my car window. I freeze, and realise this doesn't make me invisible. Why aren't tinted windows standard except for on limos and for criminals? Why can't I get a bit of privacy, too?

Kate looks at me expectantly. I have to open the door, it's the only natural reaction.

I switch off the stereo.

'Hi,' I say, getting out of the car. She looks immaculate, yet still awful, like everything has been put together in the wrong colour, or the wrong decade. She is beyond help or advice.

Then I am walking beside her, walking to life without parole.

'Rhonda told me she let you go home early yesterday.' Kate says.

'*What*?'

I stop walking. The Martyr has covered for me. She has told them she sent me home. My *statement* at the sacking of my friend has been made into an act of kindness on her part. She has turned anarchy into sympathy. I can think of few things crueller.

'That was nice of her, actually,' Kate says, twisting the screwdriver.

I am about to try and articulate how I feel about this, when I realise I'm not dealing with actual human emotion here. Still, I attempt to give it a go.

I start walking again. 'Nice? Kate... she just sacked your husband.'

'I know. But you know what?' Kate puts on her best children's television presenter face. It's terrifying. 'It could all be for the best.'

'In.. what.. way?' I say it as slowly and as un-through gritted teeth as possible.

'Well, Jim can put this silly acting dream on

208

hold again. He realises now he needs to get a permanent role if he's going to support our family.'

A *permanent* role. The exact opposite of the joyous variety of acting. The world of pretend and make-believe.

I think; in another time, another place, we could have been best friends. On another planet. If only I'd had less ideas, or compassion, we could have been so happy, crushing hopes together. Creating dictatorships.

'What family?' I say, rather obviously. I look into Kate's stupid, 21-year-old face and think, you fucking idiot.

'We're *married* now, Steph, we need to start thinking about these things.' We have reached the door and she holds her ID card up to the sinister robotic force-field. 'Marriage is a responsibility.'

I am speechless. But it's for the best, really it is.

I follow her up the stairs. She is almost skipping.

Finally I manage, 'Well, wish Jim good luck from me.' He'll fucking need it, you psycho, I don't add. I want to shake her, but I know in my heart that she's not my problem. It's Jim's stand to make, not mine.

And then we are nearing the top of the stairs, two steps behind Mr Happy and I'm Not Being Funny, but... Is my anti-climatic return sullied by arriving with Kate in tow? Do I look like I need the support? What will The Capricorn say? What will The Martyr say?

We walk up the catwalk/tightrope/corridor. I

see Sam's head turn to face me, and he looks relieved, and I am momentarily happy to see that look on his face. Kate splits off to the other side of the office, secure in her deluded daydream. She is even more of a traitor and a spineless zombie than I'd given her credit for. And I'd given her a lot.

The Martyr is at her desk. The Capricorn looks like she pitched her tent here since yesterday, waiting for the main show.

I sit, switching on the radioactive box that I intend to stare at without moving for the next 7 hours.

The Martyr turns to me and says casually, 'Hi, Stephanie.'

And that's it. She has denied me my fireworks, my floorshow. The Capricorn looks visibly disappointed.

'Aren't you going to sack her, too?' she asks, which would be cheeky coming from me, but from her sounds expressionless. I don't even feel annoyed at her for saying it, more relieved she's given me another stab at a ruction.

'Oh no,' The Martyr says. 'Stephanie's here for life.'

It's definitely a threat.

I think of cars on cliff-tops filling with poison.

I think of other jobs.

There are other jobs.

But the sound of the starter gun just seems ungraspable. Doing it all over again – new people, new rules, new building. It seems insurmountable. Undoable. The finish line seems more realistic. Just coming to an end.

Just stopping.

In my email inbox is a message from Sam.

I was worried about you.

And I want to stay... and I don't want to stay. And what if it's not the job, what if it's just me? What if every job is the same? I imagine going to a new place and it being worse, what if it's fucking worse?

I try and squash the panic back down. Put it in a box.

But I can't. I came back. I made my choice.

Wednesday

Summer is scorching. My breathing feels constricted and I'm not sure if it's hayfever or just my throat slyly trying to kill me, constricting under the weight of some invisible snake.

I am keeping my head down at work.

So far down.

Sam emails, but I don't reply. The Capricorn tries to rile, and fails. I keep my back to Jim's empty seat, running my finger down his parting gift, the scalpel. I wondered what it was for originally. I could think of something. A few things.

The Martyr is in a meeting with When Animals Attack. Time for her to cough up her ill-gotten figures.

I hate her.

The air-conditioning suddenly comes back on, and everyone rejoices. The room gets colder and colder, until I feel like a joint in a freezer. It can't be good for you, these drastic changes in temperature. Still, I like it. I could be on a slab in the morgue.

I realise that both Kate and Bowser aren't lurking either, so all the managers must be in the meeting. Time for an early lunch. I walk out, past The Capricorn.

I haven't spoken all morning.

Going outside feels like I've just got off a plane in Florida.

I sit in my car again. I finger the hole where the cigarette lighter used to go. I think of the gap inside me, the bit that is missing.

I sit in silence, staring at the sun. The painted cars glint under the heat like diamonds in a display case.

It is 33 degrees by my car's clock. It seems inconceivable. I can't think straight: my head feels so hazy.

It feels like it can never be winter again. I imagine I'm a forgotten lolly from a shopping bag, melting into the seat. It feels like another form of self harm.

I think of forgotten dogs or babies dying in hot cars. This must be a truly horrible way to die. Even I would turn my nose up at that one.

Then the tapping begins.

Not again.

I look up.

But it's Sam.

'What are you doing sitting in here?' he asks. He makes a winding motion with his hand.

I open the window.

'What?'

'Why are you sitting in your car? You got a death wish or something? Didn't you ever hold a magnifying glass over an ant as a kid?'

No, I never had. But I'd seen someone do it, burning them alive; those miniature families, just going about their business. I had watched in horror, fascinated and disturbed. It was my brother who did it. He liked destroying things. He wasn't the only one.

'What do you want?' I ask. I'm almost snapping, but not.

'Well if you're gonna sit in your car, take us to get some ciggies,' Sam says. 'Then at least you can get some air in.'

I look up at him, what I can see of him, silhouetted by the sunshine, a cardboard cut-out in front of a fire. How can I refuse him?

Ok,' I say, and somehow I smile.

Sam comes round to the passenger door to get in. He is wearing the badge I made. He has stubble – it suits him. No apparent sweat patches. He looks so big in the seat next to me. So immediate – I can't avoid him. There is something about a person like him being so close that makes the atmosphere change, as if the air itself needs to shift to make room for him.

'Garage?' I start the car. I suddenly feel glad of the distraction.

'Cool.'

He takes out a packet of cigarettes and winds down the window.

'Do you mind if I smoke?' He looks puzzled at the dashboard. 'Where's your ciggy lighter?'

'It's lost,' I say. I think of the lighter skittering across the car park. I think of the circular scar, so different from the others. Geometrically different.

Had I changed at all from then? Had I moved on mentally, even one little bit?

Yes. Please God, I *must* have.

But I think of diaries from the past, always the same New Year's resolution. Always the same hopes and fears. People never change. I was still a child, still kidding myself that something was going to happen soon, as promised. The fact I was still kidding myself was something – some shred of false hope, I suppose.

I look at the circular gap. I remember the smell more than anything. The pain was just beyond memory.

He is looking at me.

'I use that hole to charge my iPod.' I say. 'God knows where the lighter bit went. Glove box?'

'It's OK, I have my own,' he says, rummaging in his vinyl bag.

'I thought we were going to *get* you cigarettes, anyway.'

I wonder what his ulterior motive is.

'We are. I still have three though.'

'You don't smoke anyway.'

'I do sometimes.'

'You trying to look cool for me?' I ask.

'Of course!' He laughs. 'Is it working?'

'Kinda.' I smile, but he sees through it. He puts his right arm on my headrest and I feel like my space has been invaded. I think of boys who walk through town centres with their girlfriends in a kind-of headlock. Those girls probably feel quite special for a while.

'What's up, Stephsy? You've been so quiet the past couple of days. I've been pining away without ya.'

'It's hot. I'm tired.'

'It's not just that.'

'True. I guess I've been down about Jim.' I admit.

'Yeah that is a bummer. He was pretty funny. The cowardly lion.'

The memory of that makes me sad.

I pull into the garage. We could have walked it. Sam stubs out the fag he lit about three seconds before.

'You want a sandwich?' he asks me.

'Bottle of water...'

'Ok.'

I wait.

What am I waiting for? Why am I here? Why is *he* here? I feel like I should be more alert. But the sun is frying my brain and I'm frightened to speculate. Hope is dangerous, and leads to disappointment. In any event, my mind's turned to marshmallow.

He comes back a minute later with a sandwich and a bottle of water. I always feel self-conscious walking across the forecourt, like it's a stage, and I'm being judged or rated. He swaggers across, like he was born to stride. His clothes aren't the usual Topman/ chav-chic. He wears vintage stuff, surf stuff. He has his own thing going on. He is foreign, different. New.

'You wanna park up? There's a Tesco, isn't there? We can park in the shade.'

'Why do you want to do that?' I ask him, honestly.

'To eat my sandwich! What are you suggesting?' He gives me a big smile. I can't help but crack.

'Ok, deal.'

I drive round to the Tesco in silence. I park in a quiet corner, in half a patch of shade. Lorry drivers park here too, snoozing in their cabs. Dogs die in hot cars, I think.

I switch the engine off. Sam opens his sandwich and passes me my water. I lean my head on the headrest, closing my eyes. I feel exhausted.

It feels like ten minutes pass but it's probably only one. I can hear him eating. I can hear birds outside, tweeting in the shrubbery. I can hear engines in the distance.

'Pretty girl.'

'What?' I open my eyes. Sam looks at me.

'You are.'

He takes a bite of his sandwich. It's almost finished.

And then it dawns through the marshmallow... this guy is actually interested in me.

Oh!

'Why are you so sad, Stephanie?' He throws the plastic triangle out of the window. An empty shell. I want to berate him for littering, but can't bear to. I look out the window. Car bonnets twinkle all around, but I can't see any people.

'I don't know. Maybe I was just born like this.' And I can feel tears in my eyes.

He reaches forward and touches my face.

'No you weren't.'

I try to kid myself that the heat between us is because of the weather. That it is just elemental. But the air feels like it's made of gunpowder.

Then his hand is on my leg.

I don't say anything. I feel like I'm watching this on TV, or reading about it happening to someone else. It is usually that way. I can't arrange my emotions correctly. Maybe I'm just not used to feeling this... desire?

Then his mouth is on mine.

He tastes of sandwiches and cigarettes and I like the taste, and his lips are soft and wet. His hand moves further up my leg and I feel like shouting 'stop' because it's too much, and my legs are certainly flabby, and possibly sweaty – panic sets in. The bottle of water that was on my lap falls down by the pedals with a thud.

His hand is on the back of my head, and I think of the headlock again. I can feel his fingers in my hair, and the lack of control feels wonderful and horrific. He pushes me to the side of the seat, so my back is against the door, and I'm worrying that it's not locked, and that we'll tumble unglamorously onto the concrete together.

Breathe, Stephanie, breathe.

His tongue is fighting with mine, and then he moves my hand to touch him beneath his jeans. I feel cornered, but there is excitement running through it like a vein.

It's *lunchtime*.

His hand touches the seam of my knickers. He's not messing around. I want to peek to see if anyone's looking, but I can't. I am trapped.

'I need you now.'

'We can't now...' I say, feebly.

'Why?' His hand is in my knickers. His *hand*. He is feeling me, touching me. His fingers. I remember seeing them, holding the cigarette, eating the sandwich. Now they were in me.

He unzips his trousers. I feel shocked at his fucking brazenness. I can't think of a thing to say. My throat is so dry.

'Are you turned on? You are, aren't you?' he says. I can't reply, so I just nod, not knowing if I am or not.

'Sit on my lap.' he says.

So I do.

Wednesday afternoon

I am sitting at my desk in a state of shock. Less than 60 minutes ago, I was melting in my car, staring at the sun, alone. Now I am back at my desk and it feels like I've been through the looking glass. Wrenched down the rabbit hole, then vomited back out again. My world is without order.

Does everyone know? Of course, they can't do. Still, I suspect I may as well have a sign on my forehead.

I feel polarised. Like I'm in a film and everything else is racketing by at high speed whilst I am totally still inside the whirlwind. I ate a space cake once, long ago, and it made my brain slow down, but the scenery speed up. This feels the same, like seasickness, or a trip.

I can't see Sam. I know he is there, but I can't see him at his desk. He could be in Guantanamo Bay or the Big Brother house.

I realise I need him. I need him to give me a hug and say everything's going to be alright.

Even thinking this frightens the hell out of me.

Afterwards we had driven back to the office in silence. It was like we'd witnessed a car crash, or an explosion. The radio played knowing songs. I turned the blower on high to drown it out. Sam put his head out of the window to cool down like a Labrador. My legs felt wet. Even the seat felt wet under me. It felt like I was sitting in a lake of sweat and semen. I prayed that my skirt was OK, that it wouldn't betray me and scream at everyone what had happened. What *had* happened?

It was consensual sex but I would never have chosen it to play out like that. It wasn't an attack but neither was there any illusion of romance.

And now what am I left with?

I feel annihilated.

But I also feel important... he chose me, out of everyone.

For what? To fuck for ten minutes in a car park as an alternative to a Happy Meal?

Shut up.

I look down at my hand. I realise I am gripping my stapler like it's a handlebar.

I need to get my head together.

Luckily I know how to pull a rabbit out of a hat.

I arm myself and go to the toilets.

Green is for go.

I grab a handful of paper towels and wet them, pumping out orange soap onto one. My hands are shaking. I take the tissues inside my favourite cubicle for a rudimentary wash. I balance my razor blade on the sanitary bin whilst I do this. My skirt is hitched up around my thighs and I think of it, him inside me, and my stomach lurches.

For a moment, I was somewhere else, joined to someone else, involved in something. I remember him right there in front of me, his weight on my hips, black pupils, open-mouthed. I remember the feel of him inside me, we had been that close. As close as anyone can be. He had held one of my wrists above my head for a second. I had been on top of him, and then underneath him. He had smelt like deodorant and hair wax. Like a real person.

You *stupid bitch.*

I rub my skin with the wet paper towels, paranoid that I smell. I wonder if he can smell me on him and I feel mortified, just in case he does. Just in case it revolts him.

It was OK though, wasn't it? It was fun, wasn't it? I could lose weight if I did that every lunch time, I reason, flippantly.

The other part of me shouts louder. Why did I let him do it? He had used me, hadn't he? A beyond-fleeting shag in my car. His hand on my wrist. His face afterwards.

I'm easy.

'Argh!' I put my hands over my ears, but it doesn't help as the doubts are inside my head, not outside. I look at the razor blade, my skirt still hitched up, my thighs damp but clean; all trace of him removed.

Not all.

Unthinking, I slash myself fast across my inner thigh with the razor. It really hurts, and I can feel the sting of my sweat mingling with the blood. I wince, but don't stop.

I do one on the other side, around four inches long, and my blood looks so bright against my white thighs, like red pen. My skin is so soft here and the blade glides through. I am warm butter.

'Stop, stop.' I actually utter the words. Why am I doing this? I thought I'd given up. I should be happy. Someone wants me. Why am I punishing myself?

But this isn't punishment. It dawns on me that this feels more like pleasure than *that* did.

This feels like real abandonment. And I control it. I control everything in this cubicle, every slice. Not him, not anyone else.

I am responsible.

I lean back, not thinking for a while. With my eyes closed, I could be anywhere. I could be free. Finally I come back to reality, and wipe up the blood with the soggy paper towels. This virgin area bleeds for much longer than on my well-travelled arms. I pad it gently and am patient.

I can feel the cuts. But I can still feel him inside me, the ghost of him.

I leave the safety of the cubicle and wash my hands. I look in the mirror. My face looks flushed.

I walk back towards the kitchen and stop to look at the First Aid Kit. I don't need anything, and I'm cautious since I was caught the last time, so I just stare at the green case, wondering.

First Aid Kits don't contain contraception, or razor blades, or any real drugs of any kind. First Aid Kits are ultimately full of fluff.

I feel shocked at this revelation. I sit down at one of the smooth beech tables, and look out through the glass wall, at Allied Carpets. I look out onto nothing. I wish Sam would come in and put a comforting hand on my shoulder, and tell me that nothing has changed and everything's still the same, that he still likes me.

No one comes in.

I walk back to my desk. Time has slowed down again. I try and catch Sam's eye above his screen but he is tapping away. I don't want to email him. I can't think of what to say.

Nice shag?

Do you still respect me now you've stuck it in me?

Will you ever speak to me again?

Save me.

I imagine another world, outside of work, where I get to go on proper dates, and fall in love. Where I can be happy and have a real life.

I look at the pile of invoices on my desk with my name on and my vision blurs; my eyes stinging with warmth. The Capricorn is looking at me. She never stops. I turn my head to the side, and blink fast.

<u>Thursday</u>

A new day dawns.

I think, so I guess I'm not a virgin anymore.

Ha, who am I kidding? I might be a depressing loser, but I was a teenager once. Even geeks get some if boys get desperate. Even ugly girls, and I wasn't ugly. Just nothingy.

I'm wearing black leggings underneath my skirt so my cuts don't rub together. They feel soft, but make me hot.

I walk past Sam. The Capricorn has her glasses on the end of her nose. In another dimension I'm a lottery winner, and I don't have to come here.

I settle down at my conveyor belt. Assume the position.

I get another one of those dumb emails. This one is called: **Respect yourself! Shortest way to be happy?**

It proclaims:

tail spin re-eligible base box

work ticket play actorism roundabout system

mellow-toned stage door wasp-minded

three-eared coffee roaster barium dioxide

map reader induction machine thrush nightingale

oath-making wrong-ordered kinematic viscosity

dumping car well-rested turret steamer

scaly-leg mite torch singing tool miller

I like the thought of the scaly leg mite. Maybe I've caught it off Sam, because I didn't 'respect myself' as advised.

Shh.

I kill half an hour using hole-reinforcers to fix old alphabetical dividers. I'm too embarrassed to order more stationery. I don't like boxes coming with my name on. It draws attention to me. Plus I have to pick it up from the post room. Fuck that.

I go to the toilet. The light is shining in through the window and hits my face. My hair dye has faded already. I pull up my sleeve and examine the raised skin on the inside of my wrist, down to the inside of my elbow. I wonder if these scars will ever fade, knowing that they won't.

No one can ever see me naked.

It isn't just the scars though, it's every part of me. Every black thought I'd ever had had leaked into my body, distorting it. That and all the shit I'd shovelled into my mouth. I am bloated and stretched and deformed. I am terrified to let anyone see the reality. The truth of who I am.

Maybe I am destined to a life of abrupt encounters in cars, or in the dark.

My eyes shine again, and I want to hurt myself.

I just want to stop feeling.

Or to feel something.

I feel sadder than ever now that I've given myself to someone, to him.

I stand, listening to the silence, surrounded by that unknown green until the cat cough of the air freshener tells me it's time to go.

I wonder what will happen with Sam.

I know that I can't sit here, so close to him. I grab my iPod and put my phone on divert. People complain about the mindless jobs like filing and shredding, but I like the brain-off jobs. Filing and shredding can go hand-in-hand anyway; can't find the file you need? Just pop the intended piece of paper into the shredder! Job done.

The only bad part is when someone comes into the shredding room, taking up valuable oxygen.

I feed paper into the shredder. You don't even need to switch it on. The hungry teeth are always ready. It snatches from your hand like an ill-mannered child.

I have my headphones on, so don't hear that someone comes in behind me. I jump when I see Sam, doing his best big-bad-wolf face.

'What are you doing?' I ask.

'I didn't know you were in here,' he lies. He is close. I am still arbitrarily looking for a file but I've suddenly forgotten the name of it. He reaches out and grabs a strand of my hair. I am still. He runs his fingers through my fringe, his eyes warring with mine. It feels like an assault, him touching me in here. But my heart feels plugged in.

'Turn around and bend over the shredder.' He orders.

'Fuck off.' I reply. Does he think I'm crazy?

He laughs it off, as if he didn't expect me to say yes.

'What is wrong with you?!' I ask.

'What's wrong with you?' he replies,

innocently.

'Don't fuck about.' I say, but his eyes are boring into me. His arm is blocking my way out.

The door moans and Thyroid lollops in. The tension swirls out of the atmosphere like water down a sink. Sam pretends he is helping me look for something. My cheeks are burning, but she doesn't look at us, just grunts her way past. I have to flatten myself against the wall for her to get by. As Sam passes me to leave, his chest grazes mine. He knows exactly what he's doing.

I have *no* idea what I am doing.

I breathe, and listen to music, and Thyroid eventually goes. I wait for Sam to come back, but he doesn't.

I buy Jim a card at lunch. To show him he hasn't been forgotten by me, even if his wife can't be arsed to stick up for him.

I decide I don't like the card I've bought almost instantly, a cheapy one from the newsagent. I cut out the sparkly raised stars and use Pritt Stick to fix them to a piece of card. I google the Cowardly Lion and print off a suitable picture. I write 'Enjoy Lion-In' in marker. I want to pass the card around but I don't want to talk to people, or for The Martyr to see it.

I'll pass it to Kate on the sly later and get her to do the dirty work. I'm not going to beg the likes of Rambo or Thyroid to sign it. I'd done the creative part.

I would have emailed Jim but I can't because he and Kate have a *shared* home email account, an amalgam of their surnames. Whatever happened to privacy? It's sick. What I want to say to him, I don't want to say to *her*. They are not the same person; a joint-sentient being, a futuristic Frankenstein.

It's all kinds of wrong.

The Martyr buzzes like a fridge in the background. She has the tone of a harassed mother. She says 'good morning' in the afternoon and 'good afternoon' in the morning. I wonder what it must be like to have no sense of time like that. I plot every second in this place on an intricate mind-map. You could do analytics on my ploys to shave a minute off my start time and add it to lunchtime.

I decide she is annoying me too much, so I run away.

In the kitchen there is a free newspaper. I read an article that is a test for Alzheimer's. It says to write as many fruits down as you can in a minute. A normal person will get 25. Someone with Alzheimer's will get 10. I get 14. Is this an indicator of mental decline or just a bad diet? I decide the test is flawed. I wonder what The Martyr would get.

Sam comes in the kitchen. Is he following me? He does look godly today, immaculately groomed, yet it still looks effortless. He has a Ready-Brek glow, a T-shirt suntan. I wonder what he sees, looking at me. I am becoming angry with the mirrors in the toilets. They must be lying.

He pulls back a chair with a creak across the polished floor. We are alone.

'How are you, Stephsy?'

'How are you?' I answer, noncommittally. I don't mention the shredding room, and neither does he. It's like it never happened.

'I'm good, I'm good. We cool?'

I think, I'm in love with you.

No, no I'm not. That is absolute rubbish. I hate you.

'Of course we're cool. Why wouldn't we be?' I drum my badly-bitten fingers on the table. I hear him say *bend over the shredder* in my head.

Had he been serious?

I wish I could hear the other conversation we're having – the one inside our heads. The air between us is awash with questions.

Do you like me? Am I ever going to see you again? Was it just sex? What do I have to do?

Just tell me and I'll do it.

He looks up. He is looking straight at me.

The door swings open and Ruby Slippers enters the kitchen. The room exhales. We both look away.

She looks at us a little too long. I realise that we are not acting like work colleagues. Our... *liaison* is probably the worst kept secret in Officeville.

'Hi,' she says, as you are obliged to say to every fucking person you look at or walk past at work. Her ruby slippers twinkle at the end of her Lycra-lollipop legs. Our little Hong Kong Phooey. Not many people can get away with leggings as outerwear. She does.

'Hi,' we say back in unison.

She fills up a plastic cup of water and leaves.

Sam watches her go then turns back to me.

'What were we talking about?'

'Nothing.' I shrug.

He looks at the paper I've been reading and the scribbles around the edge.

'Is that your shopping list?'

'No.' I point at the article and he skim reads it.

'Oh. Is that how you spell 'cumquat'?'

'Fuck knows. But would you have thought of cumquat?' I ask and he laughs.

And then it's there between us again, that tiny flicker.

'My shopping list?' I repeat. 'Are you mad? Where's the Ben and Jerrys?'

<u>Friday</u>

I wonder if I think about dying more than the average person. Every car that goes by, every person brushing past me is a potential threat, a would-be assailant. I fantasise about it. Stepping into the road and getting my face taken off. My car blowing up. A stabbing. Everyone's getting stabbed these days, why not me? Spontaneous combustion. You don't hear about spontaneous combustion so much these days, do you? Probably because it doesn't exist, or someone would have camera-phoned it. Still, one could hope.

Strangely, I feel safer at work. Safe in the bubble-wrap blandness, nothing can touch me, except me.

And him.

But does he want to?

We are less than a metre apart, separated by two desks. If my legs were twice as long, I could touch him with my feet. If he crawled under the desk, he could put his head in my lap. If everyone would just disappear, I could just wrap myself around him, and we could hide; the world would just implode.

But would it?

Does he really want me?

I need to know. I just need to know, one way or another. But how can I ask, without sounding desperate? Of course, I'll never ask. But floating here, in this uncertainty, feels as painful as slamming my fingers in a door.

At least I know where I am with that feeling.

A blunt, tangible pain.

In the background, on the phone, The Martyr says 'I trust you one hundred and fifty percent.'

I want to tell her that's impossible. But what do I know?

What the fuck do I know about anything?

I look at Jim's empty desk. I look at The Capricorn, who must have the most perfect view of Sam, all day long, she must go to bed at night with an image of him like the flash of a bulb, imprinted behind her eyelids.

I need to know.

I just need to know.

But I will never ask, can never ask.

I wonder when and where I lost my spine. I don't know, but I know I'll never find it again. But I do know of ways to prop myself up without it. A little bit.

The word of the day on Google is **Florid**: *Flushed with red; of a lively reddish colour*. Oh, yeah. I know all about that.

No, I'd never had my heart broken. But sometimes I feel like my heart is trying to escape from my chest, via my throat. Sometimes I feel like I am going to start crying and never stop. Sometimes panic can just rise and rise in me, and the only way to stop it is to...

Stop.

I look at the clock on my screen and it's 12.01. I get up without a word.

It is still blazing hot outside. The sky is pulsing blue, a headache. Why won't it fucking rain? I walk up the tiny pathway, to the patch of grass behind the building, surrounded by the waist-high hedge. I lie on the grass and it feels

232

hot under my fingers, so I wriggle into the shade.

I don't feel like eating. I don't feel like anything.

I can see most of the building from here, brown windows like buttons on an 80s keyboard, but they can't see me, I'm hidden by the hedge.

I lie there, trying to decide whether or not to cry, when I feel a fly land on my leg. I sit up, to bat it off, and the sun blinds me, and then he is there, an outline against the sky.

Then I realise it wasn't a fly after all.

I'm slow sometimes.

'Sam..'

'Shhhh...' he says, sitting down, his back to the hedge. His finger trails along my calf, and he still feels like a fly, ticklish, and I want to flick him away. I am wearing a black maxi skirt but I'm not wearing leggings today. My legs are bare. We are both hidden by the hedge to an extent, but if anyone came...

'Here...' He pulls the newspaper from his bag and shakes it out. He puts some of it on my lap and the sports section on his. He does this like it is perfectly natural, like he's unfolding napkins for a formal dinner, and I let him, as if it is, too. His hand passes my knee, his fingers stroking my legs, crawling up, and up.

There are still cuts on my thighs. They hurt when I sweat; I can feel the salt gripping the broken skin like tiny teeth. But he doesn't know. I am almost certain he won't notice. Almost.

Is this it, then, Sam? Will this be it, the final thing that makes you like me, really like me? I want it to be, I want it to be so much, and yes, I am turned on, turned on and terrified. There's a whole alphabet of windows looking down on us, and it would only take one careful Capricorn eye to spot us...

He takes my wrist, grabs my arm, and puts it on him. I can feel he's hard through his trousers, he's pulsing like a heartbeat. The newspaper is barely covering us. And most of me wants to pull away, for twelve different reasons, but I can't. And part of me wants to go along with him. Of course it does. Then his fingers are in me *again* and we're *outside*. It's insanity, and he just goes, 'Shh...' and what am I meant to do?

'They'll see...' I say, and he shakes his head, black pupils fixed on mine. He looks high. There is some potential madness in him, something that is beyond spontaneity and closer to recklessness. He doesn't seem to care about anything.

'It's fine. Don't look at me. Look at the paper.' That infuriatingly mumbling voice of his, issuing orders.

I look at the paper.

I notice a story likening eating crisps to drinking a litre of oil. Oh, Christ.

His hand in my knickers. My hand inside his fly. I can feel the blood pumping through him. He is red hot.

This doesn't feel right, somehow. Not allowed to look at him as he touches me and he moves my wrist to touch him. It feels like unpaid prostitution, or some minor sexual abuse. If a stranger did it, you'd have them arrested. And he was kind of a stranger. He was definitely strange.

You have the ability to say no, Stephanie, my brain points out.

So why isn't it coming out of my mouth?

Two girls are walking up the path. I try and pull my hand away and Sam catches it in his, wrist side up. My sleeve has ridden up under the paper, and now my flesh is exposed.

Oh my god.

No.

I feel his other hand pull away from me, like I just caught fire.

In another dimension, the girls sit down; only a few feet away in reality, but to me they are as far away as a painting, or a view. They don't look at us, wrapped in breezy conversation of their own.

I'm not looking at the paper anymore. I'm looking at Sam, and he is looking at the train-track scars painted across my inner arm, only they aren't painted. They are tattooed on. Thank God it's not the other one. Thank God it's not the arm with the burn. But this is just as fucked if you don't know any better. To a layman, this was some serious shit.

It's all relative.

I look away, almost hearing the sound of barriers crashing down like a foiled bank raid. I want five minutes ago, like that balaclava-clad boy in my fantasy wants five minutes ago. But you can never have it – you can never just press rewind, can you?

If I could turn back time.

Well you fucking can't. Not even you, Cher. It's only bloody Botox, not the elixir of youth.

I wonder if his dick is still hard.

No.

I know that it isn't.

'What have you done?' he asks me, and his voice sounds weird, not mumbling, but trembling.

I look at the girls for a point of reference, fellow office workers, normal people, eating normal sandwiches, having a normal chat, not tangled up in this pathetic mess, this lacerated life of mine.

'Just fuck off, it's none of your business,' I hear myself saying, and still he doesn't let go of my wrist. He is rubbernecking. Even now, exposed, I feel a warped sense of pride about my scars, their neatness and accuracy. Mine was a tidy mutilation, you had to give me that much. I kept things in line.

'Why?' he asks me, and then he seems to remember where we are and lets go. I pull back from him, pulling down my sleeve. Long sleeves for the summer, always.

'I did it when I was younger,' I try.

He looks at me. No, he *stares*.

'That isn't some teenage compass scratch, Steph.' Not Stephsy. 'This is *systematic*.'

He lunges for my other arm.

'No, get off, get off, Sam...!' I try and wriggle away, and now the normal girls are staring. He's stronger than me and sees the beginning before I can stop him. He doesn't get to the burn mark, but some of the scars are recent.

Teenage scars fade. Mine had.

These hadn't.

'You fucking idiot, Steph! You fucking idiot.' Then he is holding me, suddenly his arms are around me. I fight him, but he is stronger, and then I succumb to it, because before him, it had been such a long time, such a long time since anyone had even looked at me, or said one word that made me feel like I was even the same species as them. And isn't this what I want, just normality, just what other people have, just to be cared about?

I feel a rush of pride or blood to the surface, and I don't care who sees, I want everyone to see. I realise I am crying on his shoulder, and then it comes out, I can't stop myself.

'Can I see you sometime? Can I see you in the evenings, or on the weekend?'

'Of course you can, Stephsy,' he says, and it sounds like the truth, and he's kissing my head, his hands in my hair, his hug stemming my sobs.

Just to be held, just to be understood.

It's within my reach – the dream.

Monday

It's Monday morning and already I want to die.

I can't believe I let my guard down last week, virtually begged Sam to see me. How pathetic. I want to push the words back down my throat. Hire someone to wipe his brain, and mine.

Even worse, I have to attend a meeting in the goldfish bowl room, with its tyrannical glass walls. Luckily I don't have to say anything, but it's still too much first thing on a Monday. Kate is running the meeting, and she says, 'I've got my team leader hat on today and, in that capacity, there are a number of key issues I want to talk to you about.'

I wonder what a team leader hat would look like – if someone had to manufacture it for you. I have a few 'key' issues of my own today, Kate, but I'm not making you pay for it. And you're not *my* team leader, thank fuck.

And I don't want to face Sam, but I don't like the fact the choice has been taken away from me.

The lights are dimmed for the presentation. Dimmed lights plus PowerPoint equals sleep for me. An hour into the meeting and the corners of the room are starting to look hazy. Blinking is taking five times longer than normal. It feels so good when my eyelids close. I allow myself one second. Two seconds. Three.

I need to take action so I bang the nib of my pen against the webbed skin that connects my fingers. It's an old trick but a good one. The pain is sharp but too fleeting. It fades in seconds, and then I am back in that dissolving room, back with eyelashes coated in lead mascara.

In a micro-sleep I have a vision of Sam, yanking at my clothes. He is kissing me, but his gums are bleeding, and he's biting my tongue. I can taste metal.

'Steph!'

I jump in the darkness, jolted back into the room. The PowerPoint has croaked and The Martyr is calling out to me in the dark, shooing me off to IT. Eyes are upon me. I need to wake the fuck up and sort this out fast. Slight problem; Rambo works in the frigging IT section.

I skulk over to his department, praying there is someone there to help me. Bingo; all six desks are full, girls on one side, boys on another. Unfortunately, that includes his. I explain the problem, my head still full of fibreglass.

He looks very serious. 'That's fine, but you'll need to log a call with the helpdesk.'

I look around me and up at the sign above his head that says 'Helpdesk'.

He sees me looking.

'The external helpdesk.'

My blood is definitely cooking, but I rein in my expression as much as possible. How do you ever know if you're pulling off neutral expressions well? You only ever do pull one face in the mirror. In fact, I do less than one.

'Can I use the phone here?'

'Yes.' I look at the mouse mat. Spawn of Ramboloid.

I dial. I am connected to someone Northern. I spell out my name. I spell out the problem. I spell out the name of the basement room.

'OK!' comes the chirpy reply. "I've logged your call. Someone will be with you shortly.' Someone is with me now. But no one is *moving*.

I look around at six blank faces. It's not just the Rambo tyranny; this is how they treat everyone. They have worked in IT so long they are no longer humans, but human-esque.

The phone rings. Rambo picks it up. 'Yes, yes, OK.' he says.

'Was that the person I just called, ringing you?' I ask. He doesn't even look ashamed.

'I've just got to log it...' He is typing. He is remembering everything I've ever done to him, the prick, which incidentally, is *nothing*.

'There's 15 people waiting downstairs.'

Waiting for me.

To fix this.

Two blokes stare at me gormlessly. A girl pretends she is doing something else.

I crack. 'Please, can someone help me?'

'They will.' says Rambo. 'When they're finished here.' He is smug. He is winning.

Too late. My rage-o-meter has hit the mercury, and nothing can be done.

'This is a fucking joke. Do you realise how stupid this system is?'

His manager stands up, and heads towards me. 'Calm down. We'll be with you shortly.' I can tell by his face this man knows. He knows the system is a joke, and there's nothing he can do about it, except ride the fucking storm, lick up the shit, and take home the cheque.

And in what way am I any different?

Well, I get paid ten or fifteen grand less.

I go back downstairs, empty-handed. Kate

and The Martyr fill time, badly. Several people scowl at me.

Ten minutes later, someone who isn't Rambo comes down and sorts it out. I stare at the slideshow, trying not to look through the wall, trying not to look in the direction of Credit Control. At least I'm awake now.

At lunchtime I walk out to try and avoid the shared sandwiches, vacuum-packed so comprehensively that no germs or flavour remain. Cold bread is just wrong. But not as wrong as having to attempt small talk. I don't schmooze. I don't want to be seen by any stragglers who have the same idea of escape as me, and I don't want to see Sam, so I walk, walk, walk in a direction I don't normally go.

I walk past chicken shops, chip shops, kebab houses. I walk past newsagents and off licences. The shop fronts are dressed in gaudy yellows, reds and greens with shop names screen-printed in fonts that must have been invented for a joke. I go inside a chip shop called The Codfather (not bad) and buy sausage and chips, open.

I sneak through a gate, exploring. It's not like me. But I just need to get away from that building, away from the spectre of Wembley fucking Stadium.

Improbably tucked away behind a hundred opportunities for a heart attack is a tiny, ancient cemetery, attached to a crumbling church. The stones are so old and worn they are unreadable, but still I feel warm towards them. I like the bravery of the decaying stone, the angels without wings, the statues who have lost their noses and other extremities. I admire the decomposing crosses and the long-dead bouquets. They feel real. What will we do when we run out of room to bury people? I don't want to go in the fire. I want to go back into the earth– feed the worms, feed the trees.

It sounds hippyish for me, but that's just the way I feel.

I sit down on a bench that creaks under my weight, more due to dry rot than the size of my arse – I hope.

I eat chips out of the bag, relishing the taste of the salt and fat, feeling the grease smear from my lips onto my chin. I imagine the food making its way inside me, the fried potatoes slathered in salt, and sausage drenched in batter, not one healthy calorie among them.

You can't stop lonely people eating this stuff. It is something to focus on, to look forward to. That's what food-Nazis on TV can never get, with their fucking raw food diets. The emptiness that needs to be filled, with something bad.

It tastes divine. I can't stop myself.

I feel the salt hit my heart, popping and fizzing. Clotting and furring. I fantasise about my arteries clogging. My cholesterol levels rocketing. Was it such a bad thing? What were people afraid of; living on rabbit food, pounding away at the gym, denying themselves, every single day. Who would really want to live The Capricorn's freeze-dried life for ninety years?

I'd rather die.

I fish around in the bottom triangle of the chip paper for the crumbs, the burnt bits, the flakes of batter. I want every bit, all of it. I need it. It's something to cling to.

It's all gone.

The sun is perched high in the sky. I watch a plane go by and I'm jealous. I want to go. On holiday, out of the country, across continents. Beamed up in an alien abduction. I'd go. I'd go just to have a look. If they'd have me.

I lean back, folding the chip paper into a square.

My brain feels quiet. I look at this picturesque oasis of death around me and I feel quite comfortable, like I can somehow disentangle things in my brain, like there might be a route towards making things right.

How strange that this place has existed the whole time I've worked here, and for hundreds of years before, yet I had never seen it. I had never walked far enough up this road. I had been trapped by the same square mile, the same square footage.

There's still hope, I think.

How, my brain replies.

But I don't know.

I walk back, back, back. I'll come here again, I think. But it won't be like the first time, a discovery. A treasure.

Sam smiles at me as I go by his desk, but it's an insurance salesman's smile.

I'm a done deal.

I realise I miss Jim. I miss laughing at The Martyr and The Capricorn, and talking about what was on TV last night. I miss sexist emails and four dirty cups on his desk before The Martyr cracks and goes to wash them, like his mum must have done for 18 years – and probably more.

I want to wait until the end of the week to cut, have something to aim towards, something to look forward to. But the Monday blues are just too bad. That talk has crippled me, and the graveyard, however pretty, has just been too close to the bone.

I reach into my bag, groping, and feel something sharp and metallic sink into my finger.

'Fuck!' I recoil, snapping my hand away. My finger comes out bleeding. I look in my bag expecting to see an explosion of razor blades amongst my iPod headphones and keys. Instead it's the serrated edge of a Panadol packet, the protective red plastic flipped open to reveal a glint of foil, hungry as a venus fly-trap.

'Bastard,' The cut is pretty deep and really stings. It won't stop bleeding. The Capricorn observes me but says nothing.

I get up and go to the First Aid Kit.

You're meant to be my friend, I think, opening the catches.

And then there they are, in little plastic bags, the Airstrips. *They're back.*

I put a plaster on, trapping the bright red blood underneath. What a waste, I think, as if this kit is only fit to clear up my self-inflicted wounds.

Irrational, me?

I close the catches lovingly behind me. It's not the First Aid Kit's fault.

'Are you in that First Aid Kit again? I swear you live in that thing.' I turn to see Kate and feel like saying, 'Well, it's a legitimate injury this time.'

'Caught my finger,' I explain but she's already zoned out.

'Jim says hi,' she concedes, as I put the plaster wrapper in the bin. 'He loved the card.' This seems genuine.

'How is he?' I ask, certain of the fact I will never see him again.

'He's good, he's good.' We're interrupted by the swing of the door and Sam comes in. He nods to us, and bends down to fill a cup with water. I watch him.

After he goes, Kate asks, 'Do you like him?' I'm amazed she's noticed anything outside her own Kateness. Yet she has.

'No! Not like that, anyway.'

'Oh, good.' She switches the kettle on.

I wonder why it's good, but don't want to look like I care by asking.

'Better get back.' I say, leaving her staring out the window. Planning her next move.

At least I don't want to cut now. The distraction has curtailed my craving. I've still got it ahead of me. A bit of hope. This must be how *they* feel about a drink after work on a Friday night. That tiny goal to justify this eight-hour penance. Living for the weekend.

Back at my desk I get an automated email that sounds like the most personal and heartfelt message I've had all year.

I'm afraid I wasn't able to deliver your email to the following address....

This is a permanent error; I've given up. Sorry it didn't work out.

Why can't Sam be this honest?

<u>Tuesday</u>

The light above my desk is in its death throes; it has been strobing intermittently for about a week now. I call Un-Handy Andy again but it keeps going straight to voicemail. I imagine him sitting somewhere, stuffing his face, oblivious to the fact I could suffer a seizure or an epileptic fit at any minute. What a selfish arsehole.

Maybe I'll come in tomorrow in sunglasses to make my point.

Sam sends me an email that says,

Sorry I didn't get a chance to talk to you yesterday. I like what you're wearing today.

I am wearing a grey skirt, with a purple vest and a black woollen cardigan. The air-conditioning is back on the ice-box setting.

I like what you're wearing, too. I reply, falling into the pattern, letting him drag me back in so easily. Never mind the fact he ignored me all day yesterday. Never mind the fact he has no intention of seeing me at a weekend, or an evening, or ever, sympathy-case or not, self-harming loser or otherwise.

Maybe I'm asking too much?

I should just be grateful for what I get.

Grateful for anything.

What are you doing for lunch? I've got a sandwich with your name on it. We can sit by the hedge again if you want. Or pub it? I'd like to see you.

It's not exactly a night out at the IMAX, is it? And I don't even want to go to the IMAX. It's too loud. I just want someone to want to go there with me.

The Martyr clatters about behind me like a carthorse. I adopt tunnel vision.

OK, no problem.

The Capricorn isn't in today; her kid isn't well. I try and imagine The Capricorn in motherly, nurturing mode, but can't. Maybe she has different personalities for the different roles in her life, that she puts on and takes off like a jacket. I'd like that power. The power to change.

I read the music news online. I can't be arsed with 'word of the day' this week. Fuck it.

The Martyr asks me if I'll get a file for her from the third floor. I want to ask if she's lost the use of her legs, but decide to just put up with it, as I'm not doing anything better. I stand, hoping to catch Sam's eye, but he's away from his desk.

Not long until lunch, now, though. Another sliver of hope served with my sandwich, just how I like it. Brown or white bread, it doesn't really matter.

I get in the lift and press '3' but the button jams. I whack it again and accidentally hit '5'. As I arrive, I realise I've never been up here before. Seven floors and I'd never ventured past the 3rd. I must be feeling adventurous after my graveyard adventure yesterday, so I walk out of the lift and wander down the hall, cautiously curious, fully expecting the usual key-card force-field to stop me in my tracks. Surely a robotic arm would reach out to fend off nosy interlopers such as myself.

But the door just swings open.

It is deserted up here.

Silent.

The whole floor is completely gutted, a gaping expanse. Wires dangle from the ceiling like electric vines in purple, yellow and red. Very few desks remain; maybe six or seven, and two or three empty filing cabinets. The computers and phones are gone. Almost everything is gone.

There is so much *space*: it is the same size as our floor but looks ten times bigger, like a football field – no, like a *ballroom*. It has a strange, ghostly beauty, like everyone was here one minute, then gone the next, struck by some 9/11 winged bullet, or vaporised by some nuclear bomb. It is zombie movie-esque. The windows are free of blinds, and the view is sweeping, rolling out like a giant painting: the Bayeux Tapestry of Wembley. I walk to the window and stare out, looking down on the petrol station and McDonald's on the left. I can't see Wembley Stadium on this side.

It is so quiet up here. Dust hangs in the air, filling my lungs and my nose, like a virus. The carpet smells like old boots, rotting plastic. I want to speak, hear my voice echo across the room, but I'm too self-conscious.

A noise in the distance startles me. It is far away, and like a scuttling, or a whisper.

I know I shouldn't be here.

But still I want to look.

It's probably builders. This is probably where Un-Handy Andy hides when we're all after him. It's quite useful to know, actually. Maybe I can hide up here, too.

I walk along the fifth floor, and see a pile of files at the far end, a mountain of them; green and orange and brown, like autumn leaves spilling across the floor. A tape gun with Ruby Slippers' real name as well as 'Hong Kong Phooey' taped on the side is resting on the floor and I can see some of the files have been sorted into boxes, A to E, F to K.

God, has she been up here all on her own, filing? This was a health and safety issue – she needed a dust mask, at the very least. They give her the crummiest jobs...

But it isn't *that* crummy. Away from everything sounds quite appealing. Most times even grimy loneliness beats polished company.

I hear another noise: it sounds a bit like a whine, something animal.

Rats?

I push back the double fire doors at the end of the room. In the hallway I can see Ruby Slippers' bag and iPod in a pile on the floor. I can hear the faint tinny hum from the headphones. Then I see an upturned ruby slipper. Not a slipper, a pump.

Just one.

My head tries to think of a reasonable explanation for this, and can't.

I stare at her abandoned shoe, and instead of Dorothy, I think of Cinderella. Not allowed to really live. Watching the clock until midnight. Frightened of people seeing the real her. Cinderella was just a pawn in someone else's game. Everyone was just making fun of her, one way or another. She just went from being owned by one person – to another.

Shit. Maybe someone's killed her. Ruby Slippers, Hong Kong Phooey. Maybe she's been murdered. Maybe someone's murdering her *right now*. Why else would she be missing a shoe?

Don't be ridiculous.

Not a yelp this time... a laugh.

Something is crawling at the bottom of my stomach, telling me to mind my own, to turn around, curiosity killed the cat, and all that crap. But still I feel compelled to see, to solve the mystery. I'm a slasher-movie heroine in the making, stumbling into disaster, not listening to the gut, but the heart. This is how it goes, isn't it? There's no story otherwise. How many humans had come unstuck, hearts shattered, or simply just bludgeoned by untimely deaths, by this basic human curiosity, this dumb nosiness that I was suddenly consumed by?

There are toilets at this end of the floor, just like downstairs. I can just say I am using the loo if anyone asks...

There. I have my excuse. Now I can run head-first into my fate.

I push back the toilet door. It is just as downstairs, but smells damper. Some tiles are missing nearest the door. On the floor, another ruby slipper lies in my path, and then a pair of black leggings. Further along lie a pair of hot-pink knickers, the lacy type that do up with ribbons on the sides. Frilly, pretty pants. Teenage knicks.

I look at them, then up, towards the window. She is sitting on the sinks, her legs wrapped around him, feet curled. Her hair falls over his shoulder, shiny as a shampoo ad.

She hasn't seen me.

I look at him, his back, the stripe of his short-sleeved shirt. His blonde hair. I try and kid myself: like he's the wrong height or something, but everything fits. I could identify him from any angle. I had pored over his image in my head, and on his dumb website. I had manipulated him in my imagination from every angle, as if he were a Sim. I could make him say anything I wanted – in my mind.

His back is to me.

I have never seen his buttocks before, I think.

I have now.

This isn't happening. I was at work one second ago. Now I'm watching some horrific porno. Some bad late-night soap opera. Some cheap yet disproportionately scary B-movie.

And I'm stuck.

'I don't think we should,' she says softly. Fairly unconvincingly considering the noises that brought me here, and the fact her underwear is at their feet.

His voice is low. 'I think we should, I think we *have* to... we can't turn back now.'

I try and remember if he fed me crap like this. Something similar, no doubt. He is so far from the handsome prince, for *either* of us.

It's only her that doesn't know it yet.

'It just doesn't feel right here....' she is saying.

'It feels so right to me... just let me,' he says, 'Just let me.' And I see him move closer to her, and she sighs, but it's a good sigh. Good for her but not good for me, the fucking Phantom of the Opera, or Quasimodo, mutated and lurking in the shadows.

'This is so bad,' she is saying, quieter now, but her tone says something else.

His hands are holding her little waist. I hear

him murmur, in that infuriating, mumbling accent of his, but I can't make out what he's saying.

I watch them rock back and forwards like in some grotesque dance. I think of a mental patient, rocking back and forth, finding comfort in the midst of madness. What looked so wrong and freaky to a 'normal' person, must be making them – the nutcase – feel better. Why do it otherwise?

Please. Please let me change the channel.

I imagine it all, the scene before: her filing, listening to her iPod, maybe singing. Lost in a daydream. I imagine him sneaking up behind her, and her turning, surprised maybe, but happy... I imagine him talking her into it. Leading her here.

How had it happened? When? Before me? Since?

I am trying to work out how not to be sick, or how to *dissolve*, when she sees me and screams.

'Oh my God!' She jumps up like someone just turned the hot taps on her butt. Then he turns, comically, and I can see his hard-on, and it kind of bobs up and down, and I realise I've never actually *seen* it before, just touched it, or had it in me.

Weird.

'Stephanie!' he shouts, and then she is scampering round, grabbing her things; Ruby Slippers. We made her a joke, gave her nicknames, because we were scared. Because she was too pretty to just have a normal name like us. She was otherly.

She doesn't look at me again as she locks

herself in a cubicle, clothes in her hands, pink ribbons trailing over her arms, like incisions.

I look at him, *Sam*, right in the eye. They are black with fading desire, and defiant. His lips are pink and I'm not sure if it's her lipstick or because he was turned on.

Before I showed up and ruined the party.

He shoves me out of the door, into the hall, and leans towards my neck, kissing-distance away.

'She doesn't know about us.' he whispers, his first thought for her.

'That's obvious.' I can feel his breath on me, and he looks angry. He doesn't look on the hop. He looks like he's the one who's been screwed over.

Why is *he* angry at *me*?

I think of him touching my scars. Was that the point he decided to throw me away? Or was it when I dared ask to see him at the weekend?

Suddenly he grabs my face, just like madmen do in films when the police are banging on the door, and they're having a final flip-out. I always thought I'd kick someone in the balls if they did that. But in reality, you just freeze.

'Were you following me, you bitch?' he asks.

You bitch. I can't compute this. This isn't going the way it's meant to. *I'm* meant to be the wronged one! What the fuck?

Then I realise something else – he's actually pretty ugly. His teeth are like fucking fangs or something. Had I created his beauty in my head?

I flounder. I can feel myself *floundering*; a fish on a slab.

I can hear Ruby Slippers going 'shit, shit, shit'

behind the green cubicle door and I look away
from him, back towards her, back into the toilets.

And then it occurs to me: *the colour*.

The same up here as downstairs, as on every
single fucking floor.

That colour.

It's *pistachio*!

My jaw drops. It hadn't when I'd found them
together. *They* hadn't been as much of a
revelation; as much as finally working out that
infuriating shade of paint.

Pistachio.

Of course! You idiot! Why hadn't I thought of
that before?

Focus, Stephanie! A voice in my head says.
And I stop looking at the door. But I'm still
thinking. Pistachio! Of course. How did I not get
that?

He is doing his trousers up. We've been here
before, but not like this. He doesn't say sorry. He
doesn't say anything.

I have no hold on him.

I never did.

And I want to grab something. Stick my nails
in.

'I'm gonna tell her.' I say, suddenly, knowing
I won't. I just want to fuck him over. I just want
to hurt him back.

Then he is shoving me further down the hall,
and I can't believe it. He virtually grabs me
round the throat.

And with her out of earshot, he doesn't need
to whisper any more. His face is contorted with
rage and now I have no idea whatsoever what I
ever saw in him. None. He's uglier than the Toxic

Racist. He is vile.

'Just shut your fucking mouth, freak girl. One jerk-off and a ride doesn't give you any hold on me. Neither were that good, anyway.'

'Jerk-off' stands out. What an incredibly un-English expression. What a ridiculous person he was – *is*. All along.

And I always knew this.

Always.

I look at him.

He looks at me.

Why can't I think of a comeback?

Does it even count as a 'jerk-off' if he didn't ejaculate? It was just a feel-up, really. He was overselling it.

Ruby Slippers opens the door fully-clothed and starts to speak. Her cheeks are bright red. No – more than her cheeks – her embarrassment is colouring her entire face. And I know what she's going to say, 'I know how this looks/it's not what it looks like/please don't tell anyone' but I can't stand to hear it.

I turn and run, past the ruby slipper in the hall, back through the ballroom.

After

Downstairs, I go straight to the First Aid Kit. I don't even know why. I haven't cut myself, intentionally or otherwise. Maybe it's just the *hurt*. The hurt and the cure. I need a bandage, a cuddle, a Valium. I realise I haven't got The Martyr's file. I hadn't even been to the right floor yet. Upstairs feels like I went through the wormhole. If I'd just pressed '3', the future would be different.

I'd altered destiny.

Maybe I imagined it.

But I can still feel where his fingers gripped my face, still see his angry little eyes, his mouth trying to hurt me with words.

Freak girl.

You don't say.

Imaginative points: nil.

I reach for the catches on the First Aid Kit, struggling to get a grip on something tangible, to focus on something that's not the image of his buttocks or his dick or that fucking paint.

I open the First Aid Kit.

'Stop! Stop right there!'

I jump. My nerves can't take anymore. I turn and see I'm Not Being Funny, but... advancing towards me.

'What's your injury?' she barks.

I think:

Broken heart.

Shock.

Manic depression.

I say, 'Uh?'

'Your injury.' She puts a large flat hand on the front of the First Aid Kit. She may as well have put it over my mouth. 'I'm the new First Aider. If you have an injury, you need to report to me. I will log it in the incident book, and administer the first aid. People have been dipping into this like it's a sweet shop. Not anymore.'

It *is* a sweet shop, I think, but it's like in Hansel and Gretel. The house made of sweets is a trap. It tastes good, but it drags you down and tries to kill you.

You can never have enough.

'Forget it,' I hear myself saying, but I'm in the fog, I'm looking at things from a long distance away. I'm amazed at my restraint given the circumstances, as I turn on my heel. I can hear her shouting after me, but I go, I just go. I bolt to the toilet.

I know one thing: I will never open the First Aid Kit again.

I close the pistachio-coloured cubicle door behind me.

And then I am sobbing, sobbing for my love, the embargoed First Aid Kit, and sobbing for Sam, who I never even loved! How can he ever have hurt me, this pathetic New Zealander whom I knew nothing about, who knew nothing about me. He is an opportunist. A fucking predator. He's shagging a little girl. I picture them. I can't stop.

And I always knew it would have no happy ending, and not because I'm a pessimist. But because of the person he was/is.

I had expected him to turn. Like a dangerous animal kept as a pet, it was just a matter of time.

257

You can't put a tornado in a buggy, not forever. A tornado doesn't care about your history. A tornado doesn't know any better. It just wants to destroy.

I am crying, surrounded by that ice-cream green, and I just want it to encompass me, to swallow me up, to turn me inside out. I have this feeling – this new feeling. That this can't go on.

That I can't go on.

Wednesday

I have no idea how I got to work today. Every part of me except my body is hiding under the covers. Every part.

Sam comes in late. He doesn't look at me.

I'm nothing.

I wait for Ruby Slippers to come in. She normally starts at ten. I'd always felt happy when I'd seen her before, always admired her sense of style, envied the fact she was at university, and just passing through this ghoulish place. I'd admired the way she'd deal with Rocket Science Bore, polite but kind. She seemed like a real person with her sparkly shoes, her symmetrical smile. She seemed effortlessly pretty, happy. Like someone I could have been, given a different body, a different face, and a cup full of confidence.

Now I knew the sight of her, and all those things she had that I didn't, would make me feel another way.

I'm Not Being Funny, but... walks by, probably on plaster patrol. I keep my head down. I won't cut. I won't give his action a reaction.

I'd like to cut him. Cut his dick off.

But we were never boyfriend and girlfriend.

I want to email him a rambling stream of abuse. He'd offered me a sandwich half an hour before he'd fucked her. I want to tell him where to shove his sandwich. I want to shove it there for him.

But the worst part is, he doesn't care.

He doesn't feel a thing.

The doors beep at the end of the office. Ruby Slippers walks in wearing bright green leggings like Peter Pan. Instead of her ruby slippers, she has on white trainers. We aren't allowed to wear trainers, but she is, because she doesn't have a desk, and she isn't permanent.

She's not on a contract.

Here until she's sixty-five.

I wonder how long the longest person has been here.

I look at Bowser.

It could be him. I remember him telling me to escape, like a wise old owl, or a soothsayer.

I hadn't listened.

Like a cursed giant lottery finger, it could be me next.

Ruby Slippers is walking towards us, saying 'hi' to this person and 'hi' to that person. She walks past Sam. Her lips are thick with gloss. She is consistently thin, consistently groomed.

And she had him.

And she will escape.

But still I find it hard to conjure up any hatred towards her. It isn't her fault. She doesn't even know.

I realise she is coming right for me.

'Stephanie. Can I have a word?'

Those words are enough to strike fear into the heart of anyone at the best of times. I'm just not ready to face this head-on today.

The Capricorn is watching. She knows Ruby Slippers and I have never spoken before, except when we cut that picture out as a joke, back when Jim was here.

A thousand years ago.

'I'm kind of busy,' I say, shuffling my paperwork importantly.

Feebly.

'Please.' She looks like a model. Her eyes are improbably bright, imploring.

'OK, I'll grab a quick cuppa,' I concede. I'm such a wimp. As I stand, I see Sam is giving me a don't-you-dare stare. I pretend I haven't seen him.

We go to the kitchen. Neither of us make tea.

'I am so sorry about yesterday,' she says. She talks really fast. 'Thank you so much for not saying anything. I was so embarrassed.'

What would I have said? I wondered. To whom? I suppose I could have emailed it to the staff newsletter if only I'd had my camera with me. If only I could think of a headline. Some stupid pun.

'I'm sorry I saw,' I say, quite honestly.

Although I wasn't sorry I *knew*. No more hanging on like a yo-yo for me.

'There's nothing really going on with him,' she says, like I actually want to know further details. She sits down at a beech table, long arms folding in her lap. Then she leans forwards, like we're best friends, chatting over coffee, and drops the bomb. 'He's got a *girlfriend*.'

I find my eyes drawn to the far wall. I'm changing my mind fast about not cutting. I'm wondering how deep I can go without a plaster, or a bandage, as there's no way I'm touching that treacherous First Aid Kit ever again. Not now it had been commandeered.

Condemned.

'To be frank, it's a relief to tell someone.'

I think of my tin. I've got some steri-strips in there. I can probably cut an inch down at least, and just stick it back together. My head feels like it's fizzing a bit, like some important brain circuitry just got a cup of tea knocked into it.

I look at her.

My heart is like a rubber ball; manic, lost.

'I mean, naturally, I was mortified yesterday. But now it's out in the open. I might as well be honest.'

I think of Kate telling me, or almost telling me, not to get too close to Sam. It wasn't her fault the penny got stuck in the slot. I should do the same here, reward Ruby Slippers' honesty.

'So what do you think? Do you think he'll leave her? Do you think he likes me?'

And then I realise something else. This girl is pretty stupid.

I could say,

Of course he won't. You're fucking him. Where's his incentive?

I could say,

He had his hand up my skirt by the hedge last week, mate, what do you think?

I could say,

Why are you fucking someone else's boyfriend?

But I don't.

She is looking at me. She is willing me to say something.

I open my mouth.

'I think you should go for it,' I say. 'I think you guys look great together.'

I wonder how I managed to say that with a straight face, but somehow I did.

262

'Oh my God, I'm so glad I talked to you!' She smiles radiantly. 'I knew you'd give some good advice. You're right. I should just go for it.'

'Yep.' I say. 'Just do it.'

Just like the advert.

Just do it.

I'm going to just do it. Right now.

I push my chair out, wobbling slightly, but so slightly she doesn't see. I get up and go back to my desk, straight to my bag. I shake my little tin, palm a razor and half a pack of steri strips into my pocket. God bless pockets.

I half-walk half-run to the toilets but someone has propped the doors open with the fire extinguisher and I trip over it. Only the wall stops me from hitting the carpet.

'Ow!'

This is a three-fold safety issue. Firstly, the fire door is propped open, which I believe is illegal. Secondly, it's a total trip hazard. Three, I have a razor in my pocket, although I guess I have to take some of the responsibility for that. Some.

And then it occurs to me: I'd like to burn this place down.

I'd like to hurt them, not me.

But I can't. Even a cigarette in the loos would probably trigger the sprinkler system.

I push back the pistachio-green door and put down the toilet seat, sitting down, rubbing my stubbed toe.

At what point would they actually use the sprinklers? I imagine it raining in here. A lot of people would get an electric shock. I imagine it like a cartoon, thunder bolts of electricity zig-

263

zagging though my soaking enemies.

I twirl the razor round in my fingers, thinking.

For a small fire, a fire extinguisher, archaic as it was, would be a lot more reliable.

But what if it wasn't?

'Oh, my God.'

I think of Sam and Jackass, and his mates who filled a fire extinguisher with petrol for a prank.

Some prank, I'd thought.

Idiots, I'd thought.

I look at my toe.

I think about Sam, and his girlfriend, cuddled up at night. I thought of her asking him, 'How was your day?'

Sam and his friends shared a common passion for hurting people. A common disregard for their fellow human beings.

I want to think of a way to hurt him.

And then I put the razor back. Back in my pocket.

I leave the toilet and look around to see if the coast is clear, like in a crappy film. My life has definitely been that this week. I was the star of the shittiest show in town.

I look at the fire extinguisher more closely.

It looks reasonably tamperproof. It has a pretty tag on it. But who would notice if it was missing in the *heat* of the moment?

I smile to myself fleetingly.

Who was I kidding?

This was impenetrable.

Then I think of boys, angry boys, making bombs in their baths.

How do they learn how?
How does anyone learn anything these days?
The internet.

Thursday

What am I doing? I am going to work with a 2-litre bottle of Coke in my bag. Only it isn't the Real Thing.

I have fucking lost my mind.

This thought keeps running through my head. *I have fucking lost my mind.* Then I think, is that right? Should it be, I have lost my fucking mind? I think both work. Both work, I reassure myself.

I walk past the security guard. I walk up the stairs.

I have got to do something. I just have to. The thought of one more day in this place.

I can't keep coming back. I can't face another Monday.

How can I stop myself coming to work day after day?

I have to force my own hand. Force everybody's hand.

I am mentally sub-normal. All I need to do is stand up for myself. Make a stand. Have it out with everyone. Just like they do in soaps. Isn't that the normal way? Have it out with everyone and move on. Just move on.

Let me move on.

I sit down at my desk.

The Capricorn says without emotion, 'Did you have a good evening?'

I think, I learnt how to tamper with a fire extinguisher and make it look shiny and new.

I wonder if The Capricorn has ever visited an arsonist website. If she's heard of 'Twisted Firestarter' or 'Pyromaniacs Anonymous'.

I'm not even kidding.

'Not bad,' I say. I realise she knows nothing about me. I know about her kid, her background, sketchy bits. But what does she know about me? She couldn't name a friend of mine, or tell you if I had one. A song I like. A book I've read. We don't even talk about the telly.

You're sitting in the danger zone there, I think to myself. Right opposite Sam the Man.

Am I really going to do this?

I look at my tray full of work.

I'm not going to do *that*.

I guess you could call me unprofessional.

My hands still smell of petrol, even though I've washed them forty times. I feel like a marked woman. The coke bottle under my desk is a dirty bomb.

I'm a *terrorist*.

'How was *your* evening?' I suddenly say, conscious of the fact I've not even kept up the pretence of being civilised.

I probably have this wild-eyed, vacant look about me. They'll probably call me a zombie in the papers. A mad-woman. They'll print a list of the medicines I was taking, the websites I'd looked at. They'll call me crazy. People will say I was a loner, weird. That they never liked me. That there was always something strange about me.

I am Mark Chapman, waiting, just waiting for them to arrive – John and Yoko.

I am Lee Harvey Oswald. This is my grassy knoll.

When you do something massive, you don't get a right of reply.

You just get labelled.

But at least you get noticed.

Finally.

'I had some friends round for drinks,' The Capricorn says, and I feel shocked. I can't imagine her friends, and their interests. I imagine her laughing and drinking. What do we really know about people at work, the people we only see during office hours? What horrors or wonders do they return to at night? What keeps them alive; keeps them awake?

The Capricorn has a mouse-mat with one of those things on it that looks like a breast implant. Magic jelly to support your wrist. I've always envied it.

She's probably alright really, The Capricorn.

She's probably a nice person, a good friend, a loving mother.

What if it has just been me all along?

I look around, feeling frightened. What if all this was normal, all these people were decent people, and I was just this loon, this weird freak?

Then I think of Sam.

He's not normal. He deserves it. Everything. He gets away with murder.

But what if that was normal as well, for a man to get away with murder?

Women are just meant to put up and shut up. Women are just meant to take it. Get played. Get fucked.

My head hurts. I was up too late, and now I can't think straight.

I am *not* Mark Chapman. I'm *not* going to kill anyone.

I realise I need to get this Coke bottle out

from under my fucking desk.

'I forgot to put my lunch in the fridge,' I say unconvincingly to The Capricorn as The Martyr arrives, looking flustered. Good timing.

I can't really put my Coke in the fridge of course. Much as I hate – well, everyone – I wouldn't want someone to take a swig and... die. Well, I would, if I could magically make it be Sam. But I can't guarantee that.

None of this stupid plan has the slightest guarantee, I think.

But that's not true.

Whatever happens, it guarantees I can't turn up on Monday.

Whatever happens, I'll be free.

My heart skitters a little at this thought, and I feel renewed enthusiasm. I look through the kitchen door. No one is there. I go next door to the toilets, which are also empty. I hang my plastic bag on the back of my cubicle door. I go back into the corridor.

The fire extinguisher is still propping the door open. The coast is unambiguous – inviting.

It's too easy.

The extinguisher is quite heavy, but I can drag it along with both hands. I wonder what would happen now if someone saw me. I think of the words 'gross misconduct.' They are weighty words. But it's worse than that. The police...

My heart skitters again.

Then I am here; in the cubicle, me and my pals; the moth and the flame.

Here I am, the scientist.

The arsonist.

I don't need a diagram, I don't need

instructions. The tag snaps off easily. I have everything here in my bag. And it strikes me, this is a bit like cutting. The precision. The intricacy. The slosh of the liquid.

The pleasure, the pain.

I think, if this goes off in my face, it will probably kill me. But I've played with death in this cubicle more times than I could count. This is no different.

Then the door goes. I freeze, listening. Nothing unusual... the door next to me slams, the tinkle of urine on porcelain. I can hear my heart beating in my ears. I can smell petrol on my hands, the bits of fire extinguisher laid out on the floor. Black handle. Red clip. Gold screw. The other person rips toilet paper from the roll, coughs. I am holding the screwdriver in my right hand, the pliers in my left.

I don't know how to change a tyre.

But I learn quick.

The other person flushes. I breathe in and out. Go, just go. I need to do this quickly. Taps. Water. Paper towel or hand dryer? Hand dryer. Then she is gone.

Hold upright.

Pull out pin.

Squeeze levers.

It hisses like an alley cat as it empties air down the toilet. It goes on and on, on and on. It sounds like a horrible, guttural scream, like something in pain.

The important part is not to lose the pressure. Otherwise this was going to be one unspectacular firework. Literally, a damp squib.

Then the lid of the extinguisher is off.

Looking into that hole, like a giant Thermos, is like staring into the abyss.

People are not meant to see this. But I have.

I think of the inside of the sanitary bin again. This must be how the cleaners feel. They know all our dirty secrets, how we're filthy on the inside. They must hate us.

I undo the Coke bottle with my teeth and instantly regret it. Stress is making me stupid. I gag and spit into the toilet bowl.

Two litres fills up the extinguisher over three quarters. It must be enough. It has to be.

This is a Frankenstein's monster, but I care about the detail as I screw the handle back on. I can feel sweat blocking my pores, suspended in my skin. I look at the markings on the side of the extinguisher as I go. Carbon dioxide. Chubb. I wonder what a squiggle inside a heart actually means. I even put the tag back on as a finishing touch. Perfection.

Will this work?

Do I even want it to?

I put the empty Coke bottle and the tools back in the plastic bag. I hang the plastic bag on the back of the door again. This will be the riskiest bit, dragging the extinguisher out, the smell of petrol on my hands, like blood, marking me out.

I peer my head out of the door. Nothing.

Just give me ten seconds. That's all I need. I can feel my breath scratching against my lips, my heart head-butting my ribs.

I drag the fire extinguisher along. It is lighter than before, but only noticeably so by me, I'm sure. Here I am.

I pull back the door.

'Steph!'

It's The Martyr. I am bent over, two hands on the fire extinguisher.

She looks at me.

I look at her. The sweat that was on pause trickles down my leg.

'What is up with that thing!' she says. 'You think something as heavy as that would keep the door propped open, wouldn't you? Do you want a hand?'

Jesus.

'No, it's OK, I got it.' I say, pushing it up against the door. I don't want her getting petrol on her hands. No matter how scatterbrained she is, she would surely notice that. My throat feels as narrow as a biro.

'Oh OK,' she says, then passes me, walking towards the toilet.

Fuck!

My bag is still hanging on the back of the cubicle door.

This is it.

She has two options.

50/50.

Deal or no deal?

If she picks my cubicle, it's game over. No extra life.

I go after her. She walks through the main door. Her hand on my cubicle door, why, why, it's not even the first one? What is wrong with her?

'Wait!' I shout.

She turns to me. 'Are you OK, Steph? You look a little flushed.'

'Yeah, course. I just... I think I left my lunch in there.'

'Your lunch?' She pulls back the door. The cubicle looks empty, but I know it isn't. 'I don't see it... try the other one.'

She slams the door in my face.

Oh my God.

What was I thinking, I was no criminal, no arsonist! I was going to get fucking caught, and it was my own fault, I could smell petrol everywhere, on everything!

I am going to prison.

The door flies open again. I stand, staring at her, gawping.

'Here it is!' she says, handing me a Bag for Life containing an empty Coke bottle, a screwdriver, and a pair of pliers.

On what *planet* did that constitute lunch?

For once, I had to thank God for her flakiness.

'Thank you.' I say. 'Thanks.' I feel like I'm going to puke. My hands are dripping.

I stagger to the kitchen, passing one of the call centre drones with a cup of water. Then I'm alone. I pull the lid off the kitchen bin and shove the bag in, all the way to the bottom, past everything. But everything isn't much as it's still early, so I put more paper towels on top.

I go to the sinks, and wash my hands with Fairy Liquid. My hands are shaking. My legs feel like they belong to someone else, or no one.

I'm breathing. I'm breathing; in, out, in out.

And then it occurs to me.

I got away with it.

I go to walk back to my desk, seeing The

273

Martyr pass by, looking totally normal, as normal as she ever had been. I look out into the hall, at the fire extinguisher once more propping open the door, silent and normal-looking. Benign.

I think, *shit*.

I can't go back now, even if I want to. Even if I just leave it, I am condemning people to... what? I have to go for my target. I have to finish the job.

At lunchtime I go to the toilet again, passing the extinguisher, my very own elephant in the room. I check *that* cubicle. All seems well; the cleaners may even have been in already, my unwitting accomplices. I wash my hands three times. I open the window.

When am I going to do it?

Am I going to do it?

I leave the office, go out the revolving doors. Heat hits me in the face like a smack. I swear, I've never known such a hot summer. I walk across the stepping stones to our bit of grass. Our chairs are still there, tucked up against the hedge. I wonder if there is even a caretaker of this bloody building. You think a gardener would look after the place and would have thrown them in the skip by now.

I sit on one of Amy's chairs and stare at the sun.

I wonder if I want to die, or if I just want everyone else to.

I feel inside my bag, and find the box of matches I bought two months ago, the ones with the kittens on the front, much cuter than a button. I shake them into my hand, then put them back in again, tidily.

'Stephanie.'

It's him. Is there no peace to be had, anywhere?

He sits down on his chair. These were our thrones, Amy and I, these knackered old chairs from Asda.

This is where everything will be decided. This is our Narnia.

Her words ring in my ears, but that was so long ago, I don't even know if I remember them right.

'Have a seat.' I say, sarcastically. I shake the matches in their box.

Your death rattle, I think, dramatically.

He sits, staring at the bushes. He exhales long and hard, as if he has the weight of the world on his shoulders. As if he's deciding on life and death matters like me, and not just which woman to sleep with next.

'I shouldn't have spoken to you like that the other day,' He says. He pushes a cigarette out of a packet. For a non-smoker he sure smokes a lot. Good. Get lung cancer. Get throat cancer. Get dick cancer.

'Where's Gemma?' I ask. Gemma is Ruby Slippers. Hong Kong Phooey.

'I don't know. Who cares? She'll be back at uni next month. You and I will still be here.'

Is that a threat? He leaves me so cold I feel like someone's injected a Slush-Puppy into my veins. He looks so disgusting sucking on that cigarette. How could he get so ugly so quickly? It was really weird, like he was in a soap opera and had been switched for a different actor, a substandard replacement. What else was I blind to?

'Talk to me, Steph.'

My name doesn't sound like Steph when it comes out of his mouth. It sounds like 'Stiff', which may sound exciting written down, perhaps, but aurally, it's horrible, like a little squeak coming from his nose.

And he used to call me 'Stephsy', which was even worse. I don't reply to Stiff or Stiffsy. And it's not like I ever corrected him, but now I notice every time he says it. Now I notice everything.

I look up at the building. For a second I'm sure I can see Ruby Slippers looking at us from the window of the first floor. No – it's just my head making fun of me. Playing games.

I take his hand, just in case. He looks shocked, as if it was too easy.

I lean in close to him. From the first floor, it might pass as a kiss.

'Fuck you.' I whisper.

He looks startled by this.

'Listen, I know it must have been hard for you, seeing that...'

I think of blue skies, and fire extinguishers filled with petrol. I don't speak.

'I *do* feel guilty,' he says. He gestures to my arm. 'What with your scars and everything.'

That's it, wrap the little self-harmer in cotton wool. Cover her ears. Feed her some whitewash.

I'll feed myself the whitewash, thank you. Right from the bottle.

'Don't feel sorry for me for that reason,' I say. 'That's none of your business. Did you even *say* sorry?'

'I *am* sorry.' Then he turns on those puppy-dog eyes and it feels like an attack, like a trick. Like he's caught me.

How can I do it? How can I do what I'd planned? He is a bastard, but so what? I burn down a building in response? What am I thinking?

I just have to take it. I just have to take it like everyone else has to...

This frightens me. This feeling I have to lie down. Backtrack.

Back to work on Monday after all.

I wonder how I'll get rid of the fire extinguisher. Maybe drag it out the back door, dump it in a skip. It would be tough, but what choice did I have if it came to it? I have no real alternative.

'I really like you, Stephsy.'

Stiffsy.

He touches me and I recoil. 'Gemma means nothing to me. She's just a kid.'

Oh right! And then I realise. This is cliché hour. This *is* the soap speech. The one I was meant to deliver.

Its not you it's me.

It was just sex.

Let's just be friends.

My head's in a strange place right now... oh yeah, I knew all about that one.

'What about your girlfriend?' I ask suddenly. The sun blazes in the sky behind him, giving him an inappropriate halo. I wish it would just turn its rays on him, and burn him up. He is just a speck, an ant. Surely he has enraged the planets with this bullshit. I want to see it.

'Oh God,' he says, like he's swallowed a fly. 'Did *she* tell you that? I just told her that so she didn't get too hung up on me. So she didn't go telling the whole office about us. There's no girlfriend.' He is looking obstinate now, treating her with the same worthless contempt I saw on his face for me this week.

Rewind!

I picture myself lugging the extinguisher out of the skip. Dragging it back up the stairs. Propping the door open. Giving it a little pat.

'Prove it.' I say. Does he really think I'm that stupid? Does he really expect that I'll just drop my knickers again? I'm a self-harmer, not fucking brain-damaged.

'How?' he asks, looking innocent as a choirboy.

He thought he had it all sewn up, didn't he?

But I know better than anyone, things are never that simple.

'Show me inside your wallet.' I say. 'Show me your mobile phone. Your photos. Show me your text messages.'

His expression changes. He throws his cigarette butt on the floor and pushes his face into his hands.

'OK, OK. You win. I do have a girlfriend.'

'No shit,' I reply.

I win. Doesn't feel like it, Sam. I still want to look at her picture. I still want to torture myself that one extra inch. But I don't think I'll get the chance.

Maybe he thinks I'll still shag him. Maybe he thinks I'm as thick as Ruby Slippers.

'Do you love her?' I ask, not wanting to, not meaning to, knowing he doesn't, whatever he says.

'We're getting married,' he says, and my stomach lurches. 'I've been so stupid.'

I look up at the window again. It could be Ruby Slippers, or a shadow, or a coat-stand, or a desk.

Everything is relative from this distance.

Friday

Today it is raining, clouds throwing water hard against the windows. There is enough rain to spoil your day if you had something planned, or to put out a fire. Enough rain to dampen the spirits.

But this rain doesn't dampen mine.

Every part of me itches with this crazy, tormenting yet delicious thought: *I will never come here again.*

I look at The Capricorn eating lychees. I didn't even know what a lychee was until The Capricorn arrived with her organic, macrobiotic regime.

I have obviously looked too long, because she extends a skinny wrist. 'Want one?'

I look at the pink skin, pulled back to reveal what fundamentally looks like a freshly extracted eyeball. Or... a testicle.

'No thanks,' I say, trying not to gag.

'Didn't think so.' she replies, like I have lived up to all her worst expectations. Well fuck you, I think. Eat your eyeballs. What have you got for lunch? Frogspawn?

You might not get to eat it.

The Martyr fusses. Mitesh looks at me earnestly, trying to make eye contact so he can talk about his wife, his computer, his children, anything not to feel alone. I can't see Sam. In the distance Bowser lumbers around, and for the first time I don't feel disdain or annoyance that he exists. I almost feel sorry for him, the fat old fucker, his one bit of power in life is being in charge of a quarter of the people on this floor.

280

But was *my* one bit of power any better?

The truth is – I've got two bits of power now.

Closer to our desks Thyroid sits marooned. She has dyed her fake-red hair platinum blonde, not the most natural look when you're black. Her lips are purple, and she speaks to every customer like they're fucking her off just by being alive. I remember her complaining about my laugh. I remember a lot of things. It all gets lodged inside.

Who else is there? Who else is there to miss? No one. There's Kate, who could have been the friend to save me from all of this, someone to eat lunch with, someone to support me, and for me to support.

But she was pretty vacant.

Yet who was to say I could have supported her anyway? I'd never tried.

I was just as useless, just as impotent.

Fuck this shit. Am I just going to sit here all day? It's not like I'm going to pick up my pay cheque. It's not like they're going to write me one. I might as well do it. The Capricorn has gone to make a cup of tea, so it's perfect. No witnesses.

OK.

I bend down and feel in my bag for the kittens. Bingo. I palm the matchbox into my hand. I feel further, and palm a lighter, too, for good luck.

I don't smoke. But you can use lighters for other things.

I can still smell the flesh from the car.

I turn to The Martyr. 'Rhonda. I'm not feeling so good. I'm going to go outside for five minutes

281

to get some air.'

She waves me away not looking up from her screen. No, 'are you OK?', or any sort of normal acknowledgement.

Bye, I think.

I stand, picking up my bag. Goodbye, desk. Goodbye, chair. I think.

Sam is over by the fax.

I walk around to his side of the desk. It feels weird there, like looking at things in the mirror, or in a photograph. Mitesh is on the phone, his chair facing the window as he wraps the phone cord around his arm.

Sam notices me but he's tied to the fax. 'What's up?' he mouths.

I mime writing a note. I can feel the rectangle of cardboard in my hot palm and the plastic in the other.

It is all a rough plan, a sketch of an idea. But it's mine.

I knock a pen off his desk and bend down. I cough as I spin the wheel on the lighter. I set fire to the whole matchbox and dump it in his bin, which is nicely full of invoices. I guess his confidential shredding days were over.

The box goes 'whoosh' but quietly, and Mitesh is talking quite loud, loud enough.

I think, 'fuck' and want to retract it immediately.

I want to get it out. Rescue it.

But I can't even look in the bin.

It's too late.

And no one rescued me, did they?

I probably have thirty seconds to get out before they smell it.

Sam is walking back to his desk as I go.

I lean towards him, closer than I've ever got within these walls.

'I'm out of here.' I say.

'You're not well?' he tries.

'No. I'm not going to work here anymore.'

And he must know just from looking at me that I mean it. I must look purposeful, decided.

'I left you a note,' I lie.

He squeezes my arm. 'I'll read it.'

'I know you will,' I say, and start walking.

I don't run.

I just walk away. I can hear songs playing inside my head, an orchestra, waves, Mozart, all that hackneyed crap. I think of the motivational posters – what had that one said? *The will to succeed can overcome the greatest adversity.* If a cliché is vague enough, it can be attributed to almost any situation. Like someone telling your fortune. Like reading your star sign; have you ever read someone else's star sign? They all say the same thing, just dressed up in a different way. Money, love, career, success, it's all coming your way today. Every day.

I think: this is it.

Something finally happened.

And I made it happen.

I get in the lift. The face staring back at me in the mirror doesn't look like me, how I must feel, *triumphant*, but I guess it is me. It has to be.

All I can see is ugly. And I can't remember if I'm really ugly, or if it was just an obsession that started, and I forgot how to stop it.

Ground floor. Ground zero.

The security guard nods at me as I walk out,

towards the car park. I keep expecting someone to stop me, to feel a hand on my shoulder.

Come with us.

What have you done?

But nothing happens. I walk and walk through the rain that is now just a patter, not a hurl. The sun burns like a cigarette-end above the car park.

I want to look up at the first floor, but I am too scared.

And then there he is, a scratch on the sun, the Toxic Racist – and I nearly thought 'rapist' then, and why not? He stood for sexual harassment as well as ignorance.

'Hi,' he says to me, keys jangling in his hand. 'Early lunch?'

'You still don't know my name, do you?' I say, and I can barely see him, which is a blessing. He is a smudge against a planet.

'Course I do,' he says. 'It's... er...'

Don't worry, you'll know it soon enough, I think.

And even if you don't, it won't matter.

I've just walked past him when I find myself turning and saying, 'Hey, do you want to go out sometime?'

And he turns, facing the sun now, his car crash of a face spot-lit.

'Sure,' he says. 'Sure I do.'

'Well, try being a bit less of an inbred fuck then,' I shout. 'And try being a bit less racist!'

And then I am gone, and he is just an imprint again, and even though he is shouting words at me – cunt, bitch, fat – I can't hear them. I can't hear a thing.

Besides, I have to get out of here.

I unlock my car. I get inside. I start the engine. I turn the radio off because I'm frightened of portentous songs. Triumphant gave way to scaredy-cat pretty quick. In fact, I'm not sure I even did the triumphant bit.

My heart is hammering under my breast.

Think. Just think.

Just fucking drive and think.

I drive, away from the building, away from the scene of the crime.

It's not a crime.

What is it then?

It doesn't matter. I'm never going back.

Like that's good enough. Like they won't come looking for me.

I drive towards home.

I wonder what will happen.

I imagine Sam's face burning off.

Probably nothing will happen. Probably it never even caught fire, not really. Maybe Sam put it out with a glass of water, or a cup of coffee and never said a word.

Probably the sprinklers will turn on and they will all be covered in cool indoor rain. It will be beautiful, like a music video, until the electrics go...

I change down the gears. Traffic is backed up down my hill as far as the eye can see.

On the other hand –

I wonder how it might pan out, picture it in my mind's eye.

The Capricorn back at her desk with a cup of tea. Sam notices the smell or sees a flame shoot out or just gets super-hot trousers. He jumps up, shouts 'Fire!' Probably at this point he wouldn't even remember me leaving. But it wouldn't be long.

I imagine Bowser or When Animals Attack coming to the rescue, wielding the fire extinguisher like a giant blowtorch. I imagine the shock as the whole thing goes off like a fucking bomb, my petrol surprise; a present from me to them. I imagine their faces bathed in orange light. Would they have time to even look surprised, or would they just hit the ground screaming?

Would Sam have time to realise it was me? Would he remember his little story, his friends' failed Jackass moment? Or would he be too busy rolling on the floor, putting out his over-gelled hair?

I crawled to the bottom of the hill. Mine's the next turning.

This is all bullshit, of course. The fire probably never even got started. It probably fizzled out.

A whole matchbox. Are you sure? It had *already* started by the time you were on the ground floor.

I can't know that.

I go to turn off and suddenly a motorbike roars by. There is a flash of yellow and my heart catches in my throat. Is that *him*?

Motorbike boy!

How many weeks ago was that? It felt like a thousand.

That sinking feeling as I realised he'd gone.

In another life time, he'd have stuck around. Saved me.

Just fucking save yourself, Stephanie. Just this once. You're not bloody Rapunzel. It's not a fucking Disney film. Are you a feminist or a fuckwit?

My life's not a fairytale, it's a funeral.

Still, I watch as he disappears from view. I could never have caught up with him. The traffic stands in my way, like a giant alloyed wall, shimmering back up the hill.

I still didn't know where he lived, five minutes from me. A stone's throw.

If I'd turned a different corner, would my ending be different? Or was every door on the advent calendar just another dead end?

I feel like crying, but I don't.

I'm past it.

I park right outside my house. A small victory.

At home I can finally relax.

My cat Jammy runs out to greet me, a silver smudge, and I pick her up, my key in my spare hand. She mews and purrs.

My ground floor flat. My one-bedroomed world.

This is where all my secrets are kept. Except I don't have any.

I realise I don't care what happens. Here or at work.

But is that the truth?

I knock on the door next to mine. Margaret's.

Margaret answers, Sudoku book in hand. I wonder if she just fills in the numbers, like Sam did, like I should have, long ago. I can hear the afternoon repeat of Jeremy Kyle blasting in the background. I hear him say, 'Well, well, well, what do we have here then?'

Jammy scampers into Margaret's flat and she wrinkles her nose. She appears to be dressed in a blanket. She never seems to go further than the corner shop.

Jeremy Kyle says, 'You were lying.'

I say, 'Look, I know you don't like her, and I'm not asking you to, but will you just feed her? I'm going away for the weekend.' I press my key into her hand. She doesn't like cats but I suspect the chance to poke around in my flat will seal the deal. Margaret likes to be involved.

'I'll feed her tonight before I go, so you won't need to come until *tomorrow*.' I say this part slowly.

She looks at me, her eyes as small as five-pence pieces.

Jeremy Kyle says, 'Yes or no? Yes or no?'

'Tomorrow, please.' I repeat. 'Food's in the top cupboard.'

She nods, but says nothing. The cat rubs around her legs, not fussy.

'Get out of it...' Margaret says, and shuts the door. I know she will feed her. I know she's just pretending.

Jammy scampers off down the hall, a flash of grey. She can climb outside from the balconies. I let her go.

I close my own door behind me. There is no post.

I walk from the living room to the bedroom. There's barely a wall separating them. I pick up some underwear and clothes and throw them in the basket. I walk back to the kitchen. My kitchen is smaller than most people's hallways, but I always liked it.

I check the cupboard; three sachets of Whiskers. Fine. I empty one into the small bowl, fill up the biscuits, refill the water. I wash my hands.

I go into the living room. It is quiet as a library. Books stare at me from the far wall. The TV won't tell me the news, not if I don't let it.

Everything is quiet.

I think of old women with plastic bags stuffed into plastic bags, or trolleys stuffed full of newspapers. And I understand what that's about, their life in a trolley; their possessions, their friends. Those were things that belonged to them. Their kingdom.

I think of all the women who are pregnant and don't want to be. I think of all the women desperate to be pregnant, subjecting themselves to pain upon pain.

Life, hey. It was such a funny joke that I could barely stop laughing.

I *could* go away for the weekend, I think, but I know it's just another lie, just a delay. Where could I go? Who could I go and see?

My family look at me from glass frames on the side, all four of them. I haven't seen them in such a long time. I wonder if they wonder where I am.

I wonder if they remember me.

Finally I sit in my chair. My mind is close to being empty. Close to being free.

I just have to stop fighting.

I feel down the side of my couch, and there it is. I put it there such a long time before. Every so often I would take it into the little box-kitchen, and sharpen it. But I'd always put it back safe, wrapped in a cloth, my little blanket. My little blanket from when I was a baby.

Every night since, I'd pulled it out for a while, turned it over in my hands as I'd watched television, alone.

Felt its curve in my hand.

But I never dared.

Never had a reason to.

Margaret will find me tomorrow. It's a bit cruel, but she's a tough old bird, and she can take it, and it will be a story for her to tell, over and over, glamming it up or dressing it down as needs be.

As needs be.

The police might come sooner.

No. They won't.

Maybe Sam will cover for me.

Maybe Sam is dead.

And I'm not even sure if this is about him anymore, or if he was just my excuse, my get-out-of-life-free card.

The old typewriter he gave me sits on the chair opposite me – where I left it weeks ago. If it had a spare ribbon I could write a note. I could explain all.

But some things are self-explanatory. You didn't need the extra smiley-face, Ian Curtis. You already said it all.

I look at the knife in my hand. It's different from the pissy little razor blades. It is ten times as big. And I'd never used it. Not for anything. I'd been saving it.

It was expensive, and sharp as... a knife.

I hold my arm against the arm rest, palm

upwards. It looks perfectly white. I can't even see my scars today. I've assumed this stance so many times. But this is no dress rehearsal. You don't get a practice shot for what I have in mind.

Am I really going to do this?

I think of the office. Why didn't I just leave whilst I could?

I think of the wall of cars, keeping me from Motorbike Boy, keeping me from life.

Nothing will ever change. Except now they'll come and get me. Ask me questions. I'll be the bad guy, and I'm not, I'm just not.

It's them.

I don't want the police to come. I don't want to go to the loony bin.

I'd just come from there.

OK, then.

Let's do it.

I raise the knife high and plunge it into the narrow part of my wrist – an inch below my palm – with a force I wasn't sure I was capable of. I half expect the knife to bounce off my arm, or to snap, to let me down as well.

But it doesn't.

Blood spurts across the armchair and into my lap, and I realise somehow that the knife is impaling my arm and impaling the chair, and I'm trapped in a kind of freakish handcuff. It is like something from a horror film and is the most fascinating thing I've seen in my entire life.

I try to wriggle my fingers, but they don't move. I can't feel at all, unbelievably there is no pain, but my lap is pooling with my own blood, and it is so bright. I feel like I've wet myself. Maybe I *have* wet myself? Suddenly my mind feels like it's on a piece of elastic, jiggling out of reach, whilst I am skewered in place.

God, that knife was sharp. And I was strong; stronger than I'd ever hoped. With that comes a real sense of pride.

I think, is this a rush?

I lean my head back, trying to decide.